OFFICE PARTY

by Michael A. Gilbert

The Linden Press/Simon & Schuster
New York, 1981

Copyright © 1981 by Michael A. Gilbert
All rights reserved
including the right of reproduction
in whole or in part in any form
Published by The Linden Press/Simon & Schuster
A Simon & Schuster Division of Gulf & Western Corporation
Simon & Schuster Building
Rockefeller Center
1230 Avenue of the Americas
New York, New York 10020
THE LINDEN PRESS/SIMON & SCHUSTER and colophon are
trademarks of Simon & Schuster
Designed by Ed Carenza
Manufactured in the United States of America
1 3 5 7 9 10 8 6 4 2
Library of Congress Cataloging in Publication Data
Gilbert, Michael A.
Office party.
I. Title.
PR9199.3.G524403   813'.54   81-8394
                                        AACR2
ISBN 0-671-43636-8

For my parents,
Lewis and Esther Gilbert,
and Gram,
Brushka Portnoy

PART ONE
Friday, November 27

ONE

Brackin stood in the middle of his room searching for an emotion. After eleven years in the same two-room flat he ought to be able to bring forth more than his usual blankness for this final visit. The old leather chair placed before the television, the scarred table with two chairs, one of which was never used except for standing on to change light bulbs, the worn fake Oriental rug that Mrs. Hampton would beat once a month, all were a part of a life he was leaving forever. He winced once or perhaps it was just a squint to help pierce the dim light. His long black overcoat, lengthened by his habitual stoop, finally made his long goodbye uncomfortably warm, so wiping his forehead with his palm he picked up the leather suitcase beside him and turned for the door. The case was heavy and drew him over to one side as he went down the steps, treading the rosette carpet and inhaling the scent of mothballs for the last time.

Brackin set down the case for a rest at the foot of the stairs. As usual Mrs. Hampton stepped out of her parlor with her little dog at her heels. As the dog began leaping about Brackin's suitcase alternately growling and sniffing, Mrs. Hampton began her queries.

"Off on a trip, Mr. Brackin?"

"Oh, no, Mrs. Hampton. Just putting up some shelves at the office. It's easier if we do it ourselves."

"Do you mean you're working today? On Thanksgiving?"

"Oh, well, today isn't Thanksgiving. Yesterday was, and we have fallen far behind so Mr. Gaylord asked a few of us if we'd mind . . ."

"Well, I don't think it's right at all. Still, you've no choice, I suppose. You will be home for dinner, won't you?"

"Of course, of course. Why wouldn't I be?"

The sweat on Brackin's face grew suddenly more complete as he flushed with the lie. He was sure that Mrs. Hampton's glare was not nearly so piercing as he imagined but it hastened his departure nonetheless. Lifting the case again he smiled for an instant and went out the door she held for him. The bag clanked a bit as he bumped it against the sill, and he looked up suddenly and almost fell down the porch steps. The sunshine conspired to further confuse him but his body was able to begin walking to work all by itself. The cool air helped clear his face but the weight of the bag required an exertion that produced its own perspiration. Well, he thought, when I get to the office I can relax. And as soon as the thought was processed, his stomach tightened and his throat constricted so that he remembered with a violent shudder that today would never come again. He tried a long gentle sigh that managed to relax him somewhat and trudged on, his balding head shining in the sun as he peered out before him on his way to the office.

It was not a long walk, some ten blocks or so, but Brackin was terrified of some mishap. Should he fall and the suitcase spill open before him his end would be at hand, his great mission aborted before begun. There were many hours between now and the time for action, hours that he would have to pass with normalcy and naturalness. He must constantly remember that no one had any reason to fear him, to guess at his object. He must simply behave in his usual way and the day would pass without alarm. It would be easy. See, the front gate of the plant was already in sight, the guard lounging in a chair outside.

"Morning, Mr. Brackin," said the young guard quite heartily.

"Good morning," Brackin replied without actually looking at him. He had always felt the young man was making fun of him in some way but had never been able to pin it down. There was something about the warmth of the greeting that made Brackin suspicious.

"Moving in, are ya?" joshed the guard, while Brackin signed the off-hours book.

Brackin did not get the joke. The young man had pointed to the suitcase, but since Brackin had not been looking at him, he could not see. Brackin simply said, "No," and continued on toward his building. He must make no mistakes today.

Brackin made it until four o'clock without slipping up even once and then, while he was seating himself at his desk after going to the washroom, he caught sight of his suitcase out of the corner of his eye and stumbled. He hated to stumble and quickly looked to see if anyone had noticed. Mrs. Talmage, administrative assistant to the boss and guardian of all that is right and proper in both the office and the world, looked away from Brackin. She pretended not to notice with the fine air of someone who notices everything. Brackin went back to his desk. His round face, accentuated by his thinning hair, frowned in concentration as he stared at a report. His eyes, large and vacant, never wavered from the page before him. He began to perspire slightly and knew that Mrs. Talmage was watching him.

Eugene Brackin had been working at Felton Products for eight years. Mrs. Talmage had been there twenty-six, longer than anyone in their department. This made her not merely expert in company history and method, but morally superior to and significantly less removable than anyone else in the office. But Brackin would have been

afraid of her had she been a newcomer without any senior-
ity at all. Mrs. Talmage was a judge, an overseer who with
a barely discernible movement of her head could express
disapproval in a complete and thorough manner. To such
people Brackin always fell short. He consistently satisfied
their feeling of superiority. And Brackin's torment was his
agreement. He, too, condemned himself with the judge.
This was the role Mrs. Talmage played for Brackin. That
was why he had decided to kill her this weekend.

He would not kill Sally Laird. He had definitely sworn
to himself that she would live. As she approached his desk,
he reaffirmed his commitment to protect her at all costs.
Sally was dressed casually for the office. Wearing a denim
skirt and red plaid blouse was her way of reminding everyone that they should have been off today. They were being
paid for it, to be sure, but the honor was not purely volun-
tary, so Sally's casual dress stated her attitude. Brackin,
on the other hand, wore the black suit and white shirt he
always wore on Mondays, Wednesdays, and Fridays. He
wore the black three days and the gray two since the black
was easier to keep clean. Since both suits were slightly too
large for him, he always looked a bit like a recent refugee
wearing a good-quality donation. Sally sat down in the
chair alongside Brackin's desk. She stretched her legs out
in front of her and stretched.

"You know," she said with a reflective air, "if our fear-
less leader, Mr. Lawrence Gaylord, were any more ambitious we'd have to move into the office full-time. Can't you
see us having breakfast together at five A.M. so we could
be at work by six? Mrs. Talmage could run a bedcheck at
nine each night to make sure we were all abed. Would you
like to be roomies, Gene?"

"Oh, come, Sally," Brackin answered, "it's not that
bad."

"Isn't it? I suppose not. Still, if I were running this office
instead of the incompetent eager beaver who got us here
today, we wouldn't have gotten so far behind in the first

14

place. But then I can't really expect to assume a job of that degree of responsibility, can I?"

"Why not?" Brackin asked.

"But Eugene, dearest," Sally said as she moved closer to him, "haven't you noticed? I'm a woman." She made a moue at him and laughed.

Sally was constantly amazed that Gene Brackin had no sense of humor. Whatever you said, he took it literally and seriously. Sally found that both an endearing and a trying quality. "You're right, of course, Gene," she went on, "it's not really that bad. Still, if he doesn't get transferred back to New York soon we'll all perish from overwork. Maybe he won't last that long. Maybe he'll die of something. Or maybe, Gene, I'll kill him."

Brackin was startled. He had decided he would probably not kill Mr. Gaylord, but if Sally wanted to kill him, then perhaps he should reconsider.

"Would you really kill him, Sally?"

"Gene you are impossible. You're not usually this bad. Of course I wouldn't kill him." She shook her head in wonder, and then her attention was diverted by the large suitcase behind Brackin.

"Are you going somewhere?" she asked him.

"Uh, yes," he answered, "after work today."

"Where are you going?"

"Just to my aunt in Cleveland. Just for the weekend."

"That's an enormous suitcase for a weekend. What have you got in there?"

"It's the only suitcase I have. So . . ."

"Well, in half an hour or so we'll be off. Have you seen Gaylord? Has he come out?"

"No," Brackin told her, "he hasn't come out since lunch."

"Okay," she said. "I'm going to give this to him in person to make sure he knows how much work was involved. See you."

Brackin waved goodbye and watched Sally move off. At

15

thirty-one she was fifteen years younger than his forty-six and alive in ways he envied. He liked talking to her even though he could never tell when she was joking or teasing. He often watched her very closely when he could do so undetected. Her movements were loose and easy without being sloppy, and she always had something to say to Brackin, and sometimes they even had lunch together.

Sally knocked and entered Gaylord's office, lost to Brackin's view. Her way with Gaylord was easier than Brackin's. She was informal with him while not being casual. Brackin, on the other hand, was uncomfortable with Gaylord even though he was not afraid of him. Gaylord was a boss, and so Brackin wanted to avoid him as much as possible. One of Brackin's dreams had always been to have an office. A room all to himself where he would always know who was watching him. But such was not to be. He did not get one when he joined Felton Products, and after this weekend he would never get one. Not ever.

Brackin looked at the clock on the wall and then at the double door beneath it. That was the door he had to seal shut. That door was the connection to the outside that Brackin would sever. And with that act he would be closed up, locked up, with these people until he, Eugene Brackin, decided what he wanted. It would be like a marriage—till death do us part. But he couldn't just sit and stare at the door. He had to get up and lock it. He had to begin the adventure. He was not sure he could get up. He did not know if he could force himself out of his chair to seal tight the last years of his life.

He knew he would do it. He had been able to get up and now was sure he would go through with it. He had been planning for a year and was never sure how much he meant it, how much was fantasy. A lot of the time he figured it was a game, a silly drama to keep from being so bored and lonely. Even when he got the supplies together, some food, rifle, chains, he kept mocking himself with the

16

knowledge that he would not go through with it. Well, he was going through with it. He was perspiring, he was pale, he was a little shaky, but he was slowly walking to the door.

He stopped at the kitchenette and had a glass of water. He turned back to the office and ran his eyes over the familiar scene. Mrs. Talmage noticed him and he smiled at her, nodding his head and turning away. He replaced the glass after rinsing it and left the kitchenette. Turning left he walked the ten paces to the entranceway. He opened the glass doors and stepped through. He stood in the small area between the glass doors to the office and the doors to the staircase going down. The doors leading to the outside had matching handles about four inches apart, one on each door. Brackin reached into his pocket and took out a bicycle lock. It was the sort with the long U-shaped piece, with the locking part able to slide up and down to the proper height. He put the U-shaped piece so that the two handles were in its U and then slid the lock into place as far as it would go. It was now impossible to open the door from either side. The point of no return had been reached. Brackin had not brought the key with him.

TWO

The building in which they were now secured was built in the fifties. It was essentially a concrete blockhouse fifty feet square, three stories high, with a yellow brick facade. There were sash windows on three sides which actually opened and a parking lot right behind, so all told it was serviceable. They were the only department on the third floor. Since there was no elevator, they walked the two flights up into the small entranceway. The door to the main office was always kept open during working hours unless a department meeting was in progress. These would take place in the very center of the office at a large conference table. The entrance wall, actually the south wall, also housed the separate washrooms, storage and cloak room, and kitchenette. This last was considered a treasure, enabling anyone who so desired to prepare lunch in the office. During the winter this right was exercised by almost everyone.

Entering the office a visitor would see the conference table directly in front. Beyond the table would be Brackin's desk. To the left of Brackin was Gaylord's office, the only private office in the room. Attached to Gaylord's office was Mrs. Talmage's office, but since she had a wall on both sides she would be invisible to the visitor. Turning right from Brackin's desk the visitor would see two smaller desks aligned to Brackin at right angles. These belonged to Walter Page and Judy Swick, assistants. Continuing along the wall to the right of Brackin one saw the last desk, larger than the other two, which was Sally Laird's. Neither Laird's nor Brackin's desk had walls around it. Mrs. Talmage's desk, across from Laird's, was in a cubicle formed by Gaylord's wall, the back wall, and an additional wall she had acquired through sheer persistence and political clout. She had tried but failed to get a front wall and door. So she was still exposed from the front.

Brackin returned to his desk and sat down. He pulled over his briefcase, the primary function of which had been to carry his lunch, and removed the .45 caliber automatic pistol and holster he had placed on the bottom. He was careful to keep all his activities beneath the level of his desk and so invisible to Mrs. Talmage. He slipped the gun into his desk drawer. He looked around after completing these preliminary arrangements and realized he was quite stiff. He tried to loosen up by twisting his neck about and scrunching his shoulders. As a result his attention was diverted and he was startled when Sally Laird spoke from behind him.

"Stiff neck, Gene?" was all she asked.

"Just a little tight, thank you, Sally."

Laird went by him and cleaned off her desk, an occupation also busying Mrs. Talmage.

"Come on, Gene," Laird called to Brackin, "knock it off and get on your way. Quitting time." Brackin mumbled something and waved her off. He had pondered long and hard about this moment. Should he announce that they were his prisoners? Or should he let them discover it? He knew very well they would have difficulty believing the whole business. Brackin sympathized. Faced with himself as a hostage-taker he too would be hard put to believe it, so he had finally decided that a bit of confusion would be good for his credibility.

Mrs. Talmage had her coat on and was collecting the mail to go into the downstairs collection box. There would

19

be no pickup today, but it would go out first thing Monday morning. She stuck her head into Mr. Gaylord's office and asked if there was any other mail. He rose and walked to the door with several items in his hand. He saw Brackin still at his desk.

"Gene," Gaylord said, "call it a day. Sally told me you're going to Cleveland. Why don't you get on your way?" He approached Brackin's desk and stood looking down at him. "I didn't know," Gaylord went on, "that you had plans to leave town for the weekend. I never would have asked you to come in today. You should have told me, Gene."

"Oh, it's no trouble, Mr. Gaylord. Really."

"Why don't you take Monday off? Stay with your aunt until Monday and come home Monday night?"

Brackin shot a glance at Sally Laird who was now working her way to the doors. She called out a cheery goodbye as she opened the glass inner doors. Gaylord waved goodbye in response and turned back to Brackin. He was still urging Brackin to take Monday off. Brackin was watching Sally. She reached the metal doors to the staircase and slowed down. She pulled at the doors and then at the lock. She pulled at the doors again and turned around to look back into the office. Her expression was puzzled, but not alarmed. She stuck her head into the room.

"Larry," she called to Gaylord, "the doors won't open. There's a lock connecting the two handles together. What's going on?"

"What?" Gaylord asked.

"The staircase doors are locked tight," Sally answered. "I can't get the doors open. Come see for yourself."

"Those doors don't even lock," Gaylord said while walking to the entranceway. "They're just jammed."

"They're not jammed, they're locked up tight with a bicycle lock."

Brackin missed the rest of the conversation but could see Gaylord tugging at the lock while Sally watched. Gaylord turned around and stuck his head in the door.

20

"Who put that lock on?" he demanded. "Is this some-one's idea of a joke?"

"It must be Mr. Brackin," Mrs. Talmage announced. "I certainly didn't put any lock on the door."

"Brackin, did you put that lock on the door?" Gaylord asked. Brackin replied with a nod. "Well that's the stupid-est damn thing I ever heard of. Get it off right now. This minute."

Brackin looked at Mrs. Talmage who was scowling at him. He returned his eyes to Gaylord and told him that he'd thrown away the key.

"Of all the crazy . . . if you didn't want to work today . . . I can't let you pull a stunt like this."

Gaylord reached for the fire ax hanging on the wall in the vestibule. He pulled it off and Brackin stood up. He had completely forgotten about that ax. Now Gaylord had a weapon. Brackin reached for the .45 in his desk and pulled it out. Mrs. Talmage saw it and screamed. Gaylord turned and saw the gun. He quickly turned back and raised the ax to swing. Before he could bring it down on the lock, Brackin fired.

The bullet hit the clock above the door to the entrance-way. But the crashing boom had its effect. Gaylord froze. Sally froze. Mrs. Talmage stopped screaming. Brackin was in control of the situation.

Gaylord and Laird were standing in the vestibule star-ing at Brackin. It was taking awhile for the facts to sink in. Eugene Brackin had just fired a gun at them. He had first placed a lock on the door of the office and then fired a shot when they tried to remove it. Stranger things have hap-pened in history, but not to either of them. They could see Brackin still standing, pointing the gun. Mrs. Talmage was standing off to his right with her hands held high in the air. They couldn't know that Brackin had given her no instructions as yet. She just naturally wanted Brackin to feel as secure as possible. Besides, it seemed right in the circumstances. Given the fine example Mrs. Talmage

21

offered, Gaylord and Laird too raised their hands above their heads.

Brackin signaled them to move back into the room. As they did so he pointed to the couch in Mrs. Talmage's office. Without a word being passed he quickly got everyone seated on the couch. Brackin then moved back toward the vestibule to collect the ax, after which he simply opened the window and dropped it into the bushes. He returned and waved his gun at the prisoners. He moved back once again out of their sight. He leaned against the wall and took a couple of deep breaths. A smile forced itself out of him onto his face. It was a smile of achievement; he was very satisfied with himself. He gave himself a minute to savor the situation, have a few deep breaths, collect his thoughts.

He returned to their view and signaled them all to the conference table. Since Brackin did not speak, they all assumed he wanted silence. Brackin wanted Gaylord at the head of the table with the women on either side. He was trying to communicate this with looks and gestures but it was quickly becoming comedic. A thought occurred to him: How serious do I have to be? How scared do they have to be? The silence was finally broken by Brackin's instructions for seating. But it quickly resumed when he sat at the opposite end of the table. They were clearly waiting for him to say something. Speaking, especially speaking in public, was not Brackin's forte. That's all right, he thought, they can wait. But as soon as he thought it he got nervous and cleared his throat. They looked at him expectantly.

"I'm sorry," Brackin began, "I didn't mean to scare you." That's ridiculous, he thought; of course I meant to scare them. He turned red and started all over. "I mean I don't want to hurt anybody. Really. If everyone just does what I say everything will be all right." He smiled at them.

22

"I just have to do this thing. But you'll all be all right. I mean I don't want to hurt anyone. Really."

Gaylord looked slowly to the women on his right and left and then back to Brackin. He let his breath out very slowly, took another, smiled, and began to speak in the voice of a loving uncle.

"Gene," he said, "I understand. Really I do. We all get ideas to do things sometimes. But you're a good person, a hard worker. Put the gun down and we'll forget about it. You take a couple weeks' vacation and get some rest." He turned to Sally Laird who was sitting beside him pale and hot in her coat. "You know, Sally," Gaylord told her, "it's really my fault. I expect too much of people. I think everyone is as crazy as I am and can only work, not play. I'm sorry, Gene," he continued, now turning back to Brackin, "I've been working you too hard. Give me the gun and we'll pretend it never happened."

"I don't want to pretend it never happened," Brackin replied. "I want it to happen."

"What's going to happen, Gene?" Sally asked.

"I don't know exactly. But we're going to stay here for a while."

"Then I better get my coat off and get comfortable," she said and got up and removed her coat. She went to the cloak room, hung it up, and returned to her seat.

Gaylord turned to Mrs. Talmage and told her to go and make some coffee. To Brackin he said, "As long as we're going to be here awhile we may as well get comfortable. Just like Sally said. I'll be right back. Need the washroom. Sally, why don't you draw the curtains closed."

Gaylord shot Sally a meaningful look and started to move off to the washroom. Sally began to rise while watching Gaylord. Everyone was now moving in different directions. Brackin was moving his eyes from one to the other. Suddenly he stood. "Everyone get back here. Right now. Back here," he commanded. Gaylord turned to him,

23

smiled, and pointed to the washroom. Brackin said, "Now, Mr. Gaylord," and pointed the gun at him. Once again everyone was seated at the table.

"No more of that. No one is to budge without permission. You may think I don't know what I'm doing, but I do. We're going through this. I'm going through this."

"Mr. Brackin," Mrs. Talmage said, "may I sweep up the glass from the clock? Someone is liable to get hurt." As she said this they all turned to look at the wall above the door. The glass case of the clock was completely gone and so were both hands, so that the clock face appeared to stare at them blank and naked.

Brackin let Mrs. Talmage sweep up the glass and then lifted the suitcase that had been behind his desk and placed it on the table in front of him. He opened it up and began unpacking. It yielded a remarkable sequence of articles. The first items were blankets. Four large blankets, each looking quite warm. Next Brackin took out food. There were packages of candy bars, four small boxes of breakfast cereal, instant orange juice, and powdered milk. He next removed a large radio, which he plugged into the wall behind his desk. He did not turn it on.

His audience was obviously stunned. They stared at this show of preparation with wonder, looking at each other as the items were removed. Brackin suspected they began to look at each other with increasing concern. They can see, Brackin knew, that I am serious. He continued unpacking. He pulled out a cloth sack closed with a drawstring at the top. It was fairly heavy and made a clanking sound as he put it down. He did not open it. The last item he removed was a rifle. It was a big rifle and had been placed in the suitcase on the diagonal. In fact, it was the item that determined the size of the suitcase. When Brackin drew it out and into sight he distinctly heard Gaylord murmur, "Ohmygod." Brackin smiled slightly.

He had known all along that he had to do it. At least he

thought he had to do it. When the idea first came he laughed at it, but also started making the preparations right away. He could have gotten ready more quickly, but he enjoyed picking up the items individually. He took a great deal of care in deciding what to take and in choosing the right materials. He spent many hours in his flat checking the suitcase, packing and unpacking. It had made for a very exciting year. But this was even better. He had not expected to enjoy this part so much. He turned now to the work at hand.

"Mr. Gaylord," Brackin said, "would you please go and get Mrs. Talmage's desk chair." Brackin wanted the chair with wheels and waited patiently while Gaylord fetched it. When Gaylord rolled the chair over, Brackin instructed him to sit in it. Once Gaylord was settled in the chair Brackin lifted up the sack he had removed from the suitcase and opened it. He removed from it a set of manacles with a thirty-inch chain. Gaylord gawked. Brackin approached Gaylord and told him to hold his hands in front of him. Brackin put one manacle on Gaylord's wrist, then looped the other through the arms of the chair. The second manacle went on Gaylord's other wrist. Gaylord was now locked into his chair. He still had a fair degree of movement. He could scratch most parts of his body and, by slipping his left hand under the arm of the chair and placing it on his lap, he had enough slack to eat.

Brackin was particularly proud of this invention. His prisoner was safe and secure, could offer him no surprises unless he took his chair with him, and yet he was not very uncomfortable. He stood back and looked at Gaylord locked into the chair and, once again, offered a slight smile. God, he felt peaceful.

Brackin returned to his sack and removed two more sets of manacles. These too had extra long chains. He went into Gaylord's office and came out wheeling his desk chair.

He pointed to Mrs. Talmage and then to the chair. He noticed for the first time that she looked pretty awful.

"Are you all right, Mrs. Talmage?" Brackin asked.

"Yes, thank you, Mr. Brackin. I'm really fine."

"Good, Mrs. Talmage." Brackin knew by now that he was not going to kill Mrs. Talmage. He even admitted to himself that he never really wanted to kill her. She just always made him feel so bad. But this was enough to satisfy him. She was being very careful to be nice and polite. Of course she was always polite. Somehow she could be rude and polite at the same time. Now Mrs. Talmage coughed for his attention. Brackin raised his eyebrows in question.

"Are you going to lock me up like that?" she asked, pointing with her head to Gaylord. "I've never been locked up or tied up, Mr. Brackin. Please. If you don't tie me I won't do anything. I'll just sit here and do whatever you say. I'm very frightened of being tied up like that." She was restraining herself and looking in supplication at Brackin. He got embarrassed.

"You'll be all right, Mrs. Talmage. I'm not going to put yours on like that. Here, watch."

Instead of securing Mrs. Talmage first as he had planned, he went and got Sally's chair and put it beside her. "Would you please sit in this chair, Sally." Sally looked at him with a mixture of suspicion and hostility. She hesitated for a moment, shrugged, and switched chairs. Brackin manacled Sally's left hand and secured the other manacle to the arm of the chair. In this way she could even walk so long as the chair came with her. "Stand up, please, Sally," Brackin told her. "See," he said, turning to Mrs. Talmage, "it's not so bad. You can move and everything. I would be too nervous if you weren't done up."

Mrs. Talmage looked fearfully at the chain connecting Sally to the chair. She shook her head, no.

"Mrs. Talmage," Sally spoke in a very calm voice, "it's very important that no one be nervous. It's very important that we all stay calm and not get upset. Do you understand, Joan? It's really the only important thing to consider. Please cooperate. I know it's hard for you. It's hard for me too."

Mrs. Talmage looked at Sally, then at Gaylord, and finally at Brackin. She cast her eyes down toward her feet and nodded her head. Brackin looked at Sally once, then went over and secured Mrs. Talmage to her chair.

Brackin sat down at his end of the table and smiled at everyone. He wished he'd brought a clipboard to mark off the different stages and events as they happened. Had he brought one he would now happily tick off stage one. He did in his mind. Stage one was complete. His coworkers were locked up with him in their office. Each one was secured to a chair, with Gaylord definitely incapable of making trouble. He could have sat like this for some time. But Sally raised her hand.

"You don't have to do that, Sally," Brackin told her.

"I don't know how to behave. I've never been held hostage before. We are hostages, aren't we? I mean that's what this is all about, isn't it?"

"Well, yes," Brackin agreed. "You are all my hostages."

"Why?" Sally asked.

"What do you mean?" Brackin responded.

"You know perfectly well what I mean. Why are you holding us hostage? What do you want? What are you going to ask for in exchange for us?"

"I don't want anything in exchange for you, Sally."

Gaylord interrupted now. "But Eugene, what are your demands? What's the purpose of holding us?"

"If I didn't have you here they would just come after me. Now they have to wait until I say it's all right. I thought you understood that. Why else would I take hostages?"

"You mean," Sally Laird went on, "that you don't want any money?" Brackin shook his head, no.

27

"Are you making a political statement?" Gaylord tried. "Are you going to demand that something be read over the radio or TV?" Again Brackin indicated the negative.

"Now just a minute, Brackin," Gaylord began. "We are sitting here, locked up, locked in, terrified, with you holding a gun on us. Do you really mean to tell me that you have no reason at all for—" But before Gaylord could finish, the phone rang.

They all stared at the telephone. Only the night line was working. It rang three times before Brackin rose and went to Mrs. Talmage's desk to answer it. At the end of the fourth ring he picked up the receiver. It was Robert Talmage, Mrs. Talmage's husband.

"Hello, Mr. Talmage," Brackin said.

"No," Brackin responded after a moment, "she hasn't left. . . . No, she can't come to the phone. . . . No, she's fine, Mr. Talmage. . . . Well, you see, I'm sort of holding everyone hostage. . . . Yes, I know it's absurd. No, it's not a bad joke. I'm serious. I'm holding everyone hostage. . . . Well, I don't know how to prove it to you. Would you like me to fire my gun?" There were interjections, loud and strenuous, from his captives at this point. "Well, yes," Brackin answered, "perhaps it would be a good idea to call the police. But tell them that if anyone comes into the building I'll begin shooting hostages. . . . Yes, it was good to hear you so well. Bye-bye."

Brackin hung up the phone and turned to Mrs. Talmage. "I always did like your husband, Mrs. Talmage. Is he well?"

"Yes, thank you, Mr. Brackin. He's quite fit lately."

"I'm going to be busy for a while," Brackin informed them. "Please don't move around or make any noises. The police will be here soon and it's important this part go properly so no one gets hurt." He took the phone from Mrs. Talmage's desk and placed it alongside her on the table. "Please, Mrs. Talmage, if the phone rings, just answer it and tell me who it is. Don't say anything you wouldn't normally say." Mrs. Talmage indicated she understood. "You may all talk quietly if you like," Brackin continued, "but be sure to keep it quiet." He picked up the rifle and went toward the windows on the east wall. Just as he was doing so they could begin to hear a siren. Right on time, Brackin thought.

THREE

Mattsfield is a small town with a population of about forty-five hundred. It is located in Ohio, about one and one half hours' drive south from Cleveland. Mattsfield has a high rate of employment, an active chamber of commerce, a healthy Kiwanis, its own hospital, and a police force. The members of the police force—the chief, deputy, and three patrolmen—largely spend their time checking on businesses, tagging out-of-town speeders, and directing traffic during the rush hour. Once in a while something exciting happens. Three years ago a body, never identified, was found in the nearby woods. Two years ago there was a robbery at the local bank. The robber was caught when one of the tellers tripped a silent alarm. Deputy Chief of Police Greg Smolen responded to the alarm by stationing patrol cars at either end of the street. As soon as the holdup car passed they grabbed him. No one ever fired a shot. Dep Smolen became a celebrity, and the small force all basked in their popularity.

The Chief of the Mattsfield force is Cy Turner. Chief Turner's main concerns are political. Not that he wants to run for office, he just enjoys seeing that his job is secure. As a result he largely lets Deputy Smolen run the force while the Chief concentrates on keeping the important members of the town satisfied and happy. He was pleased to take full credit when Deputy Smolen took the bank robber. Chief Turner, after all, had hired the deputy. So, as soon as the Chief heard about the hostage-taking he made sure that his deputy had been informed and was taking action. Immediately after, he set to work calling the plant manager of Felton Products, the Mayor, and the local newspaper. As a result the first policemen at the scene were Dep Smolen and Joe Sloan, the senior patrolman.

They entered the gate office where a security guard informed them that the only people in the entire plant that day were Lawrence Gaylord, Sally Laird, Eugene Brackin, and Joan Talmage. They were all in the marketing office in the middle administration building. Smolen gave some instructions to Sloan and turned back to the young guard.

"I have information," Smolen told him, "that an employee of Felton, Eugene Brackin, is holding the people in his office hostage. So the—"

"Mr. Brackin?" the guard said. "That's impossible. He could no more take hostages than I could fly, Dep."

"What are you talking about? Isn't he in there?"

"Sure, he's in there. But he's a mouse. Afraid of his own shadow. Why if he wasn't embarrassed he'd call us up and have us escort him to the gate when he works late, like we do for the ladies. Matter of fact, he lets Sally Laird call and then comes along. By accident like, if you know what I mean. He couldn't do it."

"I hope you're right. But I can't take a chance. I don't want anyone else let into the plant. No one comes in and no one goes out without my say-so."

Smolen learned that the only other way into the plant was through the rear truck gate, which was locked tight. He gave instructions to Joe Sloan to call the State Police and have the area sealed off. Sloan left for his cruiser and Smolen decided to inspect the building Brackin was in. He was still hoping it was a joke, some wisecrack resulting from their being made to work that was taken seriously. Then why had the woman not spoken to her husband? He had to go look and see. He left the guard's office and jogged along the road to the west side of the main plant

31

building. By the time he got to the rear corner where he could see Brackin's building he was out of breath. Have to do something about that, he thought.

There was not much to see. The whole area was a huge grass strip about as long as a football field but not quite so wide. There were paths connecting the three identical buildings to each other and the plant. Each path was wide enough to take a service vehicle. There were some benches and even a couple of picnic tables in front of each building. Must be a nice spot to have lunch in the summer, Smolen thought. Could use some trees, though. It was very hard to believe that a hostage incident was taking place here. Maybe it wasn't. Maybe it was all a mistake, or, he still hoped, a bad joke. Hell, he'd settle for a malicious, nasty prank before a hostage-taking.

Brackin, watching out the window, could see someone at the corner of the plant building. He considered taking a shot but decided to wait. He turned back to look at his hostages, all of whom were now chained up like Gaylord, making movement more restricted. He got himself comfortable and fiddled with the rifle, which he had never before fired. Looking out the open window he could see the man was still there. He was alone. Brackin was sure he was a policeman. Things were starting to roll.

Smolen was getting impatient. He also had forgotten to tell Joe Sloan to bring field glasses and walkie-talkies. Five minutes later when Joe turned up with both field glasses and radios Smolen nodded his approval. He took the glasses and located what should be the windows of the office while Sloan gave his report.

"Everything is set, Dep. The Chief is getting in touch with all the bigwigs and the press. He figured we better tell them before they find out for themselves."

"Shit," Smolen responded. "I wanted to have the area

sealed off before word got out. We'll have to get the auxiliaries here right away."

"What's happened, Dep? Has he shot? What did he say when you called him?"

"I haven't called him yet. Wait. There he is. I've got him. There's a rifle muzzle sticking out of the window on the third floor. Middle window. Here, take a look." Smolen handed the glasses to Sloan and changed positions.

"Damn straight. It's a rifle barrel, all right. What you figure it is?"

"I don't know. It's probably enough."

Brackin saw the men change position. He could sense, rather than see, the field glasses on him. It was time. He peered through the scope on the rifle until the cross hairs centered on a spot very close to the two men. He moved the rifle so that the front man was in the center of the scope. Then he moved it slightly away. He had still not made up his mind if it was necessary to kill someone. The debate had raged long and hard for six months: Did he have to kill someone to be taken seriously? Would they believe him if he just shot at random? He had finally decided that if he came close, if he looked like a killer who was a bad shot, it would probably do. But he was a bad shot, so there was no telling what might happen. Giving a mental shrug and aiming at the last minute at the brick wall just beside the men, Brackin closed his eyes and tried to gently squeeze the trigger. The noise was less than he had expected. Also, he thought his shoulder would get hurt from the kick, but it was a fairly quiet sound and the kick was not bad at all. He was so pleased that he fired three more shots in quick succession.

Smolen and Sloan were not pleased. The first shot had missed the brick wall and hit the grass about eight inches in front of Sloan who was still holding the binoculars. Both men leaped back out of sight of the rifleman. As they jumped and caught themselves the next volley of shots whizzed by them. These went higher than the first, passing to the other side of the gate. Smolen looked at Sloan and grimaced. "Well," Smolen said, "he's not just fucking around. Let's get back. I want this entire area sealed off. Anything in range. The whole area is to be evacuated. I'll lay it out on a map back at the security building."

They got back to the security hut and Smolen grabbed the phone. He fumbled the dialing and had to start again, concentrating this time. He got through to Mrs. Talmage. Brackin was at the window with the rifle, taking potshots. He was keeping his eyes open now but still lacked accuracy. It was fun.

"Market Analysis, Mrs. Talmage speaking. May I help you?"

"Mrs. Talmage. Are you all right?"

"Yes, of course, sir. Who do you wish to speak to?"

"Is Brackin there?"

"Yes, but he may be busy at the moment. Who may I say is calling?"

"Deputy Chief of Police Smolen, ma'am."

"One moment please, Deputy." Mrs. Talmage put Smolen on hold and called out to Brackin, "Mr. Brackin, there's a Deputy Smolen on the phone for you. Can you take the call? Or shall I tell him you're busy?"

Larry Gaylord's eyes were popping out of his head. Brackin turned back into the room, put the rifle down on a desk, and nodded to Mrs. Talmage. "Thank you, I'll take it." He took the phone and said, "Hello, this is Eugene Brackin."

"Hello, Mr. Brackin. This is Deputy Chief Smolen. Is it true that you are holding three people hostage up there?"

"Yes, it is."

"That's a terrible thing to do, Mr. Brackin. You're going to get into a lot of trouble. You're already causing a lot of trouble."

"I'm sorry, Deputy. I don't mean to cause you any trouble."

"Like hell you don't. What do you want, Brackin?"

"I don't want anything."

"What do you mean, you don't want anything?"

"I'm sorry, Deputy. I really don't want anything."

"Then what are you doing up there with three hostages?"

"I'm holding them. What else would I do with them?" Brackin was getting as confused as Smolen.

"Just a minute," Smolen said. "Let me see if I've got this right. You're locked up in a building. You've been shooting at me with a rifle. You've got three hostages. And you don't want to make any demands? Is that it?"

"Well, no. Not really. And I'm sorry I shot at you. I just didn't want you to come closer."

"Sure. Great. Shoot at me anytime you want to. Just tell me what your demands are."

"I demand that no one come into this building. No one. If anyone comes into this building I'll shoot a hostage. I mean it."

"You got it, Brackin. No one goes into the building. See how easy it is? What else do you want?"

"I mean it, Deputy. I have excellent ears, and if I hear anyone or anything in or around this building you're going to have a dead hostage."

"Brackin—take it easy. I'm going to do whatever you say. As long as I can I'm going to give you what you want. Got it? Just stay loose."

"All right. Now listen to me. There's a flagpole that runs from the roof of this building to the ground. The line for it is about three feet in front of the window. Did you see it?"

"Yeah. Right. It sticks out from the center of the building. What about it? You want some strange flag up there? PLO or something?"

"No. And don't make jokes. I'm serious. I want to use

35

that rope to bring in food and anything else I want. Right now I want four dinners. Everyone is hungry. Put them in a basket or something like that."

"What kind of dinners do you want?"

"I don't know. Hang on a minute." Brackin put Smolen on hold and turned to his audience. They had stopped talking when Brackin had started shooting.

"Are you going to kill us?" Sally Laird asked Brackin.

"No,". Brackin said with hurt in his voice. "I already told you I won't kill you if you do what I say. Don't you believe me?"

"What if he won't cooperate? What if the cops make a mistake?"

"Well, that's not really your fault, is it? Do you think I should kill you if they do something?"

"No," Gaylord almost shouted. "You're absolutely right, Eugene. You have a very fair attitude. Don't you agree, Sally?"

"Oh, of course, Mr. Gaylord. I think it's very fair of Gene to capture us like this. Now I don't have to make that awful drive home tonight."

"But you live nearby," Brackin said.

"What are we having for dinner?" Sally asked to change the subject.

"What would everyone like?" Brackin asked.

"What have you got?" Gaylord asked him back.

"Well, I don't know," Brackin answered. "Whatever we want, I suppose."

"How about some roast chicken?" Mrs. Talmage inquired. "That's what I was going to make tonight."

"Doesn't really turn me on," Gaylord told her. "What about some Chinese food? They have a good takeout place on Cleveland Street."

"I'd rather not," Sally said, "I get flushed and woozy from Chinese food. How about hamburgers?"

"I don't know," Gaylord mused. He was about to go on

36

when Brackin interrupted him. "I'm going to see if we can get steaks. Everyone likes steaks."

Brackin took Smolen off hold and requested four steak dinners. It took awhile to get the orders right since everyone wanted his steak done differently. Gaylord was especially concerned that it not be overdone. They all wanted baked potatoes, but two wanted sour cream while two wanted only butter. Deciding on two French, one Thousand Island, and one Roquefort finished off the exercise.

"All right," Smolen finally said after repeating the order, "here's the deal. You have your dinner party, make a speech, and come on out. When you come out tonight make sure I expect you. I don't want anyone getting hurt by accident."

"No. Not tonight. We're spending the night here. Definitely."

"Look, Brackin, I'm being very nice and patient. I'm cooperating here and I expect you to do the same. You've gotta come out tonight."

"No," Brackin said. He was getting excited now and started to turn red. "No, we're not coming out tonight and that's final. Don't ask again."

"Brackin, if you don't come out tonight this whole thing is going to get very complicated. We're gonna have to do all sorts of things and call all sorts of people who—"

"Stop it," Brackin screamed into the phone. "Don't tell me what to do. I won't have it. I demand you stop that. That is my demand."

"Right, Brackin. Whatever you say," Smolen soothed. "You got it. I didn't mean to upset you. I'll go get your dinners. Don't go away."

Brackin turned back to the room. His three prisoners were holding their breath. Sally Laird had turned quite pale. For the first time they began to appreciate their plight. Gaylord's eyes had widened and his head was pulled back to his chest. Mrs. Talmage was biting her

37

lower lip to keep the tears back. Brackin looked at them and then away again. He shook his head back and forth a few times and waved his hands. He suddenly had a thought and got out the keys to the manacles. He smiled his biggest smile and began to unchain Sally and Mrs. Talmage. He secured them in their original positions. "There. You'll feel better now," he told them, as he stood over them beaming. He picked up the rifle and hefted it in his hands; it had been fun to shoot. "Don't you feel better already?" he asked.

No one answered.

FOUR

Smolen had a lot to do. The guardroom was too small and crowded to serve as a headquarters, so he sent Joe Sloan to get a trailer from a local construction firm. They would set it up near the truck entrance and seal the main gate. He also wanted to fix up a television camera on the roof of the plant buildings with a monitor in the HQ trailer. He didn't know if that was necessary or not, but once he thought of it he wanted to do it. Besides, he knew that Chief Turner would like it. The auxiliaries had sealed off the area to vehicular and pedestrian traffic, and state troopers were on their way. Smolen had absolutely no intention of letting the staters take over his show, but he could use the manpower.

He had just sent out for the dinners when the Chief came in. He, naturally enough, wanted to know what the hell was going on. Smolen gave him a rundown of everything that had taken place so far. He held back any evaluations and just gave the details. He was right about the Chief's liking the television camera. That was the only statement on which he commented.

"So what do you think?" Chief Turner asked his deputy.

"I don't like it, Chief," Smolen answered. "He doesn't want anything. That's what scares me. He's just up there with a gun and some hostages and he's not even sure of what he's doing."

"Can we flush him out?"

"Not without risking the hostages. The door is locked

39

up and he says he'll shoot if he hears anyone in the building. I'd be afraid of the risk."

"So what do you want to do?"

"The only thing we can do is sit tight. Give him what he wants and hope he gets tired of it. The stuff I've read says to talk to him as much as possible. Establish a relationship."

"Establish a relationship?" Chief Turner echoed. "How do you do that with a nut case?"

"He doesn't sound very nuts, Chief. He's not a killer, if you know what I mean. He doesn't sound so crazy unless he gets upset."

"For God's sake, Greg, don't upset him."

"No, don't worry. I'll be careful. I'll just talk to him as much as I can. See if I can find out what's happening."

"Okay. Any way I can help?"

"Yeah. The staters are coming and I don't want them running all over my program. See if you can get them to take orders."

"I'll try, Greg. I've got a bunch of reporters out there at headquarters. They all want to come in and see for themselves. I've got to let someone in or they'll scream bloody murder. Any favorites?"

"Why not Ida Crane? She always gives us a fair shake. If she gets in on it she'll owe us a bunch."

"Good. If we picked anyone else they'd scream. Great." Chief Turner looked around and took in the surroundings. He waited for a moment and then spoke again. "Look, Greg, I don't need to tell you to be careful here. I trust you all the way. You got here first, so you'll stay on it. I'd rather have it that way. But these Felton people are very big in town, and a day's work to them is a lot. So if it's possible to get it wrapped up quick . . ."

"Sure, Chief."

Chief Turner grimaced and left. He was already preparing his statement to the press and deciding who else had to be called now that it looked like a siege.

40

Smolen took telephone calls from the Captain of the State Police, a vice president of Felton (his name was Barry Newman and he was the only VP in town for the weekend), and the Mayor. He made each call as brief as possible, referring all inquiries to the Chief. When he was finished Smolen sat down in a chair and thought. How do you establish a relationship with a madman? He has to be a madman. Only a lunatic would lock up three people and hold them hostage. But he had to have a reason. Some reason. Maybe God told him to do it. Maybe green banshees threatened to eat him if he didn't do it. Maybe it just seemed like a good idea at the time. But if he decided to do it, then he can change his mind. Even a madman can change his mind. But if he's nuts you never can figure out why he changes his mind. I've got to get his confidence, Smolen thought. I've got to get him to believe me. He's got to trust me. How can I get a madman to trust me? If he's really mad, then I can't even figure out what to do. So figure he's not mad. Or figure he's not very mad and see what happens.

Dinner had been a relatively cheery affair in the Marketing Analysis department of Felton Products. Aside from Gaylord's mutterings about the overdoneness of his steak and the discomfort of eating while chained, the repast was very cordial. The transfer of food had worked quite well. Gaylord had been unchained and, while Brackin held the rifle on him, he caught the line which connected to the flagpole. The line was now secured inside the office and would, as Brackin had planned, be used for further deliveries. Brackin was pleased and enjoyed the role of host. He never entertained at home. His small apartment in an older, once-grand private house did not permit it, though, as he knew well, living in a mansion would not have changed anything. Brackin had no friends. There was no one who would come to his home to spend time. No one who would enjoy an evening spent with Brackin. People

41

go out to someone's house for pleasure, for amusement. They never go when they expect to have a bad time. Unless they have to. If they have to, if the boss invites them or something like that, then it is a different story. Then they come whether they like it or not. Even if they have to pretend they are enjoying themselves.

"Is everything all right?" Brackin asked the company at large.

"Oh, just fine, thank you, Mr. Brackin," Mrs. Talmage answered, smiling around the table to indicate her satisfaction was shared by all. "Will I be able to phone my husband after dinner?" she inquired.

"Not tonight," he replied with regret. "Maybe tomorrow."

The phone rang and Mrs. Talmage answered it. She extended the phone to Brackin, telling him it was from Deputy Smolen.

"Had a nice dinner?" the Deputy asked.

"Very nice, thank you," Brackin replied. "You have been very accommodating, Deputy. I am grateful."

"I'm glad to hear you say that, Mr. Brackin. I was concerned the food might have been cold by the time it arrived. By the way, may I call you Eugene?"

"Oh, certainly," Brackin responded graciously. "I would be delighted. And the food was not cold at all." Brackin held his hand over the receiver and asked the group if anyone had gotten cold food. All indicated the food had been just right.

"Well, I'm glad you're pleased, Eugene. Really, I am happy that you're happy. Those people in there mean a lot to me and I wouldn't want to see anyone hurt."

"No, no," Brackin insisted, "no one is going to be hurt. I wouldn't hurt anyone."

"Good, Eugene, I'm relieved. Well, it sure sounds like you're having a better time than I am."

"Are you having a bad time, Deputy?"

"Sure am, Eugene. Everyone from my boss to the Mayor to the captain of the state troopers to the vice president of Felton Products is on my back. What do you think of that?"

"There's a vice president there?"

"He's the least of my troubles, Eugene. You've got to help me out."

"Is the Mayor there now? Is the Mayor with you?"

"Look here, Eugene, these people are giving me a hard time about this. Are you going to help me or not?"

"Why should I help you?"

"Well, didn't you say I'd been so nice to you?"

"Sure, but not because you wanted to. I'm not stupid, Deputy. If I called you up from my home and asked you for a bunch of steak dinners you'd lock me up. That's what you'll do to me when I get out of here. You've been nice to me so I won't kill anyone."

"Brackin, listen to me. You've got to come out now, tonight. This thing has got to end right away. Immediately."

Brackin had eased out his chair and put his legs up on the table. He was shaking his head sadly. "No, Deputy. That's not my plan. That's not my plan at all. We're staying here until I decide we move. Not you. Not the vice president. Not even the Mayor. I, Eugene Brackin, will decide the fate of what happens." And he hung up the phone.

Brackin looked around at his captives and put the .45 caliber pistol on the table in front of him. "I'm going to let you stay unchained for a few minutes. Mr. Gaylord," he said, "you can go to the bathroom and stretch a bit. I'm also going to let you two ladies stay unchained. But no one must get up or move without asking first. Do I have your agreement?"

They each indicated assent, and Brackin went around and undid Gaylord first. When Gaylord was unchained, he told them, he would unlock the women. Gaylord went to

43

the bathroom and had a wash-up. He came out quickly and did some stretching and bending. He walked around for a few minutes and then shrugged at Brackin. He was once again chained to the chair, but this time only on one side. When the ladies had been to the toilet and returned they found themselves seated round the table in a not unfamiliar pattern. Gaylord was sorely tempted to make a joke about getting to work but instead he looked at Brackin, cleared his throat, and spoke.

"Eugene," Gaylord began, "it's time you told us what's going to happen. We've been very cooperative and so on, and we really want you to tell us what's going on."

Brackin surveyed them defensively. What did everyone want from him? Why didn't they believe him? There was no secret message he had. If he knew anything they didn't he would tell them. He turned away from Gaylord and went over to the window. He pulled back the curtain and peered around. Even in the dark he was afraid to put his head outside the window, but by leaning against it he could still make out the corners of the buildings. He could see lights in the trailer on his right near the truck entrance.

He thought of shooting at them with his rifle but doubted that would help. He had a sudden memory from long ago, from when he was a child. He was standing in a field next to an adult. The adult was pushing him on the shoulder and he was stumbling ahead with each push. He was eight years old then. Maybe nine. He could smell the spring mud, strong and heavy. The grownup, he was pretty sure it was one of his foster fathers, was wearing denim overalls. Old ones. Brackin would wait until the man was alongside him. Then when he could see the denim, when he could grab at the overalls, the man would push him ahead. The man wanted Brackin to flush birds, ducks or pheasant or something from the bushes. But Brackin was scared the man would shoot him. He couldn't remember the man's name or face, probably never knew either. Brackin was brought back by Gaylord's insistence.

"Eugene, you've got to tell us now. You've got to."

Brackin had picked up the rifle while at the window. He had been holding it loosely in his hands, and while his mind ranged back he had cradled the rifle in his arms. Now Gaylord was still at him. Got to, Brackin thought, always got to. Brackin slowly turned toward Gaylord, the rifle in front of him. He stood, now, with the rifle muzzle pointed directly at a suddenly silent Gaylord. Gaylord was perspiring. He looked steadily at Brackin. Gaylord did not know what to do. He had taken no leadership as yet. He had not led the others aside from demonstrating the need for cooperation and calm. But he felt somewhat cowardly. As if there were more he could be doing. He must not be afraid. He must assert his leadership by showing that firmness and calm would keep them alive. He knew in his heart that Brackin would not kill them. How could he kill people with whom he worked? How?

Gaylord sat upright in his chair. With the rifle pointed at him he looked directly at Brackin. "I know, Eugene, that you can kill me. You can kill all of us. But that is entirely up to you. We have done you no harm. I feel perfectly free in my mind that I have been scrupulously fair to you. Even on that promotion business I felt I was doing the right thing." Why the fuck did he mention that? What did he have to bring that up for? "You have got to let us go. Now." Gaylord had not meant to make a demand for release. But Brackin was looking at him so calmly he thought it might work. "Please unchain us this minute." Command mixed with supplication.

Brackin felt so calm. Brackin felt so sure of himself. He raised the muzzle of the rifle very slightly. He was beginning to feel comfortable with the weapons, as if the simple possession of them made him competent. He sighed softly and felt the wood stock firm in his grasp as he fired the

45

rifle. The bullet did not touch Gaylord. Go find your own damn birds, Brackin thought.

"Eugene!" Sally Laird screamed at him. "What are you doing? You're not a killer. Stop it." She was shouting at him. Standing by the table with her fists balled up in front of her. Behind her Mrs. Talmage was also standing. Shaking her head back and forth as she moved around the table toward Brackin. "Joan, don't," Sally said to Mrs. Talmage with alarm. "Don't. Come back here."

Mrs. Talmage continued to approach Brackin. She walked slowly up to him and stood before him. They stared at each other for a long time. Mrs. Talmage had pink blotches on her cheeks from heightened emotion. A slight tremor went through her body as, without making any conscious decision of her own, she slapped Brackin hard on the face. The imprint of her hand was clear on Brackin's cheek. Once again his mind became his memories and the feeling of the slap was familiar. But this time he kept in contact with Mrs. Talmage. She was bringing round another slap, which Brackin blocked with the rifle. Mrs. Talmage hit the rifle with her hand, hurting herself. Brackin put the rifle down on the desk next to him. He reached out before him to Mrs. Talmage's dress front. He laid his hands on the clothes of one of the most modest and primmest people in the world and pulled down on the collar with all his might. The dress came away from her with a rending. Brackin pulled at the material again and again until it was completely free in his hands. He tossed it to the side just as Mrs. Talmage went for him. But she was too late. Had she not slapped and really charged before, she might have stood a chance. Brackin was not a very strong man and Mrs. Talmage had once been a gymnast of sufficient ability to think of the state finals. She was still trim and fit for all her sixty-two years. Before she could lay a hand on Brackin he pushed her away. His hands pushed against her breasts, covered now by a beige full-length slip. He noticed as he pushed the softness of her breasts and the pliancy of her flesh. She went down. Brackin watched her on the floor. The slip was very lacy but the skin it revealed was older and worn. He was curious and repulsed at the same time.

Sally Laird went to Mrs. Talmage. She was as concerned to prevent any further attacks by her as to comfort her. She knelt down and asked if she was all right. Brackin had taken the dress and thrown it out the window. "That's the way you'll stay," Brackin told her while pointing at her with an accusing finger. "And you're going to be chained up again. Now. Quick." Mrs. Talmage made no move, despite Sally Laird's efforts to help her up. Brackin picked up the rifle and pointed it at Gaylord. "If you don't move right now I'll shoot Gaylord." Mrs. Talmage got up and sat back in her chair. After signaling Sally to sit in her seat on the other side of the table, Brackin chained up Mrs. Talmage. "You both turn around," he told Gaylord and Sally, who turned away toward the windows. Brackin put the rifle back on the desk behind him. He removed the pistol from his holster and placed it firmly against Mrs. Talmage's head. "Are you going to do that again?" he asked her. She shook her head, no. "Are you sorry?" She hesitated and Brackin pressed the pistol closer. Mrs. Talmage nodded her head, yes. Brackin reached his free hand down over her shoulder. He put his hand on her left breast. Her breast filled his hand and he squeezed softly. He released his hand and tightened again. Brackin could feel her nipple on his palm. Reluctantly he let her go and went back to the head of the table.

FIVE

Deputy Smolen was well set up now. The trailer, parked alongside the eastern office building, jutted out past its protection just enough for one window to afford a clear view of the open space between plant and offices. The TV monitors—Sloan had gotten two of them—showed the window of the office and the front of the building. Both cameras were set in fixed positions without cameramen. Smolen had refused, however, to place a state trooper sniper up on the roof. Lieutenant Garlas from State Barracks had been insistent but Smolen stood firm. Smolen's opinion was that the more guns there were around the more somebody was likely to get hurt. Smolen had just gotten off the phone with Chief Turner, who was warning him of an impending visit by the Mayor. He had just finished his 9:00 P.M. check with all outposts when Joe Sloan, watching the monitors, called him over.

"Look here, Dep," Sloan said, pointing to the monitor covering the front of the building.

"What is it?" Smolen asked him.

"I don't know, Dep. I was watching the window monitor when I saw that thing fly out. It looks like clothing. Women's clothing. What the fuck is he doing in there?"

"I don't know. Let's try and find out." Smolen went to one of the radio phones and called to a cameraman to get on the roof and focus on the garment lying on the ground in front of the building. The cameraman got as tight a shot as possible and asked if that was good. Smolen told him to

48

freeze on that shot. He could now clearly see the dress for what it was. "The bastard is raping them," Smolen said and went for the phone.

This was the first time Smolen had really felt anger at Brackin. Before, the strongest emotion he could arouse was annoyance. Why was Brackin intent on spoiling a nice fall weekend? But that was the extent of it. He had not really dwelt on the possibilities. Had not really taken the time to consider what he might or might not do. But now he was angry. Angry and scared. The son of a bitch had him by the short hairs and there was little he could do about it. But if the bastard was going to rape or hurt them, then they would go in. Tear gas and all. He would not stand around playing amateur psychologist while Brackin raped and maimed. No way. The phone was picked up on the third ring. Brackin had to reach over and get it himself since Mrs. Talmage was no longer capable. "Hello," Brackin said.

"What's going on up there, Brackin? What's that lying outside the building? Have you hurt anyone?"

"No, Deputy, I haven't hurt anyone. But someone tried to hurt me. Did hurt me. But I haven't hurt anyone."

"Let me talk to them, Brackin. I want to hear them all."

"Of course, Deputy. Everyone will say hello."

Brackin got up and carried the phone and receiver around the table. As he reached each person he held the receiver for them while they checked in with the Deputy. Mrs. Talmage, speaking first, told the Deputy she was fine and had not been hurt. She just answered his questions, not trusting her voice. Gaylord was more voluble. He explained to the Deputy that Brackin had gotten upset when they had pushed him too hard. He was very eager that Smolen get his message. "Brackin," he said, "seems to have grown more short-tempered this evening. Understandably, of course." Sally added no information to Smolen's store of knowledge except to tell him, by answering questions that Brackin could not hear, that no one was raped and that it was Mrs. Talmage's dress.

Brackin took the phone back and asked Smolen if he was satisfied.

"How did the dress get out there, Brackin?" Smolen asked.

"Mrs. Talmage got very warm," Brackin joked, "almost hot." Brackin looked over to Mrs. Talmage who was now blushing furiously.

Smolen hung up the phone and turned around. He had acquired an audience during the conversation. "There's been no rape," he told them by way of a greeting.

"Well, that's certainly good to know," Mayor Brian Kowal said. He turned to Chief Turner and Ida Crane, the remaining members of the group, and asked if anyone had known there might be a rape. They all indicated it was news to them. The Mayor turned back to Deputy Smolen. "Well, Deputy," he said, "why didn't we know?"

Smolen told him what had just happened. In fact, he briefed them very fully right up to the present time. One of his tricks with politicians was to brief them the same way he would the Chief. They were never able to stand that much detail, so they got bored and went away. It worked this time with Mayor Kowal, and he took the Chief back out with him. Ida Crane, as Smolen had hoped and expected, stayed. He sent Joe Sloan out for some coffee and offered her a seat.

Ida Crane was as close as Mattsfield ever came to a celebrity. She was a very young sixty-one-year-old and had been a newspaperwoman since she graduated college forty years ago. After working her way up to the job of editor in chief of the Mattsfield *Voice* she finally bought the paper. Even though there had only been three people between Ida and the editorship, everyone knew she would have made editor at *The New York Times* if she had wanted to. The adult population of Mattsfield was about three thousand; discounting families there is a possible readership of about two thousand, maximum. But the Mattsfield *Voice* prints and sells ten thousand copies every week, many going by mail to old Ohioans all over the country. To everyone in town she was Ida and, unless you tried to bullshit her, she was always your friend.

"Glad to see you here, Ida," Smolen told her.

"Chief tells me you got me the exclusive, Greg. So thanks to you."

"I'm just being selfish, Ida. I want to pick your brains."

Smolen gave Ida Crane the whole shot, all the information he had. When he got to the part about Joan Talmage, Ida whistled but did not interrupt. When Smolen had finished she explained.

"Joan Talmage and I were in school together. In high school she was bright and pretty. A real athlete, too. Was a crackerjack gymnast; she made it to the state finals when she was in Mattsfield High. She and I were the only two girls then to go to college from Mattsfield, you know. Weren't many who went in those days. And when they did it was to junior college, not Cleveland State University. I hope she's all right."

"I think she's okay," Smolen told her. "She sounds like she's had a shock, but I don't think she was really hurt. Are you still friends with her?"

"No, not really. We run into each other now and again. Once in a while when we do we'll talk about having lunch, but nothing ever comes of it."

"Did something happen?"

"No, nothing in particular. You see, Greg, when she and I were young if you behaved the way we did you were kept at a distance. So we had this bond, really an artificial bond, if you see what I mean. All we had in common was the character to do what we wanted. In those days that was

51

enough. But she quit before she graduated and married right away. Instead of finishing her education she became a secretary. That would have been all right with me, but she never got back on the track. After a while I realized I had been sort of snubbing her for not keeping the faith or something like that. But when I stopped it was too late. Every time she saw me she'd be embarrassed. My fault, I guess, but I was young. I had tremendous demands on myself and everyone around me as well."

"Ida, I'm playing it real easy with this guy. Do you think that's right?"

"What are your choices, Greg? Shoot it out? Blow him up? Even if you didn't mind killing him, which you should, you'd still have dead hostages."

"But what if he's bluffing? What if they all come out and demand to know why we didn't go in? What if they know he's full of it? How'll I look then?"

"Who cares how you look? All you care about is getting those three innocent people out alive. And if you can also get what's-his-name out alive too, great. Don't forget that for a minute. Not for a second. This whole business is not being staged for anyone's benefit. It's just happening."

Brackin and his captives were sitting around the conference table. The episode with Mrs. Talmage had thrown a pall on what was earlier a surprisingly relaxed evening. Sally Laird had been wondering at how they were able to adapt and go on being human in a singularly inhuman situation. They had been sitting around, chained to their chairs, under threat of death by someone they worked with, and they had all been careful not to interrupt each other, to ask politely that the milk for the coffee be passed, and to appear attentive to whoever happened to be speaking. The threats behind breaches in this form of behavior were much more severe and deep than any Brackin could offer. His had to be flourished every little while. They would forget constantly that they were in danger of losing their lives. Even Mrs. Talmage, sitting in her beige slip, the lace at the top not quite masking her cleavage, had begun to relax.

Sally was particularly interested in Larry Gaylord's difficulty. Mrs. Talmage was sitting to his left in her underclothes. While she was, Sally allowed, undeniably on the wrong side of youth she was far from deformed or even unattractive. I wouldn't mind, Sally thought, being as trim as she when I'm her age. She wondered how someone who was so blatantly prudish could have so much obvious concern for her body. Why not? She doesn't have to hate it, just be a little ashamed of it, that's all. But Gaylord, poor thing, didn't know where to look. If he avoided looking at Mrs. Talmage altogether, Sally thought as she suppressed a smile at the pun, he makes her near nudity very obvious. On the other hand, it wouldn't do to stare at his assistant as she unwillingly sat before him in her slip. Gaylord's solution was to look directly at Mrs. Talmage's face when he looked at her at all. She wondered if he was aroused? She wondered if he could be aroused. He was such a sexless twit. He had nothing going for him except being a man, and at Felton, Sally knew, that was enough. Gaylord had been their department head for six months. And for six months Sally seethed as she watched him botch the job that should have been hers. The contempt she felt for Gaylord was enormous, sometimes seizing her by the throat when she had to address him. But she was not without friends at Felton, and they knew very well just how angry she was.

Sally was cognizant of her own reactions. She was not nearly as frightened as she ought to be; there was something about Eugene Brackin that just failed to terrify her. And at the same time she was fascinated by the show that was unfolding before her. Years ago, as a child, she would sometimes foment trouble between friends, cementing her role as leader of the clique. She was always entranced when

53

these episodes occurred, watching with disinterest the results of her interventions. But this was not a result of her actions, not something arising out of a plan of hers, and yet she retained the same feeling of being an observer rather than a participant. She would participate, she knew, but only when she had a sense of the outcomes, of the results and how they might affect her. Her most disconcerting moments occurred when she noticed the nude clock face staring down at her without time to tell. There was something about it that spooked her, that made her feel that they had been catapulted out of time into a world of their own. She forced her attention away from the clock, back to the scene around her.

Gaylord was once again trying to persuade Brackin to make some demands. He was still recovering from the shot Brackin fired at him. At him? About him. Gaylord had never been truly terrified, had never fought in a war, been really afraid for his life, but when Brackin fired that shot he thought, for a moment, that he was going to die. He felt impelled to action, and the action available to him, both through circumstances and inclination, was speaking. He was being very careful not to push Brackin, but to lead him into a discussion of being rich and traveling. He wished to hell that Sally was more helpful. He was, to be frank, disappointed in her. She was normally very resourceful and innovative, and if there was one thing they could use at this moment it was resource and innovation. But Sally had been sitting quietly, seemingly absorbed and distracted, in a world of her own. It was as if she were an observer of the ordeal rather than a participant. Gaylord continued talking to Brackin, going on about the joys of wealth and the peace of mind a great deal of money could bring. He was careful to include both women in the conversation. He tried hard to make eye contact with Sally and draw her into the circle, get her to help him. Maybe she would realize that if Brackin made no demands, changed nothing, they could be here forever.

Mrs. Talmage was beginning to come around, Gaylord noticed. He also included her in his chat, and she was beginning to respond. Her breathing was settling down, and the lacy edge of her slip moved slightly up and down with each breath. He tried hard not to look at her chest, but you could only control your eyes so much. He had never thought of her as attractive, or as unattractive for that matter. But there was something now that every once in a while made it slightly difficult to swallow. On his other side was Sally. Every once in a while she would move her chained arm to reach for her coffee cup. That chain was driving Gaylord mad. On the one side he had Mrs. Talmage, not exactly ravishing, in a slip that befitted a real turn-on and which was not really wasted on her. On the other side he had Sally, who had always done it for him though he had been careful to conceal it, locked up in chains. The situation had possibilities. Or, rather, other similar situations had possibilities. If he were in control instead of Brackin the possibilities would be limitless. Gaylord suddenly cut out this line of thought and brought his full and complete attention back to what he was saying. But it was too late. He had an erection.

Shit, Gaylord thought to himself, not now. What'll happen if he makes me stand up? And why the hell isn't Laird being any help? But Sally Laird was too caught up in Gaylord's dilemma to notice anything else. She somehow sensed exactly what happened and when it happened. She looked at Gaylord and, for the first time in two hours, made eye contact with him. She smiled very slightly with a minute tightening of her lips, and Gaylord knew that she knew. I'm not, she thought, being much help. Here's poor Mr. Gaylord trapped between near-naked and chained women and all I can do is watch. The dreamlike quality to everything that had passed so far stood between her and action, between her and thought. It was as if everything was happening in a slow motion replay for her observing pleasure rather than going on right then and there. But it is, she thought, and slow motion or not, I should help.

Gaylord now openly broached the topic with Brackin. As long as he had three nice healthy hostages why not ask for money? Why not ask for a plane to fly him to Algeria? Why not ask for two million dollars? But Brackin was not interested. Oh, he wouldn't mind having a lot of money. Though he had no particular desires to indulge, it seemed to be the sort of thing one always wanted. That was not why he would not ask for it.

"Why not, then?" Gaylord asked. "Why don't you make them come up with some dough? You've got them where you want them."

"They'd kill me," Brackin told him. "If I ask them for anything like that, if I try to get away, they'll kill me."

"No, Eugene," Gaylord contested, "they'd let you get away to save us."

"Never," Brackin said. He had thought this out quite fully and was not going to be swayed. "Don't you see, Mr. Gaylord, everyone who gets killed when they take hostages gets killed escaping. Sometimes hostages get killed then too, you know. I don't want to get killed."

"But what about us?" Gaylord insisted. "You can't keep us here forever. You've got to let us go."

"Oh, I'll let you go. Don't worry at all about that." But then Brackin looked at them sharply and added, "If you cooperate and I don't have to kill you, that is."

"Look, Brackin, I don't understand. You keep saying—" Gaylord began.

"It's really very simple, Mr. Gaylord," Sally broke in. "Eugene is not going to hurt us. He has no intention of harming us at all. Right, Eugene?" She looked at Brackin with a soft smile and he nodded back. "You see, Mr. Gaylord, Eugene is doing this with us because there was no one else. He is going through with this, and when it is over we will be released. Unharmed." Brackin was nodding and smiling through Sally's explanation.

"But why?" Gaylord implored. "Why is he doing it? That's what's driving me nuts. Why?"

"Why would you do it?" Sally asked Gaylord.

"What are you talking about? I would never do something like this."

"What if you did? Imagine that you did it. What would be your reason?"

Gaylord looked at Sally. He was desperately happy that she had returned to life, but did not know what she was up to. Why would he hold hostages? Well, the evidence he had, which was, thank God, subsiding, indicated the situation was not anathema to him. In fantasy, of course. But that's not why he would take hostages. Once he had them he might be tempted to indulge his fancies, but he couldn't be sure if he would or not. Would probably depend. But he wouldn't do it in the first place for sex. He wasn't a rapist, he just had an active fantasy life. But why would he take hostages?

"Answer Sally, Mr. Gaylord. If you were in my spot, why would you have done it?" Gaylord noticed that Brackin's question was not a demand. There was no hint of threat in the statement, just interest.

"Very well," Gaylord began, "why would I take hostages?" He cast his eyes away and up to his right, inclined his head slightly to the left, and leaned as far forward as his restraints would permit. "The only reason I can really think of is money. Maybe if I was really broke and out flat, really trounced on for a long time, I would pull a big stunt. I would ask for about half a million. Maybe start at two million and work my way down. And it would be planned to a T. I would know just how I was getting away, and where I was going."

"Do you think you'd get away with it?" Sally asked him.

"Probably not," Gaylord admitted. "Those schemes always seem to fall apart at some point or other. You get the whole thing set, arrive in Brazil or somewhere, and they take your money and throw you in jail." Gaylord looked across at Brackin. "No," he admitted, "I wouldn't expect to escape." He was about to ask someone else what they would do when he had another thought. "But one thing I'll tell you," he insisted, "I'd never actually do it. I'd never really kill my hostages." He was careful to look at Sally and not at Brackin. "No matter what, it would only be a threat to get what I wanted. Never touch them."

"What if you had to?" Brackin asked him. He had been sitting and listening to Gaylord with fascination. "What if you had to defend yourself?"

"Oh, well, sure," Gaylord hesitantly concurred, "I suppose if I had to defend myself, then I might have to hurt someone. But I'd never kill anyone." Gaylord was pleased to see Brackin nod his agreement.

"That's a poor reason, Mr. Gaylord," Mrs. Talmage intoned. "Putting people, innocent people, in danger for money, for your own selfish ends, is hardly worthy." She was looking directly at Gaylord; sitting straight in her chair with her head up she looked much revived.

"Then why would you do it?" Sally asked her.

"To make a statement. To bring attention to some great injustice. To focus people's minds on the anger and hurt someone is experiencing. That's the only reason."

"But you would take hostages," Gaylord pointed out, "and maybe have to hurt them."

"I would take hostages," Mrs. Talmage agreed, "but I would hurt no one. Under no circumstances would I hurt anyone. That would be perfectly clear to me."

"How would you control them?" Gaylord pushed, "How would you get them to do what you said?"

"I suppose I would have to frighten them. I imagine I might have to closet them up in some way. Yes," she said with a glance to Brackin, "perhaps chain them up. But if it came to it, if I was forced to choose between hurting one of them and giving myself up, I would end the game."

But Gaylord was not satisfied. "What if one of them

58

attacked you? What if one of them got the drop on you? What then?"

"No difference. Under no circumstances, for no reason, would I harm them." She turned her head now and looked squarely at Brackin. "They did not choose to join my adventure, they did not want to come with me, and they should not suffer because I had something I must do." She turned back to Gaylord. "Do you understand that, Mr. Gaylord? It's a question of letting people make their own choices."

Gaylord looked at her thoughtfully. "I think I understand, Mrs. Talmage. Remember, this is a game. I never would take hostages in the first place. But tell me, what statement would you make? What would be so important that you would do something like that?"

They were all slightly surprised to hear Brackin answer. "That doesn't matter," he said. "Now you," he pointed at Sally. "You tell us why you would do it."

Sally felt real for the first time since becoming a captive. She finally felt her body and the chair and the people around her. She lifted her chained arm up to the level of her head. The chain drew against the chair as she did so. She looked at each one of them and settled finally to stare intently, with wide-open eyes, at Brackin. "There's only one good reason to do it," she said and waited three moments for the suspense to build. "Power. That's what it's all about. You do it for power." Brackin let out his breath. He was alone in a universe with Sally.

"But would you kill?" Gaylord was asking. "Would you hurt anyone?"

Sally Laird continued to stare at Brackin as she answered Gaylord's question. "Of course," she said, "if you have to."

"Christ almighty," Gaylord muttered. "You're nuts, you know that?"

"No," Sally answered him, "just realistic."

SIX

Brackin had turned on the radio. He and his hostages were sitting around the conference table and this was the first report they listened to. They were tuned to the local station, which would, at this time, have the best coverage.

Good evening, ladies and gentlemen. This is WMAT in Mattsfield, Ohio, with the late evening news. The big story tonight here and across the nation is taking place right in Mattsfield. Earlier today, about 4:00 this afternoon, a man armed with guns took three hostages at the Felton Products Plant in the Western Industrial Park section of Mattsfield. The gunman has been identified as Eugene Brackin, an employee of Felton Products for eight years. The three hostages, all coworkers of the gunman's, are listed as Lawrence Gaylord, Joan Talmage, and Sally Laird. Police as yet have no clue as to why the hostages were taken.

The report went on to describe the events of the day with a degree of accuracy and lack of sensationalism that gave Deputy Smolen, who was also listening, confidence in his choice of Ida Crane as liaison. No one else could have gotten the media to take it easy. The report included the story of how Robert Talmage had discovered the kidnapping and reported to the police. Chief Turner came on assuring people that everything was under control, that no one was hurt, and requesting that people stay away from the area. He added that extensive roadblocks had been put up and there was nothing to see. The final part of the report was an interview with a psychologist at the University.

Hostage-taking, the psychologist explained, is a severe form of antisocial behavior. It exhibits an inability to cope with reality and use the means of communication available to normal people. Such people tended to be desperate and, yes, potentially dangerous and violent. Did he think that all hostage-takers were insane within the meaning of the law? Not within the meaning of the law, the psychologist answered, but that showed an error in the law, not sanity in hostage-takers. This last especially pleased Brackin, who had decided that hospital would be better than prison. But either would be better than anything else.

As soon as the report ended the phone rang. Brackin did not seem surprised to hear from the Deputy. Smolen told Brackin that he had spent an hour on the telephone with other police departments, his own headquarters, the vice president of Felton, the Mayor, and various media people.

"Eugene, I'm doing the best I can to hold everyone off, but their patience won't last forever. I think you better come out tonight."

But Brackin was adamant. He would not stop now, but yes, he promised the Deputy that no one would be hurt or molested. Brackin was not quite sure what the Deputy meant by molested, but he agreed anyway. Brackin noticed that the Deputy sounded tired and suggested rest. Smolen wanted to take Brackin's advice but decided to try one last shot. He asked to speak to Gaylord and, for some reason, was not shocked when Brackin just said, sure.

When Gaylord was on the phone Smolen asked how everyone was. Gaylord told him they were all right, or as all right as could be expected in the circumstances.

"Listen, Mr. Gaylord," Smolen said, "do you have any

idea of how long he wants to keep you? Has he said any-thing?"

Gaylord looked over to Brackin and smiled. He had not been told to watch what he said, but he did not want to rile Brackin. "No," he answered cautiously, "I have no idea."

"Do you think there's any way in? Could we storm the place? Is the door really sealed?"

Dammit, Gaylord thought, he's asking too many ques-tions at once. "Yes, it is. The door is sealed very securely." He looked once more at Brackin and saw nothing but a slight smile. Emboldened, he continued. "I think it would be impossible for you to get anyone in here without our getting hurt, Deputy."

"All right, Mr. Gaylord. You sit tight and I'll try to keep the hotheads at bay." Then they exchanged good nights and rang off.

Brackin now set about bedding down his company. It took a fair bit of locking and unlocking, placing and re-placing, but he finally got it all organized without a hitch. Gaylord was firmly planted in the narrow area between the ladies' room and Mrs. Talmage's office. One of his arms was secured to a radiator, the other was free. He had a blanket large enough to roll up in and provide minimal comfort on the uncarpeted floor. Better, Gaylord thought, than being dead. He helped as Brackin took away his jacket and watched as he emptied his pockets, carefully turning them inside out. He needn't have bothered. Gay-lord had absolutely no intention of trying an escape. Not tonight, anyway.

Mrs. Talmage was chained by one arm to the couch in her office. She too rolled up in her blanket, assisted by Sally Laird. Mrs. Talmage refused to let Brackin come near her, so he got Sally to help him. Finally, he ushered Sally into Gaylord's office where he told her she would be chained to the couch. Gaylord's office was the prize suite with a large soft couch and, most important, privacy.

"How come I get the honor?" Sally asked him. Brackin smiled at the floor and blushed, but did not answer. "Come on, Gene," Sally encouraged, "what made you give me the nicest spot?"

Brackin still did not look at her full out, instead sneaking a glance from underneath. He cleared his throat and said very softly, "Because you're the nicest person."

Sally looked at Brackin as he blushed furiously, and smiled. "That's very sweet of you, Gene. I think you're very nice too." Sally watched him struggle for a moment and then decided to move the proceedings ahead. "Do me a favor, please, and hand me that blanket before you chain me up." Brackin gave it to her and she wrapped it about herself. As Brackin watched, Sally's blouse and then skirt appeared. Each garment was laid carefully atop Gaylord's desk, followed by a brassiere and pantyhose which were more simply plopped atop the pile. Brackin tried not to stare at the clothes. "I couldn't sleep with clothes on, Gene. I hope you don't mind. You can lock me up now." The blanket went right round Sally, falling down over one bare shoulder like a sari. Sally held her exposed left arm out to Brackin as she lay down on the couch, ready for bed.

Chained and alone, Sally lay awake thinking about the day. Tomorrow, she knew, would be long. Tomorrow would be a day for action. Not like today. Today was for watching, for trying to understand and figure out. She was not like Gaylord whose solutions had to be immediate and obvious, simple and aggressive. No, Sally would watch and know what to do when the time was at hand, when they woke up hostages and faced a day together. When they weren't in a state of shock. And when she was not so confused, so unsure of what was really happening and why. I'll get out of here alive, she thought, but I may be able to do

63

even better than that if I can figure this whole thing out.

On the other side of the wall from Sally, Mrs. Talmage lay shivering in her blanket. It was not cold and it was not from a chill, at least not that kind of chill. She muffled her sobs and fought to control her breathing so that Brackin would not hear her crying. Deep, long, slow, regular breaths. Like when she was preparing for an event. This is certainly an event, she thought, an event that was entered and now could not be lost. This time she had to follow through and win. When dinner had come she had noticed the rope to the flagpole. If she could get to that rope she could slide down it. Or at least she could have forty years ago. But it was not possible now, and, anyway, they couldn't all get out that way. She wondered how the others were doing but had no way of communicating. But it would have been no use since both Sally and Gaylord were already asleep.

Brackin, after he had turned out the lights, had climbed atop two desks put end to end. This, with a blanket, was to be his bed. He did not want to be comfortable. He was never a sound sleeper, but especially tonight he must stay alert. He did not expect to fall asleep very quickly and lay there staring at the ceiling with open eyes. He could hear Mrs. Talmage across the room, and occasional noises as Gaylord moved in his sleep. Brackin's own breathing was short and shallow. His mind was racing and spinning through the most important day of his life. Was it really the most important? he wondered. There had been other days that were important. He couldn't remember them just now, but this was not the only one. There was the day he stopped being a virgin. He remembered that day very well. He hadn't made the choice then either. Like now it had been made for him.

He was in Cleveland in order to attend four days of seminars at a marketing convention. He had been thrilled when he was chosen and then became anxious for the three weeks until he went. Brackin's life was completely a matter of routine, and traveling upset that routine. When he arrived in Cleveland he spent all his time at the seminars. Many of those attending would skip some sessions and hang around the hotel or go out drinking or shopping. There was a lot of talk of getting some action. Brackin was afraid that if he missed any sessions someone would find out and he would get in trouble. And besides, he had never had any action and now was afraid he would not know how. He did not want to look foolish.

Brackin was enjoying himself at the seminars. He liked the big hotel with his clean and efficient room. He enjoyed taking his meals in the restaurant and especially enjoyed signing the checks with his room number. He even went to the bar the second night and had a drink there. He did not mind at all that no one spoke to him. Why should they? They did not know him. And anyway, he enjoyed watching all the goings-on. He enjoyed watching old acquaintances run into each other; he loved listening to people being introduced; he sat for a long time pretending to read while absorbing the conversations around him. You could learn a lot being at a convention.

The third night Brackin decided to go for a walk after dinner. He left the hotel and began walking this way and that. He knew if he got lost he could just take a cab back and so did not concentrate on his route. It was a big city, so Brackin stayed on well-lit streets to avoid trouble. But many of the well-lit streets had very little traffic on them and did not really feel very safe. Brackin began to feel uneasy. He had a sudden sense of isolation as if he were totally alone in an alien environment. What could he do if there was trouble? He did not even know which way to run. Then suddenly he heard footsteps behind him. His whole body went chill and he became rigid. He was terrified of moving his head or of showing any indication of fear. Then, just as suddenly, the footsteps stopped. Brackin could feel his body let go and now desperately wanted to get back to the comfort of the hotel.

He turned around with the thought of trying to retrace his steps and nearly walked into a large black man. Brackin could hardly speak but managed a swallowed "Excuse me." The black man looked him over slowly, his eyes slightly hooded, his head tilted to one side.

"I know," said the black man slowly, "what yore lookin' fo'."

"I want to find my hotel," Brackin said, almost pleading. "I'm lost."

"Yore not lost," said the black man. "Yore in just the right place. Here, man, come with me."

The big black man took Brackin by the arm and led him up the street to a small side street. They turned along the smaller street and Brackin stopped. He was nauseous now and thought he might throw up. He wanted to run. He wanted to tear himself away from this man who would kill him, hide somewhere safe, somewhere secret. He turned to the man to plead for his life, to beg that he just take his money and let him go. The black man looked at him and smiled.

"Doan worry, man," the black man said, "ain't nothin' bad gonna happen to you. I know this place. It's a good place. You be fine here." The black man smiled at Brackin and then said, "Gimme twenty dollars, man, you be just fine. Lotsa fellas get cold feet, but you be just fine."

Brackin reached for his wallet and took out two tens. He handed them to the black man who just kept smiling at him. Brackin was staring at the man without blinking. He knew this man could kill him. He knew this man had killed many other men. He had killed many other weak white men who had lost their way and violated his territory. The twenty dollars was a toll, a tithe paid to pass through because the black man saw that Brackin meant him no harm. The black man could sense Brackin's harmlessness. Brackin let his body relax. He let his arm go free in the black man's grasp so the man would see that Brackin was weak and not worth killing. The black man smiled at Brackin and led him on up the street.

They entered a poorly lit hallway past a sign that said Duke Hotel—Rooms. Brackin grew confused and frightened once more and he started back at the door. But the black man just increased his pressure and continued making his reassuring noises. Brackin followed in tow up two flights of stairs to a door with the number 11 on it. They stopped in front of the door and the black man knocked twice. There was some shuffling around inside and then the door was opened by a black woman with red hair, wearing a red kimono. It was tied loosely around her waist. Brackin could see the beginning of her cleavage and the rise of her breasts. For an insane moment Brackin thought the black man had brought him home to his wife.

"This here is Rose," said the black man, indicating the woman before them. "She'll take good care of ya. Won't ya, Rose?" He rolled his eyes to the top of his head so Rose would know he had a real peach for her. Rose was smiling at Brackin now. She could see he was terrified and thought she might be able to get another ten from him. Ten bucks that her man did not know about was ten real good bucks to Rose.

"Sure, honey," she said with a smile, "you just come in here with Rose and we'll have a good time."

"I'll be waiting downstairs," said the black man and, letting go of Brackin's arm, he retreated down the hall.

Brackin was relieved to see the man go. He stared after the huge figure and tried to swallow. He felt like he was strangling. His throat was so constricted he could barely breathe. As he told himself the man was not going to kill him he relaxed marginally, and just at that moment Rose touched his arm. Brackin spun to face the new terror before him. She certainly could use a knife. All these women were expert with switchblades. He spun his head from side to side looking for an escape route but saw only the staircase with the enormous black man waiting at the bottom.

"Don't you worry, honey, no one can see you here. You're perfectly safe. Your old lady won't never find out nothin'. You come on in here with Rose and we'll get comfortable." She pulled him into the room and stood him in front of the bed. With a little push at his chest she made him sit down.

Brackin looked at Rose again. She was very attractive. Her face was hard and her eyes had a hungry needy look, but her body was slim and muscular. She let the robe fall open and Brackin could see her bare breasts. They were full and creamy chocolate like the rest of her skin. They stood out at Brackin like two enormous bulging eyes watching him carefully. Brackin's own eyes must have looked just as large and protruding. He had begun to realize his circumstances and what Rose was. He could not stop staring at her. She had slipped off the robe completely now and stood before him stark naked. He tried to keep his eyes away from between her legs but they were drawn there against his will. He drew his head back slightly and looked almost directly across toward Rose's bushy black crotch. She stood with legs apart and drew her hand slowly up along her leg to her crotch where she let it stay. The sight of her hair through her fingers was startling. Brackin tried to swallow. He had never been with a naked woman before.

Rose looked at him and shook her head. She didn't know if he was a virgin but was damn sure he wasn't a big shooter. What the hell, a buck is a buck. "Come on, honey," she said, "stand up and I'll give you a hand."

Brackin did as he was told. Rose drew him nearer to her and began to take his jacket off. "You just relax," she cooed, "and leave everything to Rose."

Brackin was completely helpless. He could neither think

nor move. Rose had removed his jacket and was unbuttoning his shirt. All the while she was soothing him and touching him more and more. Brackin's terror was at war with his fascination. One moment he was ready to bolt and the next he was weak and transfixed. Rose moved her hands to his belt. He flinched at the sensation of a strange hand at his pants and pulled away.

"Don't get scared now, honeybabe," Rose whispered, "you doin' just fine. Rose ain't gonna hurt you. Rose ain't hurt you yet, has she, honeybabe?"

Brackin weakly shook his head no.

"See, honey, you safe with me. Rose knows how to make you happy."

She put her hands gently around his neck. Her arms were outstretched and she moved toward him very slowly until her breath touched his face. She began to touch her face and hair to his shoulders and lightly moved her hands down around his back and under his shirt. Brackin shuddered and Rose drew him slightly closer.

"There, honey, I told you it would be all right. Rose never hurt anybody."

Rose moved her hands down his back to his waist, continuing along his waist to his belt buckle. This time Brackin did not flinch. His pants dropped away and Rose moved her body next to his. Brackin could feel her heat and smell her musk. He was paralyzed. He felt her nipples against his chest like two points of pure intensity. Rose stepped back and once again sat Brackin on the bed, while she kneeled to untie his shoes. As she knelt before him she placed her two hands at his waist and ran them down, over his shorts, along his leg. She removed his shoes and socks and pulled the pants off. Once again she made the stroking gesture along his thighs and legs. The third time she easily hooked her hands into his shorts and pulled at them. She pushed him flat on the bed with one hand and then removed his shorts all the way. Brackin was, for the first time since a child, naked with a woman.

Twenty minutes later Rose looked at Brackin lying next to her on the old frame bed.

"Well," she said, "you sure doan say much, and you sure doan do much, but at least you work okay. You better get dressed now, honey, it's time to go. Come on," she said while pulling him up, "I got work to do. Sylvester'll take you back to where you safe. Let's go, upsy daisy."

Rose helped him dress and relieved him of twenty dollars. He watched her take the money and wished she would take it all. But he said nothing. Rose was ushering him out the door now muttering all the while about the strange folks she met in her line of work. Brackin stopped and looked at her. He looked at the floor for a moment and wet his lips. He had found some saliva again and was willing to risk speech.

"Thank you," he whispered.

Rose smiled at him and told him he was welcome. Brackin watched her close the door as he slowly headed for the stairs. He did not even dread meeting Sylvester again. He was tired in a way that was not familiar. It was a new feeling. He went down the stairs and Sylvester met him there.

"Doan you look the satisfied one." Sylvester beamed. "C'mon man, I'll take you to your hotel."

Sylvester steered a dreamy Brackin back to the hotel. Brackin got his key and went to his room. He undressed and lay on his bed. He did not want to shower and lose the scent of Rose on his body. He fell very sound asleep and did not stir until morning.

PART TWO
Saturday, November 28

SEVEN

Brackin was having a nightmare. Not the sort that wakes you screaming and shouting; not even the sort that finds you suddenly sitting bolt upright feverishly establishing your whereabouts. This was just the sort that makes you want to wake up and leaves you staring off to one side with eyes wide open and body filled with despair at such self-punishment. He slowly sat up and looked around. He moved quietly to the window and looked out at a sky alive with flying clouds. He checked his watch by holding it up to the light of the moon and saw that it was five o'clock in the morning. He sighed softly and went to sit on his bed of desks. Wrapped in his blanket with knees pulled up against his chest he studied the room around him.

It occurred to him that he alone could get up and walk to the window, examine the night sky, and stretch his legs. And as he sat on his desks in a bundle, he laughed to himself, and was suddenly taken by an idea. He should immediately release them. Right now he should rouse them, release the chains, break open the door, and send them out. He'd go with them. Wouldn't Deputy Smolen have a shock. Imagine the four of them dropping in on him. The idea tickled him immensely and he came close to moving and doing it. But then he knew it wouldn't work. He hadn't had them long enough. He wasn't ready to give them up. No, it wasn't worth it just to have a joke on the Deputy. He'd kill them instead. First he'd kill Sally. He didn't want her to suffer, to know that he'd killed the others and she'd be next. He'd shoot her in the head, no the chest, no the breast. No the head, that's the quickest, least painful. He'd sneak in while she was asleep and shoot her in the head. Right between the breasts. But then the others would get up and start screaming. He'd use the rifle on them. He'd get Gaylord next. He'd sit right here on his desks, maybe even with the blanket pulled up around his legs. Comfortable. Then he'd start shooting at Gaylord. God, he'd jump around. Not being a very good shot it might take awhile. Like at the fair. But he'd practiced a little with the rifle and would probably get him with a few shots. Then Mrs. Talmage. She'd beg. She'd plead for mercy and promise him anything if he'd spare her. Why should I spare you, he'd ask. Who are you for me to save? He'd watch her beg and plead, maybe for an hour. He'd shoot around her, high and low, purposely miss her just to get her good. That would be a lark, Brackin thought.

Suddenly, as instantly as the light going off, Brackin knew she wouldn't beg. Mrs. Talmage would just stare at him and tell him to do what he wanted. Well, he had never intended to kill them anyway; even her, really. He admired the way they were all taking it. It had to be hard, being chained up all the time. He would have been bawling a long time ago. A slow wave of depression came over him and he laid his head on his knees. When he next moved it was light out, and he could hear the clanking of Gaylord's chains.

It was about seven when Gaylord slowly opened his eyes and, without seeing anything, closed them again and began to stretch. As he spread his arms out from under the blanket he could feel the chain of the handcuffs attached to his wrist. He stopped moving and turned his head over to the right where he could see the chain. In a sudden panic Gaylord jerked hard at the chain, struggling at it with all his strength. He put his free hand on the chain and pulled against the radiator, but could not budge it.

74

The panic slowly gave way to a feeling of despair and then melancholy. It would have been nice to awaken and find it was all over. To learn that somehow Brackin had left and the police were waiting for them with breakfast and reassuring smiles. There would be many interviews and the police would ask them thousands of questions. But then there would be peace. He'd see to it that they each got a week's holiday to recuperate. Definitely. He could swing that for sure. He'd go to New York. See his kids and his wife. Eat good. Be a celebrity around the main office. Might even speed his return to New York. Maybe this whole thing will turn out all right. Maybe this will get me out of exile and back to the real action. Brackin won't kill us. He's obviously nuts so no one better take any chances, but he won't kill us.

Gaylord turned over on his side. He ached from sleeping on the floor and couldn't really get comfortable. He remembered getting word of his promotion. Great promotion. Get to live high and wild in Mattsfield, Ohio. Why did his bitch of a wife have to have an affair with a vice president? Why with his vice president? And, let's get down to basics, why did he have to call him on it? Why couldn't he keep his big mouth shut? This was all his own fault. He didn't care who his wife slept with, no more than she cared who he slept with. So why complain? It was all too much for Gaylord and anyway he had to pee. He clanked his chains a couple of times like a cranky ghost and waited to see if Brackin responded.

Gaylord remembered the scene with his wife after he got the word. It was like a Japanese ritual dance. Choreographed. The two of them making movements all around each other without ever touching, without ever making contact. He had told her that he got a promotion, but that it meant going to Ohio for a year or so. Then he'd probably come back as an assistant VP. He knew she really loved New York; so did he. Did she want to come with

75

him? He'd understand if she said no. Well, she'd come with him, of course—if that's what he wanted. Did she really want to live in Ohio? No, but she'd go with him anyway. Really, though, he'd be all right. He could understand her not wanting to go. Really, it would probably be better if she didn't, he told her. He'd have nothing to do but work and run such a great shop he'd be back in no time. Perhaps then, she conceded, if that was what he really wanted, it would be best for her to stay. The children wouldn't have the shock of moving or changing schools. Sure, he agreed, it would be best that way. Now Gaylord had to shit real bad as well as pee, so he leaned up and tried to peer around the corner to find Brackin. He saw him over by the window folding his blanket.

He clanked his chain again and this time got Brackin's attention. Saved at last, he thought. Brackin came over, chained Gaylord's hands behind his back, and then released him from the radiator.

"I have things to do, Eugene, that are very difficult with my hands behind my back."

Brackin stared at him. He was not getting the point. Gaylord tried again. "Eugene," he whispered now, "I have to take a crap. I can't wipe my ass with my hands behind my back. I'd also like to wash up and get my jacket and tie back on."

"I won't let you loose."

"I'll make you a deal, then. Release the chains and cover me with your gun while I go into the men's room. There are no windows in there, so you don't have to come with me. When I come out I'll reconnect myself for you. You won't have to do a thing. Those things just snap together, right?"

"Yes, they do. Okay," Brackin said. He could see no other way and it did not seem very risky.

"Thank you, Eugene," Gaylord said. "I assure you I have no intention of trying to escape. In fact, I'll tell you a secret. I'm a coward."

While Gaylord was in the washroom Mrs. Talmage awoke. Brackin approached and told her she would be able to wash up when Gaylord was finished. They studiously avoided eye contact with each other and their conversation was excessively polite. Joan Talmage knew that would not do. Nothing that created additional stress beyond the very nature of their circumstances should be allowed. It was, therefore, beholden upon her to break the strain. She must not push Brackin or make him feel uncomfortable. Please God, she thought, let him feel relaxed.

"Mr. Brackin," she began, "you and I had an unfortunate run-in yesterday. I want to apologize for my part in that encounter. I was frightened and should not have attacked you. I promise to watch myself more closely and try not to alarm you."

"Oh, dear," Brackin said, "it wasn't all your fault. I shot at Mr. Gaylord, remember? That must have been terrifying. I think you have all shown great restraint and cooperation."

"Thank you. It is comforting to be appreciated. I hope, now, that we will be on better terms."

The rest of the world was also awakening. Deputy Smolen had already been in contact with the Chief. Twice. It seems that quite a few people were upset about the incident. And they were especially upset it was not yet over. Since the Chief of Police is in charge of maintaining the public safety they naturally turned to him. He felt the attention uncomfortable. He liked to be pleasantly inconspicuous. Especially when people were unhappy. So he put the heat on Deputy Smolen. He in turn asked the Chief what in hell he was supposed to do. The Chief hung up.

It was nine o'clock in the morning, and if Brackin wasn't up it was time he got up anyway.

"Hello, Brackin, this is Deputy Smolen."

"Hello. Good morning, Deputy."

"Is everyone all right?"

"Yes. Fine. What do you want?"

"What do you mean, what do I want? I want you out of there. I want those people released. Now, Brackin. It's time to let them go. You've had your party. Let them go."

"Not yet. Not today."

"Today, Brackin. Now. Right now."

"No. Not today."

"Brackin I'll come in there. I'll come right in there and kick the shit out of you. Do you hear me?"

"No. Not today. I won't let them go today."

"Brackin, do you know what will happen if I come in there? People will get hurt. People will get killed. Your friends. You. Me. We might all get killed. Then you'd be responsible for all that."

"Tomorrow, Deputy. I'll let them go tomorrow. I swear."

"And Brackin, if you're dying, no one will care. No one. No one will even pay any attention. Do you hear me, Brackin? I swear it."

"Tomorrow. I said tomorrow. Stop it." Brackin was raising his voice.

"Everyone will hate you if I have to come in there, Brackin. And everyone will ignore you. Completely."

"If you don't stop that right now someone will get hurt, Deputy. I mean it."

"You're not going to hurt anyone, Brackin. You don't want to hurt anyone. You told me that and I believe you. You don't lie. Do you?"

"No. Stop it." Brackin had been feeling good and now the Deputy was confusing him. He pulled the phone away from his ear and stared at it a moment. Putting the receiver back to his mouth, he said in a large voice, "Someone is going to get hurt and it's going to be your fault. Your fault. Now stop it for once and for all." Then he slammed down the receiver and broke the connection.

Smolen sat with his arms on the desk in front of him. He lowered his chin to rest on his arms and stared with pursed lips at the telephone. He had no idea about what had just gone on, but he knew Brackin was faking. Brackin was not as angry as he pretended. His anger was an excuse to get off the phone. He was sure of that, but was much less sure what it meant. Probably the hostages were safe for a while.

Brackin turned to Gaylord and Mrs. Talmage. He avoided their eyes and walked to the kitchen. Holding up a package of four boxed cereals he asked which kind they wanted for breakfast. He put up water for coffee and kept himself busy in the kitchen. He had not received a reply to his breakfast inquiries, so he placed the little boxes on the table. He also laid out teaspoons (the only kind available), cups, milk, and sugar. Gaylord took Rice Krispies and Mrs. Talmage helped herself to the Special K. Brackin fetched the boiling water, poured it into their cups, sat down, and took a Raisin Bran.

"Did you mean it?" Gaylord asked him.

Brackin pretended not to know what he was talking about. He gave Gaylord a puzzled look and turned to his cereal. It was hard eating with a teaspoon, but it was easier to pick out the raisins. He liked Raisin Bran but always ate the raisins and the bran separately. First a raisin, then a spoon or two of cereal.

"Did you mean it when you told the cops you wouldn't let us go today?"

The cereal flakes were beginning to get wet. Brackin could never make up his mind whether he preferred them dry and crispy or wet and soggy. The chewing was better when they were crisp, but the feel of them soft and mushy was nice in his mouth. Maybe if he had two bowls, one with dry cereal and one with milk.

"Brackin, we need to know. You can't keep us in sus-

pense. You said you don't want to hurt us. But not knowing is hurting us very badly."

"Not today," Brackin said. He finished his cereal and
took his bowl to the kitchen. Returning to the table he
picked up his coffee and went to his desk. He took the rifle
off the top of his desk and began to play with it. The rifle
never pointed at his hostages, but Gaylord asked no more
questions. Instead he reached over and turned on the
radio. It was almost nine thirty and the news should be on
soon. Gaylord kept the volume down in order not to disturb Sally, who was still asleep in his office. Gaylord envied
her the couch. It was a large couch, long and wide. Good
for sleeping on.

But Sally was not really asleep. Brackin's conversation
with Smolen had woken her. She lay on the couch warm
and comfortable. There was no reason for her to get up.
Why should she go out there? What could she do? There
would certainly be nothing to do, and at least in here she
had some privacy. Besides, she had not figured out how this
whole situation affected her. She needed time to work that
out. She didn't want to make any mistakes; she needed to
know how to use any opportunities that arose.

She had gone to bed wearing only panties, carefully
draping herself with the blanket Brackin gave her. She had
considered getting to him last night, but he seemed too
distraught. She would have to reassure him today. Later
today. But now, as she went to scratch her belly, the chain
of her manacle rubbed against her breast. The metal was
cool against her flesh and her nipple was instantly erect.
Sally drew the chain gently back and forth across her
breast while her free hand found its way down below her
waist.

Sally amused herself in that early morning softness with
the feel of the chain against her skin. She thought of chains
and being chained and then of chaining. Who should be
chained? Hmm. Chain Brackin? For what? Heh. Don't
need chains for Brackin. Chain Gaylord. Gaylord covered

80

in chains. Chains from his wrists and legs and around his waist. An image arose of Sally dressed in her smartest tweed business suit with her high Spanish boots, the skirt coming down just over the top of the boots. She looked smart and authoritative, crisp and efficient, and good, sexy. Gaylord is in her office, chains hanging from him like seaweed from a mermaid. She sits at her desk and beckons him over, legs out before her, leaning back in her desk chair. She gives him instructions for the day: Mind yourself today, Gaylord, no nonsense, see to it that you act smart or you'll pay for it dearly. Hmmm. Go get me a coffee now, then shine my boots, and then, then I may have an interesting use for you, little boy. Unnn. Yes, ma'am, yes, ma'am, whatever is your wish, ma'am. Oh, you are such a good eunuch, Gaylord, such a happy little boy. Oh, uhn, hmmm.

With her gentle and very quiet masturbation completed the chain held no further erotic appeal. Nor did the prospect of another day with her charming colleagues led by their new leader, the one and only, stark raving mad, genuine certified looney, Mr. Eugene Brackin, Sir, please. Sally did not know if she could stand a whole day of his watching her. He was continually looking at her, as if she could somehow tell him what to do. He almost always looked at her before he spoke to anyone else, especially if he was answering a question. If only she knew what he wanted. If she were holding everyone up it would be for money. A lot of money. A couple of million dollars. At least enough money to get away and start something big. She was impatient waiting for Gaylord's job; tired of hoping he would go back to his holy New York so she could take over the department. Better to go to Argentina and buy a plantation or a factory. Could you still go to Argentina? Maybe you have to go to Algeria, which would not be so nice. Maybe she should get Brackin to take them to Argentina. Maybe she should get Brackin to take her away and get caught in the process. Fantastic. She'd talk him into running away together. They'd collect a ton of money and run away to Fiji or someplace he'd like. Then while they were getting out and the others were safe . . . or should he knock off Gaylord so she could get her promotion . . . no, cancel, I didn't think that. Anyway, she'd be a hero or, rather, heroine. They'd probably give her anything she wants. Make her a VP or an assistant VP, at least. And probably get killed in the process, of course. No, I don't think I'll muck around with crazy people this month, she decided. But I damn well better be nice to him, maybe confuse him a little. And I better let Gaylord know I have a plan so if anything good happens I can take credit for it. No, I didn't mean that. I just want to get us all out of here. Still, she was aware of her fascination, aware that there was some strange attraction for her about the situation. A mingling of fear and, yes, excitement, that made her want to see the adventure to its conclusion. Adventure, she thought. What a word for this horror show.

Getting Sally out of the office was, at this moment, the topic under consideration outside. They had all finished breakfast and listened to the news. The radio promised a ten o'clock special report on the Mattsfield hostage-taking, but in the meantime they had, except for Brackin who seemed fascinated beyond all reason with his rifle, nothing to do. Which was not at all true. Gaylord had nothing to do. Mrs. Talmage, as always when not on the job, was reading a large paperback novel, and while it looked almost finished, she was comforted by the presence of a fresh four-hundred-page gothic romance in her purse. She would be well occupied this day. She had wheeled her chair near the window where she sat, comfortable and apparently content, reading in the sunshine. She still wore only her beige slip with the lace bodice. Her knees were well exposed and it seemed to Gaylord that she made little effort to hide her legs from Brackin, though he was fairly convinced his imagination was overworked.

Gaylord had been covertly observing Brackin. Unlike the others who had shed their clothes, Brackin had slept in his. His trousers were rumpled and his shirt creased. His suit coat, off during the night, was not in bad shape, but it was never in good shape, so that was not saying much. Brackin needed a shave and a hair combing. He was bald at his pate and the hair along his sides was all askew. Every so often Brackin would run his hand along the side of his head and smooth the hair down. It did not help. Brackin had a slight tic on the upper side of his right cheek, Gaylord noticed. It was not very bad and most of the time you could not even notice it, but it was there all right. Every time he twitched Brackin would look up, slightly startled. That meant it was a new tic, not one he was used to. As long as his hands stay steady, Gaylord decided, I don't care if the rest of him flies apart. But I don't want him pointing guns with twitchy hands. Or maybe I do. Maybe he meant to shoot me yesterday and missed. I could be a dead man as far as Brackin is concerned. Saved by a twitchy hand. But still, it was Brackin's fascination with his weapon that was bothering Gaylord. Yesterday Brackin had hardly touched the thing except when he had to, but today he seemed very involved with it. He'd pick it up and sight through the things on top and squeeze the trigger. But mostly he just kept moving his hands along it, up and down, slow, slow. Not a very subtle bastard, is he? thought Gaylord.

"I think it's time to wake Sally," Gaylord announced.

"Why not let her sleep if she wants to?" Mrs. Talmage chimed.

Gaylord looked at Mrs. Talmage with hooded eyes, quickly reminding her that he and not Brackin was in charge of this office, her job, and her. She immediately received the message and looked surprised, as if she'd forgotten where she was. "I want," Gaylord answered, "to get some work."

"Well, actually," she said, "it is a quarter to ten, and

Sally will probably want to hear the special report. Perhaps we should wake her."

Brackin looked around at them and at his watch. He gave a slight shrug and stood. "Nobody is to move while I get her, is that understood? If anybody moves you'll both spend the whole day completely chained." He meant, of course, more chained than they now were. Both acknowledged his threat and did not move.

Brackin went to the door of Gaylord's office and quietly knocked. He heard Sally's invitation and peered in through the door he partially opened. Sally lay on the couch with the covers pulled around her.

"Is it morning?" she asked gaily.

"It's almost ten, Sally. There's a special news report about us soon, and Mr. Gaylord wants to get into his office for some things. I was hoping you'd wake first, but we thought it was time now."

"Thanks, Eugene, I've been up for a while. Come in, don't stand in the door. I can't get up without you, remember?" Brackin entered the room and, while he was approaching the couch, Sally moved over and indicated he was to sit on the edge beside her.

"Come on, don't be shy, I want you to tell me what's happened today. Sit down and don't worry, I don't bite." As Brackin sat she leaned over toward him a bit and whispered, "You don't want me to bite, do you?" Brackin shook his head, no. "Then you'd better do what I tell you. Now what happened this morning?"

"Well, everyone got up and had breakfast. Mrs. Talmage is reading a book and Mr. Gaylord, I think, is planning to work. That's why he wants to get you up. And oh yes, I spoke with the Deputy this morning. He was very rude to me. He shouted and said some terrible things. I thought he was nice, but I'm not so sure now. I wish he was here, then I could kill him."

Sally felt the blood drain from her face and made an

effort to relax her arms to keep from shaking. "Are you going to kill us?"

"Oh gosh, no. I told you I wouldn't kill you, Sally. I like you very much. You're the nicest person here. Maybe the nicest person in my life. Sally, don't think that. It's not like that, really. I just can't let you go. Do you understand that?"

"Of course, Eugene, I understand. Please don't think I was worried. I just get a little nervous, that's all. Come, you've got to help me dress."

When Sally pulled back the covers Brackin's mouth fell open. His eyes were glued to her chest where the skin was exposed and still lightly tanned at the neck, becoming pinker and whiter as his eyes moved down. "Now hop to it, Gene, get me unlocked. Get your key out, darling, and slip it in the lock." Brackin fumbled for the key and got the cuff unfastened. He went around to undo the other end for which he had to get onto his knees. He had simply fastened the chain to the leg of the couch. He turned around and stood up face to face, body to body, with Sally. "Would you get my things, please. I don't want to walk in my bare feet." Brackin went over to Gaylord's desk and picked up the small pile of Sally's clothing and shoes. "Good," Sally said with approval. "Now hand me my bra." Brackin found it and gave it to Sally. She put it on while chatting to him about her plans for the weekend. He did not hear her.

"You know," she was saying, "I had a lot to do this Saturday. You may have had nothing better to do than lock people up and play with guns, but I had a lot of shopping to do. The pantyhose, Gene dear. Thank you. I was supposed to meet a friend of mine to go shopping in Cleveland and get some things. Blouse. Thank you. Actually I hate to go shopping, but it has to be done. Skirt. There's nothing in Mattsfield. Shoes, please. There, we've done it. Now put your eyes back in your head, chain me up in the fashion of the day, and let's go join the troops." So saying, she offered him first her wrist, on which he snapped a chain, and next her arm, on which she placed his hand. With Brackin on one arm and a three-foot chain on the other, Sally went to breakfast.

EIGHT

Deputy Smolen had been busy since his chat with Brackin. The Ohio State Police in the person of Lieutenant Sidney Garlas was making itself felt. Garlas could not act without the permission of the Mattsfield Chief of Police, but that meant to Garlas that he could not break into the office with his revolver in his hand and personally shoot Eugene Brackin in the head and carry off the fairest of the damsels while comforting the other, less fortunate hostages. Aside from Smolen's incomprehensible and unforgivable lack of cooperation, Garlas had been able to accomplish much. This he was explaining.

"You may be perfectly prepared to sit around and let a nut run your town, Smolen, but I'm not."

"It's not your town, Garlas, remember that."

"It's in my fucking state, Smolen, remember that." Smolen and Garlas were old friends.

"I've done a lot of work for you, Smolen. I hope you appreciate it."

"What are you talking about? Come on, make it quick, I'm busy."

"I'll say you're busy. Busy making up excuses to hand your boss and the Mayor. All right, I may be able to pull you out yet. First thing, I've got the rest of the HIKS squad coming down. With their equipment we'll have the whole area covered by closed-circuit TV. No one will be able to get in or out. Not even a ghost."

"Garlas, you fool, no one wants to get in or out. What

are you talking about? And the last thing I want around here is the HIKS, you got that? Call them and tell them, no. OUT. You made a mistake. Send them to a riot in New Jersey."

"Smolen, the Hostage, Insurgency, and Kidnapping Squad is a group of experts."

"The HIKS are a trained group of killers and I don't want them in my town. If they come anywhere near the area I'll have them arrested."

"You're a very old-fashioned man, Smolen. A little man, that's you. You don't understand modern police methods. Today everything is the team. You need the right experts for each job. Not one lucky guy sitting on top of it all."

"Sounds like a committee to me. I don't like to work by committee, especially not police work. Is that it? You finished?"

"No, I am not at all finished. We'll see about the HIKS. But there's more." Garlas sat down uninvited, stretching out his legs and placing his hands, fingers interlocked, behind his head. "I've brought in a high-powered rifle, Greg. In fact, I've brought in just about the biggest, best, most sophisticated high-powered rifle in the world: the Monster. It's up on the plant roof right now."

Smolen stood and looked down at Garlas. "Do you mean to tell me that you put a rifle on the roof without telling me first? Is that what you're saying?"

"Well, you were awful busy and I hated to bother you, so I just went ahead and told your boys it was all right. Knowing you, Greg, I knew you'd approve."

"And what if Brackin had seen it? What if Brackin had seen it and had shot someone in the head?"

"Well, my men are always prepared to face the risks of the job."

Smolen was leaning over Garlas who, with his feet out before him and hands behind his head, was in a very vulnerable position. "What if it wasn't one of your lunatic heroes? What if it was one of the women he's got in there?

88

You asshole. What if he shot a hostage because you wanted to play with your frigging toys? What about that, idiot?"

"Geez, Greg, take it easy. We were careful. You gotta see this thing. It's unbelievable. Hey, come on, calm down, we'll go up and I'll show you the rig. It's real sweet."

Smolen relaxed and, moving backward, he shook his head and reached for his hat. No matter where he was, what he was doing, there were always people like Garlas ready to make things difficult, ready to take a chance with someone else's life. "Let's go," he said, "and see this Monster of yours."

The two men went out and around to the front of the plant. They entered and took a staircase up to the roof. The roof was gravel and the outside wall rose about three feet above the level of the roof. Smolen was relieved at the cover and hoped he could get everyone off without being spotted.

Across the roof from them, directly opposite the center window of Brackin's office, was a box. In front of the box was a man wearing ear protectors. He was lying down on a mat of some sort staring at what appeared to be a television screen. Smolen had seen three other men downstairs in the plant sitting around drinking coffee. He imagined they were all together but couldn't figure why. As they approached the man Smolen looked for the rifle but failed to see it. He turned to ask Garlas where it was but Garlas shushed him with a finger to his lips. When they reached the trooper, Garlas touched him on the shoe and the man turned around and acknowledged their presence, then turned back to the television screen. Smolen could now see that it was a TV monitor. There were cross hairs on it and a control box in front of it. The top of the whole machine was flush with the top of the roof so that only three or four inches of it was visible. He had to admit it was unobtrusive; what he also had to admit was that he did not know what it was. He decided to wait for Garlas to explain. He did not have to wait long.

"Something else, huh?" Garlas said with pride.

"Something else is right. But what?"

"Smolen, you're a hick. Look, see the TV screen? It's focused on the window. The man here watches the screen all the time during his shift, which is ninety minutes. He's relieved after that so he won't get hypnotized."

"That's reassuring."

"You're a riot, Smolen. He has controls in front of him. There's a focus control and the whole thing can switch to infrared at the touch of a button. But that's not all. Here, see those two large knobs? They control the cross hairs. One moves up and one moves across. The rifle is controlled completely by remote control. Now, you ready? If anything moves in the field of the screen the camera automatically zooms in until the new object fills seventy percent of the screen. The operator uses the aiming knobs to zero in on the forehead, releases the safety switch, which requires two hands, and presses the fire button. Zap, no more hostage-taker. That, my man, is science."

"Suppose one of the hostages takes a breath of air, Garlas? Zap, no more hostage."

"No way, Gregory, no way. These men are specially trained. They each do two hours of meditation a day. They've been studying the personnel photo of Brackin and are now completely conditioned to react to him and him alone. These men are an integral part of the machine and just as flawless."

"No one is flawless, Garlas. No one. Get it off the roof. Now."

"I wouldn't do that so quickly, my friend. Your mayor seemed very impressed by this little device. Very impressed indeed."

Smolen glared at Garlas with bunched fists. "Damn," he said, then turned on his heel and marched away.

Sally just had time to get herself a cup of coffee before the broadcast came on. She made no comment on not being chained. She was not sure if Brackin did it on purpose or just forgot but she was not about to ask him. Gaylord also noticed and, when Brackin's back was turned, raised his free wrist to Sally. She nodded back to acknowledge the message and turned her attention elsewhere. They were all comfortable and impatient for the newscaster to finish with the rest of the world. The Cleveland station they were tuned to, WUZY, was a large network station with pretty good local reporting.

"The major local news," he began, "is still in Mattsfield, seventy miles south of here. Yesterday at about four or five in the afternoon, forty-six-year-old Eugene Brackin took three coworkers hostage. They are being held in an office of Felton Products and, according to the police, are as yet unharmed. We have a reporter who has been on the scene in Mattsfield since word was received of the event yesterday."

There followed a series of brief interviews. The first, with Deputy Smolen, was reassuring. Everything was under control, communication with the hostages was sound, their needs were being met. Smolen evinced confidence that the alleged perpetrator would not harm the hostages provided no foolish actions were taken.

"You see," Brackin told them, "the Deputy isn't worried."

"I can't tell you," Gaylord answered, "how comforting it is to know he's not worried."

The next interview was with the guard at the gate who expressed enormous surprise at the idea of Brackin taking hostages. Those were his exact words: "He was always so polite and considerate, almost timid you'd say. I'd never have thought it. I'm enormously surprised."

The last interview was with Lieutenant Garlas: "Well, we have a very sensitive situation. There is a maniac with a rifle holding three people. One thing we know is that we can't predict what will happen. These types are unpredictable."

91

"Do you mean then that the hostages are in real danger?"

"Certainly. Give a maniac a gun and anyone near him is in danger."

"Why is he holding hostages, Lieutenant?"

"Well, the likelihood is that he had a bad childhood. You see, most of the time this sort of thing happens you find a bad childhood. More maniacs come from bad childhoods than any other cause. That's a fact."

"What actions are you taking to free the hostages?"

"Well, we have the place covered, of course. Some of the best men in the state are here to help with the operation. I may say that no effort is being spared to release those poor people from the clutches of that madman."

"Thank you, Lieutenant.

"The situation here is tense. You heard for yourselves that the mild-mannered, meek, and polite forty-six-year-old, Eugene Brackin, referred to as a maniac by police experts, is unpredictable. As we begin this vigil on the second day of captivity things are very uncertain. We will keep you up to date with the latest bulletins on the event. This is Norm Boloski in Mattsfield."

No one said a word. Brackin sat slouched down in his seat, his head almost down to the top of the chair, his feet out before him. His lips were in a slight pout and his hooded eyes looked at his hands folded on his lap. Without moving he raised his eyes and peered out at his captives. Looking down again he said, "That man called me a maniac." He looked around at them again. "He thinks I'm a maniac. I guess you must all think I'm a maniac."

Gaylord cleared his throat, squirmed just a bit, then spoke. "It's not that, Eugene. It's just that no one really understands why you're doing it. Most people don't take hostages. You have to look at it from their point of view."

"I think they're wrong," Sally said. "Eugene is no more a maniac than I am. Or you," she said quickly before Gaylord fell to temptation. "How can that jerk decide Gene is a maniac? He never even met him."

"Of course, Sally," Mrs. Talmage agreed. "Mr. Brackin is not a maniac. But Mr. Gaylord is right in pointing out that taking hostages is not common behavior, don't you agree?"

"He's just working something out. Haven't you ever had to work something out? Haven't you ever had a problem? A real beaut you can barely manage, so it takes you over and that's the only thing in your life, the center of your existence? Hasn't anything like that ever happened to you?"

Mrs. Talmage looked down at the table. Her face was blank and her shoulders suddenly seemed weighted down. "Yes, I know what you mean. Sometimes something happens, something happens and as soon as it does you want to make it not happen. You wish with all your soul to make it unhappen and it doesn't, it can't. Nothing ever unhappens." Mrs. Talmage was roused out of her reverie by Gaylord who pointed out that Brackin would surely prove them wrong by not harming any of them. He turned to Brackin with a smile but received no response.

Brackin was still brooding in his chair. Finally, he looked up. "That's what I want them to think." They all turned to him and Gaylord asked what he meant. "What I mean is simple. This is going to end sometime. I know I have to finish. I know when I finish I'm going to jail. They'll lock me up, probably for the rest of my life. Don't you think I know that?" Brackin sounded weary, but his voice was becoming tense. "If they think I'm crazy then they'll put me in a hospital, and I wouldn't mind that so much. Life out here isn't so great. But first, I've got to finish this. You think," he said, turning to Mrs. Talmage, "that I wish it would go away. You think I want to make it not have happened. Well, you're wrong. This is the way it is and this is the way I want it, the way it's supposed to be." Brackin was standing. He had his arms out in front of him in a plea for comprehension.

Sally was conscious of the air in the room. She could see the room from any angle, any view. She was not at all restricted to a particular perspective. The nude clock floating on the wall above kept her suspended out of time, out of place. She was observing this strange, strange group, herself not least of all. Who knew the right thing to say? What were the magic words that would release them, that would free Brackin from his vision? And would she say them if she knew them? "You do what you have to do, Gene," she said. "No one can tell anyone else what they have to do, no one can judge it."

"What the hell are you talking about?" Gaylord asked Sally. "He has no right to keep us like this. No one has the right to do that. No one has the right to keep three people, three innocent people, locked up in chains. We have rights too, and they say we don't have to stay like this."

"I just mean, Larry, you can't fight what's happening."

"Bullshit. I can fight to get out of here and fight to see that things like this don't happen. I have the right to protect myself. What about my rights? What about Mrs. Talmage's rights? Not everybody here is enjoying themselves. What's going to happen next, Sally? What if he has to kill us? What if he has to kill one of us? The poor man, the poor misunderstood darling is forced against his will to kill one of us. What then? Will you understand then?"

"I'm not going to kill anyone, Mr. Gaylord, I already told you."

"Well, just in case you change your mind, remember if you kill Sally she'll understand."

"Mr. Gaylord! Please think of what you're saying," Mrs. Talmage said.

Gaylord recovered himself. He wet his lips and turned back to Brackin. "Let us go."

"No. I can't."

"But you've done it. You've done whatever it is you

94

wanted to do. You've got us here, you've had us here as your prisoners overnight. You have half the cops in the state outside. You're famous. You were a special report on the radio. You'll probably make the national news. Damn it, man, if you let us go, Walter Cronkite will tell everyone about it tonight. You've done it. You can relax and let us go."

"No. Not yet. I haven't finished yet."

Gaylord took a deep breath, and ran his free hand through his hair. He lowered his voice and began again. "The only thing you haven't done is kill us. That's all that's left."

"Oh, no," said Brackin softly.

"The waiting is hard, Brackin."

"Stop it."

"You can let us go, Brackin."

"No. Stop it."

"Let us go now."

"Stop it. Stop it."

"You can. You can. You can let us go."

"Shut up. Shut up," Brackin was shouting and backing up. He tripped and stumbled on the chair behind him and grabbed it to break his fall.

"Damn you," Gaylord charged him with his finger out-stretched, "you are a maniac. You can't—"

Brackin had pulled his pistol out of the holster. Two shaky hands held it pointed at Gaylord. "If you don't shut up," he shouted, "I will kill you. Do you hear that? I will. Now shut the fuck up."

It was the first time Brackin had cursed in sixteen years. He immediately turned bright red with embarrassment and turned to the ladies. "Oh, I'm sorry . . . I didn't mean to . . . I never . . . oh, I am sorry."

Sally looked first at Gaylord, seated again and looking as if he had just run a marathon, then at the floor. "You should be," she muttered clearly.

NINE

Smolen sat with his eyes closed. Visions, almost too many and too changeable to pin down, swam before him. He could make out TV cameras, desks, people, skeletons, people changing into skeletons, and faces. The faces would change as soon as he tried to recognize them, as soon as he got close. Except for one face. One plain, lonely, frightened visage stood before the others, flowing in and out between and among the others, pale and strained; it seemed to Smolen the face wanted sympathy. Smolen was sure it was Brackin. He had, to his knowledge, never met Brackin, never done business with him, but still the image was strong, stronger than it should be from the pictures Smolen had seen. Brackin came to him from all angles, moving, changing his features. Why did he feel so strongly about the man? Why was he so sure of his hunches when he had nothing to go on? Smolen felt as if he knew Brackin, as if Brackin could not make a move without him; as if he could conquer Brackin with time, withholding the pain and pressure that Brackin must expect. Smolen was sure he could get Brackin in his debt, and if he did that, then he would win. He was sure of it.

He was sure of nothing. How the hell could he know Brackin that well? He didn't know what he was doing. Garlas had as much right to his own stupid ideas; he could make his guesses as well as Smolen. If I was forced, Smolen admitted to himself, I wouldn't bet a year's pay on anything Brackin might do. But maybe a month's. He really didn't know and still he felt really sure, and he was going crazy. Maybe that's why I understand him, he considered; we're both nuts. Smolen's musings were interrupted by the phone. Sloan answered it and immediately held the phone away from his ear. From where Smolen was sitting he could hear the Chief's voice. Well, thank the Lord for little things, Smolen thought as he reached for the phone. Maybe after hearing the radio he could get the Chief to put some pressure on the staters to quit the town.

"This is Greg, Chief. Sounds like you heard the radio."

"You're goddamned right I heard the radio. What're you going to do about that? You have any idea how that looks? You think the Mayor—"

"Can't you get rid of him? Can't you just get him out?"

"It sounds like we don't . . . out? Get who out? Brackin? You're supposed to be getting Brackin out, not me. At least that's what I—"

"For God's sake, Chief, I mean Garlas. Can't we get that asshole out of town?"

"Garlas? Get Garlas out of town? You idiot, the Mayor wants to give him a medal. You're going to get us all fired. If you don't start—"

"What are you talking about, Chief? Didn't you hear the radio?" A slow sort of numbness, a feeling as though thousands of grains of sand were falling against him, beginning with his legs and working up, consumed Smolen. Soon he would feel nothing, like lying on a beach for a long time until sense of place and occasion disappear.

"I heard the radio just fine. Me and the Mayor heard it together, and you know what? I'll tell you what. The only one who sounded like he was doing anything was Garlas. You know what the Mayor said? 'That's more like it,' he said. 'There's a man who's made for action,' he said. 'Why don't you put him in charge, why don't you do something?' " the Chief shouted.

"Oh, no."

"Oh, yes. And you know what else? I think the sonofabitch is after my job. You hear that? My job. He keeps sucking around the Mayor. The two of them keep drawing little pictures together. And they plan, they're constantly planning."

"No, Chief, he's not after your job."

"Well, just so you don't get too casual about it, Greg, let me remind you that if he gets my job, he'll be your boss. Think on it."

Smolen was experiencing free fall. His body, completely numbed by the cold vacuum of outer space, received the message from command central only distantly. An alien spacecraft, some four thousand miles off in the distance, noted his position on its celestial sonar; the beat of Smolen's heart was registered on a sheet of paper by little jumps of a pen. Another satellite from the water planet, they concluded, and went on about their business.

"We're meeting at the trailer," Chief Turner went on, "at half past twelve."

"Right, Chief, half past twelve."

"And Greg, think of something flashy."

"Sure, Chief, flashy."

Smolen hung up the phone and sat down. His right hand was clenched and hurting. His neck muscles were rigid and he had to concentrate on loosening them before he could move his head.

He looked over at Joe Sloan and then around the trailer. His eyes went around the room and stopped. "Where did you come from?" he asked Ida Crane.

"More or less the same place you did, I expect." Ida Crane sat in the corner of the trailer amidst cables and an assortment of odd sizes of wood. Her brown jacket and long dark green corduroy skirt blended into the background almost perfectly.

"How long have you been there, Ida?"

"Long enough, Greg. What's going on?"

"You mean you don't know? I don't believe you."

"Humor an old woman, Greg."

So Deputy Smolen gave her a complete rundown. He began with the morning's jaunt to the roof and ended with the call from the Chief. He went on to add a lengthy postscript describing the personal habits and intellectual background of Lieutenant Garlas. "How could he be so stupid? How could he think that shaking things up would help? If he gets that man really upset and scared there's no telling what he'll do."

"You can say that at the meeting. You've got a chance this afternoon."

"They won't listen to me. Not with Garlas telling them to bring in the marines. Wait, I've got it. Maybe I can get Garlas' mother to come in and testify that he's a mental defective. If it wasn't for that power-mad car jockey, this thing would work itself out by tomorrow."

"It's not Garlas, Greg. There are always people like him. And remember, to Garlas, Smolen is Garlas, so let that be your consolation."

"It might help if he weren't holding so many cards. Come on, Ida, help me."

"I can't help you. I don't even know why they're holding the meeting."

"Because the Mayor is scared. He wants to go on to bigger and better things, and he's afraid if this goes on too long he'll be embarrassed."

"What are you going to do?"

"I don't know. I really don't know."

"What do you know about Brackin?"

"Nothing, really, except what was in his personnel file, and that's not much."

"Then find out more. Inundate them with information about Brackin. Show them you know what's going on. Find out about his life, find out about his history, what makes him happy, what makes him angry."

"What good will that do?"

"I don't know, but it'll give you something to talk about."

"You're a great help, Ida. And what do I tell them after all that, provided I can get it, of course. What am I really going to tell them?"

Ida cast her eyes down and pursed her lips. "Damned if I know, Greg, maybe the truth."

"What?"

"Hell, boy, what do you want from me? I'm not a witch; I'm just an old woman. If you can't think of anything, just tell them the truth."

"Great, Ida, just tell them the truth. Is that from the Boy Scout manual? The chapter on getting out of tough situations? 'When your ass is in a sling, and your back against the wall, tell the truth, boys.' "

"Maybe, but I told you I couldn't help. And now I'm getting out of here while the getting is good. I think I'll skip this party. See you later, son."

Inside, things had settled down quite comfortably. Gaylord would have preferred Brackin to do almost anything rather than continue playing with that damned rifle, but he did not feel imminently threatened. His stomach kept turning over, and waves of nauseous anxiety would compel him to first hold his breath and then slowly let in air. These frequent attacks occurred each time his psyche remembered the circumstances that same psyche permitted him momentarily to forget. Make up your mind, he scolded himself; panic or relax, but doing both at once is killing me. In lieu of a decision he reached for his glass of water and turned back to the work before him. Brackin, who was aware of Gaylord's unease, smiled to himself when he was sure Gaylord would not notice. He did not wonder why his superior's discomfort pleased him, but it did so. He knew Gaylord was frightened, and that fact made him feel good. Brackin was very familiar with fear; it was an old friend of his and he hardly ever traveled without it; he knew its demeanor and its habits, its risks and its gains. With Gaylord afraid, Brackin was safe, as safe as the whole world had been while he was still afraid. Only when the fear left did Gaylord pose a threat.

Then he really ought to be terrified of Sally and Mrs. Talmage. They sat in similar positions before the closed but unshaded window with legs in front of them, feet resting on a third chair in between. Mrs. Talmage had quickly finished the first romance and passed it along to Sally who, with nothing to read, was bound to get in trouble. Both women seemed perfectly content and relaxed, whiling away the time with a pleasant read. Periodically Sally would giggle and insist on reading a passage out loud. "Joan," she would exclaim, "listen to this:

> Love had been a stranger to Laura Lee, never descending from its highest orbits to dwell within her youthful heart. Yet somehow, through perhaps some magic or alchemy, she knew in an instant that Captain Archer was hers. Now, with cheeks aflush, her body warm with anticipation, she approached the enemy and bowed.

"Hey now, you never told me this stuff was so exciting. Really, Joan, does it get better?"

Mrs. Talmage turned a comely shade of pink, but still she gave a slight yet eager nod to Sally. She looked across at Brackin, blushed one shade deeper, and turned back to her book. Brackin continued to stare at her while she read. It was strange, her skimpy attire, since it went unnoticed most of the time; then it would become obvious all at once that the woman was in her underwear. Really, it was a ridiculous sight, four grown people three of whom were fully dressed and one in a slip. And yet no one laughed, not even once. Somehow it seemed almost natural, as if they were a family spending Saturday at home. In a family you could wear what you pleased; you didn't have to get

101

dressed or put up appearances; you could relax in what-ever you liked. But also in a family you did not notice how nice someone's legs were. When that happened you turned your eyes away, in this case to Sally. For a long time Brackin had thought of Sally as a younger sister. If he had one he would like her to be a lot like Sally. So looking at her now, with her one leg out and the foot of the other resting on her shin, Brackin felt a stab of conscience. This was not, as might be thought, from maintaining as a cap-tive the object of both his affection and his respect, but rather from the stirrings he felt when he considered her form. As he watched her she used one foot to rub the other leg, oblivious to the way her skirt slid fractionally further along her thigh. Unbidden came a vivid image of Sally early that morning, almost naked and yet so comfortable. She did feel like a sister toward him, that he could tell. Why else would she be so open before him, so trusting and secure, unless she knew perfectly well that he was in-capable of harming her? That she had this knowledge was a great comfort to him.

Brackin's contentment filled him with the warming em-brace of arriving home in foul weather. Brackin remem-bered once when he had to walk home in a terrible snow-storm. It took him almost two hours to complete the mile walk, and he arrived at his apartment frozen and wet. He ran a hot tub and got a small brandy while he shucked his damp things. Getting into that bath was a wondrous feel-ing, and that same feeling of having arrived at some des-tination to an appropriate and earned reward was what he now felt. If he could maintain the balance between fear and comfort, it would all go so well. And yet completion, he knew, could not be held off indefinitely. Soon he would have to think about stopping. Ending. And that was not a subject he relished. He frowned now and scowled at his rifle. Why go on to think about that? Why bother with the rotten parts? Just look, just take in this scene. Remem-ber the way the sun is coming in and being used by the two women, so relaxed with their reading. Keep forever the way that Gaylord continually examines me to test the waters, my waters, my feelings, to know what I think, what I need, how happy I might be. Yes, remember all that. And remember he did, so that when the phone rang, Brackin was feeling very content.

Mrs. Talmage started for the phone, stopping when she remembered her chain, so it was Gaylord who reached over and answered it. Deputy Smolen recognized the voice as other than Brackin's and asked one or two questions about the captives' health. He received assurances from Gaylord that they were all well, and then being afraid to keep Gaylord on the phone too long, asked for Brackin. Brackin took the phone and said hello.

"Brackin, this is Deputy Smolen. I want to talk to you."

"I am not interested in talking to you, though."

"Well, I have some questions and so on I have to ask you, and I thought this would be a good time."

"You spoke very terribly to me this morning, Deputy, and I don't want to talk to you. I don't want you to try and frighten me again. I refuse."

"Wait just a minute. We have to make arrangements for lunch, don't we? You have to eat, right?"

"Mr. Gaylord will make the arrangements with you," and so saying, Brackin handed the instrument back to Gaylord.

Smolen was upset because he had decided that for want of anything better to do, he would follow Ida's advice. He wanted to pump Brackin for as much information as he could, and since he had decided that it was the only thing he could do, it had assumed a great urgency for him. He quickly asked Gaylord questions, all answerable with a yes or no, about Brackin's temperament, demeanor, treatment of the captives, and statements about their release (of which there were none). He learned that they were all chained up, it being too difficult for Gaylord to tell him that Sally was not, and that Brackin always kept a weapon

103

close to him. Those were the bits he had to know, but now he had to get Brackin back on the line.

He instructed Gaylord to tell Brackin that there was an important matter concerning Brackin's personal safety, and Smolen could speak about it only to Brackin, that if they didn't speak Brackin might get hurt. Brackin refused at first, demanding to know what it was, but Smolen in turn refused to tell anyone but Brackin. He said to Gaylord that Brackin was the only one to whom he would give this information. That must have struck the right chord because Brackin reluctantly agreed to take the phone. "What is it, Deputy? I hope it's important."

Smolen was conscious of a difference in Brackin's voice and manner. He seemed to be less tremulous and hesitant, slightly more in control of himself. He wondered if that was good or bad. "Brackin, listen to me, please. I'm sorry about this morning, but it's not easy out here, you know."

"I'm not interested in your apology or excuses, you—"

"Wait. I can prove to you that I mean you no harm. Isn't that what you want to know? That you can trust me?"

"I don't trust you."

"I can prove it. I can show you. Do you want me to prove it to you? You've got to tell me, yes or no." Smolen had decided that Brackin must ask for the proof or else he might not hear it. Brackin thought for a moment and then told Smolen that yes, he did want the proof. So Smolen told him about the rifle on the roof. "Be very careful, Brackin, and go to the center window and look across at the factory roof. Don't show yourself in the window, understand? Just peek around the curtain, okay? When you do, look along the ledge of the roof and you'll see a place, just across from the window, where there's a rise about three feet long on the ledge. Go take a look and tell me if you see it."

Brackin put the phone down and cautiously made his

way to the window. He stood with his back to the curtain and slowly peered around to the window while holding the curtain in front of him. He looked like some strange voyeur peeking out instead of in. He followed his instructions and identified the spot to which Smolen referred. It looked like someone had laid a three-foot plank on the ledge. He returned to the phone and reported his sighting.

"Do you know what that is, Brackin?"

"No, what is it?"

"It's a rifle. A special rifle intended to shoot only you. If you were to look out the window at the plant for fifteen seconds you would be shot dead."

"I don't believe it."

"Try it, then. Go on, take a good look out the window. It's a pretty day. Go and enjoy the view if you don't believe me."

Brackin looked at the window. He moved over a ways to get further out of the line of sight. "Why do you want to kill me? Why did you put a rifle there?" Hearing this, Sally and Mrs. Talmage looked out and then quickly drew back themselves. They did not know for certain what was going on, but it sounded deadly, and it definitely involved both windows and rifles.

"Eugene, I've been trying to tell you all along that I don't want to kill you, but there are other people out here who are very angry at you. Can you understand that? Do you know why they are angry? It's wrong to take hostages, Eugene, and they are afraid you'll hurt someone."

"But I've told you so many times I won't; can't you believe me?"

"I do, but they don't. They haven't spoken to you the way I have. That's why I need to talk to you some more. I want to persuade them that you won't hurt anyone, and to do that I need your help. Will you help me?"

When Brackin agreed, Smolen could have cheered. But the job was not over yet, and he needed to get Brackin talking. So he began to ask Brackin a lot of questions as if there were a form in front of him. Where was he born? What were his parents' names? Where did he attend school? What jobs had he held? How long? And on and on. He learned quite a bit, actually.

Eugene Brackin had been an orphan since the age of two. He had been raised by an elderly aunt for the four years following his parents' death. She was kind and pleasant but became too ill to look after him when he was six. For the next five years he was in four foster homes, the longest stay being two years, the shortest three months. All of his departures were due to circumstances of movement, illness, and in one case, divorce. In two of the homes he was expected to do a lot for one so young, but was not ill treated. At eleven he was taken in by a large family with seven natural children. The foster child allowance appealed to them, and it was assumed that no one would notice one child more or less. Brackin stayed with this family for the next five years, and when he remembers his childhood it is this period he recalls with fondness. There were so many of them, and there was always so much going on. The family was run by the eldest daughter with the eldest son backing her up as enforcer. As long as everyone pitched in, there was a fair allowance made for miscreant behavior. Not that Brackin was mischievous; it was just that he had a habit of forgetting where he was, or what he was about. This was generally tolerated as being considerably easier to handle than, say, the third youngest's fondness for setting fires. The true wrench to Brackin's life, were he to write his autobiography, would not be the death of his parents, nor his comings and goings from foster homes, but the dissolution of that family when he was sixteen. Absentminded, awkward, terribly shy, it was natural for the other children, once having decided he was one of them, to protect him. The removal of his defenses to the world, when the father died shortly after the eldest daughter married, was heartbreaking to him. The now-married daughter took two of the youngest to live with her, the eldest son went away to seek work, and the mother, never mother to Brackin as much as the sister was, could cope only with the remaining three at most. And after all, Brackin, being sixteen, would understand. He spent the next two years, quiet and withdrawn, in a state school.

Smolen did not know what to make of it, but it might be helpful. It did not sound like a terrible childhood, though certainly not an easy or pleasant one. Surely almost everybody had bad times when they were young and still did not end up taking hostages.

"And you've been living in Mattsfield for eight years?"

"Yes, Deputy, eight years. And before that I was living in Lingstan."

"Yeah, nice town, Lingstan. Okay, let's see where we are here."

"Is there much more?"

"No, not much. Here we go. What makes you happy?"

"What?"

"I want to know what makes you happy. You know, birthday parties, sunny days, football games, that sort of stuff."

"Well, I don't know. I guess that stuff makes me happy."

"Okay, we're doing great here, Eugene. You're a great help. Let's see. Oh, I've got it, what makes you angry?"

There was an extended silence during which Smolen did not know what to do. And still Brackin held his tongue. Smolen had not a clue what to do. Should he prod? Leave it be? Just go on? He figured the sadness bit would not get much more action than anger. He wished he knew what he was doing. "I'll tell you," Smolen found himself saying to Brackin, "what really makes me angry. What really puts me out is when I—"

"You asked me, didn't you? Why are you telling me if you want to know? I mean, why can't you just listen to me?

107

You can bet that gets me angry; you can bet it gets me angry when someone asks me a question and then doesn't wait for an answer. But I'll tell you, Deputy, what really makes me angry is being taken for granted, you know, being used. Or seeing someone else used, that too." Brackin's voice was tighter now, matching his grip of the phone. "When I remember some of the times people used me, just wanted something, just didn't care anything about me, that's when I get mad."

Smolen tried to find out more, but to no avail. No matter what he asked Brackin, regardless of how he phrased the question, the answer was the same. Being used made Brackin angry, and it also made him sad. Smolen could get no details, no reminiscences, no fantasies, no descriptions of what he meant. But he at least got that. Brackin hated to be used. Maybe it would come in useful, maybe he could use it. Who knows? He made final arrangements for lunch and rang off.

Inside, Larry Gaylord was having a go at Brackin. It was very understandable that Brackin got upset at being used, Gaylord explained to him. After all, treating someone as if they didn't matter, as if their feelings and emotions didn't count, was a pretty rotten thing, wasn't it? Well, wasn't it? Of course it was. But here was the funny thing. Here was the thing Brackin maybe hadn't thought of because he'd been so busy. Brackin didn't want to use anyone, did he? No, certainly not. But just think for a moment. Wasn't he using the three of them? Wasn't Brackin really using his friends for his own purposes, regardless of their feelings, their emotions? Had Brackin realized that? Wasn't he doing just the thing that he most hated? Shouldn't he stop?

"Leave him alone, for Chrissake." This from Sally.

"I'm just trying to raise a point he might not have considered. C'mon, Gene, admit it, aren't you using us?"

"This is different," Brackin said, and then he went over

to the desk, picked up the rifle, and peered cautiously out the window. Gaylord looked after him and continued talking.

"Really, Gene, if you think about it, you're making a terrible mistake."

Sally began to fume. There was no need to badger him like that. There were better ways to handle Brackin, and she knew them. Fucking Gaylord always thought he knew the right answer. Him and his New York. Well, the sooner he went back, the happier she'd be. For one thing, she'd get his job; that was an open secret in the administrative part of the plant. And she'd run the place a lot better than he. Not that he wasn't a fair manager, you know. Credit where credit is due after all, but the man thought he was perfect. Look at him picking on poor Gene.

"Larry," Sally finally interrupted him, "lay off, will you? You're not doing any good. You'll just make things worse."

"Oh, Mrs. Freud knows what's best, does she? What makes you the expert? All the times you've been held hostage before?"

"I don't have to be an expert to know that just badgering someone is no solution."

Gaylord was about to retort when Mrs. Talmage asked Brackin for permission to use the telephone. She wanted to call her husband. She also wanted to stop the bickering between Sally and Gaylord, but once she thought of calling her husband the idea appealed to her. Robert was always steady, bless him, and it would be good to hear his voice. Better than these two going at each other. She was frankly a little shocked that Sally should talk to her employer that way, not right at all. But again, this was a confusing situation. Who was boss now? Gaylord? He was chained to his chair while Brackin roamed about with guns. Perhaps the bosses had changed after all. Maybe they were boss of different things. She didn't know anything anymore, except that it would be good to talk to Robert.

Brackin told her to go ahead, and immediately the others started planning their calls. Sally to her mother, Gaylord to his wife. The sudden expectation of personal contact with the outside world stirred excitement in the room. Now smiles were visible and bickering had stopped. Mrs. Talmage congratulated herself on a wonderful idea and wheeled over to her desk. The others moved away to ensure symbolic privacy.

Mrs. Talmage spoke to Robert for quite a while. By the time she finished Sally was eager to get on the phone. She put a call through to her mother, who, it turned out, had not left the phone since learning that her daughter was a hostage. Her mother began to cry immediately and tell Sally how desperately worried she was. Sally tried to reassure her, but to little avail. After a bit Sally had her calmed down and could tell her she was all right. They exchanged news but quickly drifted into an uncomfortable silence. They were moderately close, but what, after all, do you say to your mother when you are being held hostage by a man with a rifle and no demands. You cannot say, please raise the money, or free the prisoners, or publish the letter. All you can say is what Sally tried.

"Mom," she began, "I don't know what's going to happen in all this, and it'll work out just great, I'm sure. But if something should go wrong—" which was as far as she got before her mother broke down and started wailing.

For the first time since her father died fifteen years ago, Sally wished he was around. Her mother was great in the clutch if there was something to do, but if it was a reassurance you wanted, if all you needed was support and a few don't-worries, then you were barking up the wrong parent. Her father, useless for most things except dominating her mother and herself, though he never really succeeded in commanding Sally, was great if you needed words and no action. Action for him always meant getting someone else to do it, but the words were always his own,

110

and sometimes, if you really needed to hear them and accept them, you could close your eyes and almost reach that point where you believed what he said. But even that wouldn't last long enough to do much good. So Sally calmed her mother down once again and told her she had to leave the phone because the police might want to get through.

Sally's eyes were a bit red, and she took a moment alone by the phone to collect herself. The others had heard her side of the conversation and were avoiding looking directly at her. Sally turned and saw everyone deeply engrossed in some object before them. "Well," Sally announced in a controlled voice, "you'll all be relieved to know that my mother is coping with the stress, and that cousin Licia had a seven-pound baby girl. Larry, the phone is all yours." Gaylord grinned in acknowledgment and dragged his chair back to Mrs. Talmage's desk, where he had been working.

Gaylord picked up the phone and dialed his apartment in New York. The phone rang three times and then it was picked up. Gaylord was delighted and beamed his pleasure around the room. "Hello," a strange accented voice answered, "Mrs. Gaylord's residence." Gaylord stared at the mouthpiece as if it were some strange object that had just squirted water, cold water, at him. He asked to whom he was speaking. He learned that he was conversing with Mrs. Gaylord's maid. "Mrs. Gaylord's maid?" he queried. "And where might Mrs. Gaylord be?" Well, it seems that Mrs. Gaylord was off in the country for the weekend with friends. The children were out at the park. Would the gentleman care to leave a message? No, no message, thank you.

Gaylord hung up and looked at the others. "I'll bet you didn't know I had a maid, did you? Mind you, I don't have a maid. I have a one-bedroom apartment in a high-rise overlooking a barren wasteland. My wife, the fortunate Mrs. Gaylord, has a maid. It must be nice for her," he

111

mused aloud, "to have a husband who can give her all the finer things." He sat back in his chair and put his hands behind his head. "I don't know how you do it," he said to Sally.

"How I do what?" she answered. "I didn't do nuthin'."

"You know what I mean," he carried on, "how you women get men to do everything you want them to do, and then still go on to drown them in guilt for one crime or another." His voice was calm and matter of fact, but Sally could sense the hostility pent up behind the words. Once again she recalled rumors that his very presence here was engineered by his wife. Well, Sally was prepared to fight Gaylord anytime and anywhere—and win, but this was ridiculous. She wouldn't have a clue what she was fighting about or for. So, much to her credit, she did not rise to the bait.

"I'm sorry your wife wasn't in, Larry," she said. "Isn't there someone else you can call?" Gaylord stared at Sally a moment longer, pursed his lips, and said, yes, he could call the home office and see if Armour, the VP he worked for in New York, was in. Saturday or not, Armour usually showed up for work, and the weekend switchboard would be on anyway. But when Gaylord tried Armour he was told that Mr. Armour was away for the weekend. Why yes, he was in the country. Who was calling, please? Gaylord hung up.

"Hey now," he said to the group with an aggressively cheerful voice, "seems like a good weekend to get out of town in the Big Apple. Doesn't seem as if there's anybody left to talk to me."

TEN

They came into the trailer an hour late, the Mayor, the Chief, and Garlas. Everyone was glaring at everyone else. Smolen did not like it one bit. No one was smiling, no one was joking, they hardly said hello. They sat down in the chairs around the deal table, and everyone stared at Smolen. They wanted him to start the meeting. But Smolen had nothing to say yet, and he just looked back at them for as long as they looked at him. It was the Mayor who finally broke the ice.

"What the hell are you doing about this, Smolen?" Not Greg, not Dep, not even Deputy; just plain Smolen.

"I'm taking care of it."

"And how," the Mayor asked, "are you taking care of it?"

"I'm talking to him. I'm gaining his confidence, establishing a relationship. I'm getting him to trust me."

"I don't care if he trusts you, Smolen. I don't even care if he likes you. All I care is that he gets the hell out of there."

"Look, Mayor Kowal, I've been talking to him regularly. I just had a long talk with him at noon and got his whole history, everything."

"How'd you get him to open up, Greg?" the Chief asked.

Smolen took a deep breath. Maybe he shouldn't tell them, he didn't know, but what the hell. "I told him about the gun on the roof."

"You what?" Garlas exclaimed.

113

"I had to show him that he could trust me, Garlas. It was the only thing I could think of. Look, Mayor, give me a break. At least listen to the tape of the conversation. He just doesn't sound like a killer."

Garlas spoke before the Mayor could reply. "We don't need to listen to anything, Smolen. You're through here." But that was a mistake.

The Mayor turned to Garlas and looked at him with ice in his eyes. "That decision, Lieutenant, is mine and mine alone. Don't forget that." Then he turned to Smolen. "Play the tape."

Smolen did just that, and the Chief and the Mayor listened with fascination to the man who was holding their town at bay, to the man who had ripped off Joan Talmage's dress, to a man who, Smolen hoped, sounded like anything but a cold-blooded killer.

When the tape had ended, Smolen sat silently awaiting their reactions. "Well," the Mayor said, "he sounds like a nut."

"But not like a killer," Smolen added.

"I don't know, Greg," the Mayor confessed. "I really don't know."

The Chief had been quiet through most of the meeting, but now he spoke. "I think we should leave it with Greg. I think he can pull it off." The Mayor did not reply, but sat thoughtful, looking at Smolen through half-closed eyes.

Garlas could take it no longer. "What the hell does that tape mean? Nothing, that's what. We still don't know what he's going to do. He's still a maniac. And he's still in there, tape or no. Just tell me, Smolen, what are you going to do next?"

Smolen looked at the Mayor. "Do you want me to answer that question?" The Mayor nodded his reply. "I don't really know," Smolen said, "but it'll be the best I know how."

"Maybe," Garlas spat, "that's not good enough."

"If you go in there," Smolen told him, "and try to take him, some of those hostages are going to die. Do you care about that?"

"If it's done right, no one will die."

"I asked you if you care about that."

"Of course I care about that."

"I don't believe you. I think the only thing you care about is getting Brackin, dead or alive. Preferably dead."

"You don't know what the fuck you're talking about."

"You don't care about Brackin. You don't care about the hostages. You don't even care about Mattsfield. You just want to see Brackin wasted. If you cared about anything else you'd never want to go in there. He's got that place sealed up tight. We don't even know if he sleeps. Maybe he's so strung out he stays awake all night."

"He can't do that forever."

"No, but he might be doing it now, right?"

"If it were done in the right way no one would get hurt."

"You don't know that, Garlas. You can't know that."

"All right," said the Mayor, "enough. I'm going to let you have your way, Smolen. But not forever. I don't know when, but sooner or later I want him out. And it better be sooner."

The Mayor rose to adjourn the meeting but lagged behind as the others filed out. "Greg," he said softly, "a lot hangs on all this. More than you imagine. I know you don't want to be a deputy all your life, and I have no intention of being a mayor for all mine. Do you understand me, Greg?"

Smolen pursed his lips and nodded. The Mayor smiled slightly and stepped outside the trailer.

Inside, lunch had been finished a long time ago. Gaylord was at work using Mrs. Talmage's desk, whose owner was once again reading in the window with Sally similarly disposed opposite her. Brackin was off by himself in a corner, sitting behind a desk, rifle laid before him. Things were going according to plan and he was pleased. In his heart, before he had committed himself, even after, even when he could not turn back anymore, he had still not known if he would carry it all out properly. His doubts, fears about himself, nagging inner thoughts that despised his weaknesses, rose to his consciousness, bringing racks of anxiety and the certain knowledge that he would fail. But now, now it looked good. Now he could hear his heart keep a normal pace, a sane rate, while he assayed the kingdom before him. There was no fear now, no crawling feelings licking at his guts, no driving fear twisting his head around to search for observers too quick to see. No. None of that. Brackin looked quickly to his left. Nothing there. It was vital he not be caught off guard. All of his collapses, all of his errors, not to mention retreats; oh, had there been retreats, all of them were from poor vigilance. That must be his password. He must trust no one, least of all himself.

He looked now at his enemies. He gazed at them with a cool detachment, a critical judgment such as he had read of but never before experienced. They would not look at him while he first looked at them; that would be wrong to a king in his realm. When a king sought you out for inspection, you simply stood the review with eyes averted. One did not stare back at the head of state, especially not in full dress, and no emperor without clothes was he. Mrs. Talmage should be an empress, an empress without clothes, for so she sits, dignity intact; her sensibility somehow brought in front of her as she read of romance in her slip. What a defense for a king; it is her sensibility, her presence, that is kingly. Mr. Gaylord has no such presence. What will protect him when only kings are spared? His intensity? His concentration? Or maybe his distance. Gaylord is right, thought Brackin; distance must be maintained. Look at his regal style, his aloof bearing. I trundle,

Gaylord marches. I sit with every nerve ending screaming at me—yes, screaming—and Mrs. Talmage reads.

Brackin was close to tears. His face was contorted and his hands spasmodic. He was blinking furiously. This was not the way it was to be. This was not flying and singing and running and flowing and he, Brackin, at the center of the final, complete circle. He looked round him quickly, pushing himself back into the corner. The desk was good protection, but not enough. He moved his pistol holster from the right side of his belt around in front of him, right in the center—where the circle should be. Brackin looked round again and again, but all he saw was what he knew and he did not know what he needed. His hands, especially his right, were opening and closing. It was strange and unsettling, but also calming since he stopped to watch his hands. He looked up from this wonder and met Sally's eyes. She smiled at him and gave a little wave with her fingers. She probably thought Brackin waved back since she didn't know his hands were in spasm, but she may well have sensed his urgency. She stood up and put down her book, coming over to Brackin with a smile and a lilting gait.

"Hi, Gene," she tried, "having a think after lunch?" But Brackin just stared at her, giving no indication he even heard her words. Sally sat on the desk, put her back against the wall, and pulled her legs up, tucking her skirt in beneath her.

"You certainly seem to be in a funk. What's happening, baby?" she mimicked. Still there was no reply. "Scared?" she asked.

Brackin rolled his head around and looked at Sally, then stood and came beside her. She was beautiful. She sat there smiling and easy, so easy so casual so free, while he sat with cramps that bound him like straps. "No," he answered her, "I'm not scared."

"Why not?"

117

Brackin looked as if he did not understand, and his stare of confusion led Sally to repeat her question. Brackin looked at her again. He continued to stare at her so long that Sally had a fantasy about his going catatonic on her right there and then. "Do you think I should be scared?" he finally answered.

"Well, I would be if I were in your shoes." I'd also be if I were in my shoes, she thought, and I am, so I am.

"Do you mean that? Would you really be scared if you were me?"

"Absolutely. Eugene, I think what you are doing here is extraordinary. I know it's supposed to be wrong, but there's a poetry to it, a kind of beauty. Do you understand what I mean? We go on and on doing what we must, doing what we're supposed to, and it takes a very special person to break out of that box." Brackin was watching Sally carefully as she spoke, her eyes sparkling, her brow creased in concentration. She clutched his arm as she continued. "You are doing something I have always ached to do but haven't had the courage, to tell the whole mob to fuck off. There's nothing wrong with you, Gene, you're not a criminal, you're a hero. A hero, goddammit. Do you know how many times I've been screwed over and not done a thing about it? Let people kick me around and walk away from it? But now I feel like I found a liberator." And she reached her hand out and touched his cheek. Sally turned and looked at the armless clock. "You've even liberated us from time," she said. What was it about that stupid clock that got at her, she wondered even as she spoke. She was becoming as strange as Brackin. The crippled leading the maimed, she thought.

Brackin looked at her worriedly. "I'm not a liberator," he told her. "I'm only doing what has to be done. What I have to do."

"Very few people can do what they have to do. The circle is very small, Gene, very, very small."

Brackin couldn't believe his ears. She saw it. She under-

118

stood the whole thing. "Yes, yes, I know what you mean. It's the circle. The perfect circle. It's not something that can be easily or carelessly done. And you're right, very few can do it." Brackin moved closer to Sally. He was looking up at her, her whole body a package on the desk before him. He leaned toward her. A moment's reluctance wafted through his body, but he rolled his head and spoke. "I am not sure, but I think I am special." He quickly averted his eyes from Sally but stayed close to her.

She looked up at him. "You are," she told him. "You are very special."

Brackin looked down at her and asked, "Are you sure?"

Sally took a deep breath and slowly let it out. "I am sure," she said, and pointed her finger at Brackin. Her eyes were very intense now, boring into Brackin's skull, seeking out his attention. "I must tell you, Eugene, there is more. You are not alone. I am with you. Do you understand?"

"There must be more."

"There is more, and I know it. I know the rest of your mission, Gene. I know what must be done."

"Tell me. What must be done?"

"Not now."

"Now. Tell me now. I demand it."

"You demand nothing from me."

"I'm sorry. I didn't mean it."

"I understand. I appreciate your strain. I have the greatest admiration for you. Do you believe that?" Sally had put her left hand over Brackin's. She applied gentle pressure with her words. "We have very much in common, don't we?"

"Oh, no," Brackin answered, "almost nothing. You are very self-assured, possessed. I never know what I'm doing."

"But you do now, don't you? You know exactly what you're doing. You planned it perfectly, executed it exactly, and you are staying in control. I'm very proud of you, Gene."

Brackin beamed. "Thank you, Sally. I didn't believe

119

anyone could understand. Everyone keeps asking me questions, but you have none. Do you really see the beauty?"

"See it? How could I not? It's—"

But Sally was interrupted by Gaylord. He didn't know what the hell was going on over there but it stank. Whatever she was up to, it looked like no good. Brackin could manage to hold them without amusements from Miss Sprightly. If she was cooking something up he wanted to know about it. In fact, he wanted to know about it before she did anything. He was responsible here, not she. This was his office, not hers. If she had a plan, she had to clear it with him first and that was that. With that in mind he interrupted Sally's tête-à-tête with their jailer.

"Hey, Sally," he said with measured jest, "how about doing some work now. Double time for hostage days, ha ha."

"No, Larry, I don't work on Saturdays. Especially Saturdays when I'm being held hostage."

"Well, come over here and give me a hand for a minute. This stuff is confusing."

"No, I don't want to work, please."

"It'll just take a minute, Sally, that's all." Both their voices had gone flat and were rapidly acquiring a bit of an edge.

"Dammit all, Gaylord, I told you I'm not interested. Buzz off."

"There is absolutely no reason to get nasty. All I'm asking for is a little help and cooperation. I don't see what you're getting so excited about. Do I have to remind you this is an office? My office?"

Sally leaned over to Brackin so she could whisper, "Tell him to leave me alone." Brackin looked at her. He reached around her to take his rifle, which she had moved over when she sat down. Rifle in hand he stood up and looked at Gaylord. "Mr. Gaylord, do your work and stop bothering Sally."

Brackin sat and Sally covered his hands with hers. "You did that very well," she said. "He doesn't understand at all, you know. He has no sense of imagination, no ability to rise beyond his level. I was supposed to be the department head until they had to find a place here for Gaylord." Her voice now had an absent matter-of-fact air as she explained to Brackin how she, Sally, and not Gaylord was supposed to be his boss. She had been told that the position would be hers, that there were plans for her to have more responsibility. "I'm very highly thought of, Gene." When Brackin asked what happened, Sally had to say she was not sure. For some reason Gaylord was banished to Ohio. "Can you imagine, Gene, what they must think of us if they punish people by sending them where we choose to work and live?" The rumors say it had something to do with sex, but no one found Gaylord the type. "But do you know," Sally went on, "two VPs apologized to me when Gaylord got the slot. Two of them who want me to be happy, who want me to be successful." Sally's dreamy voice was a tonic for Brackin who drank up her inflection and cadence far more fully than her meaning. Sally looked to make sure that Brackin's face was blocked from view by her own body and then reached up to his cheek with an open hand, stroking once, very lightly, from his ear to the point of his chin. "Two vice presidents, Gene, one in public relations, the other in marketing, both impressed by me enough to make promises. What do you think of that?"

No one ever made promises to Brackin, especially about promotions that, he would quickly admit, he had no desire for. "I don't think," he told Sally, "that I've ever spoken to a vice president. You must have a great deal of ability, a great deal of promise for them to be so interested in you."

"Eugene, it's not ability. It's knowing what I want, where I'm going. That's how you could do all this. You knew every step exactly and precisely. You were certain you could do it and knew you would succeed. That's what it takes. I know you have the vision for this, as you must have for whatever you want, whatever you really need. Do you understand?"

Brackin puzzled for a minute. Sally was trying to tell him something and he was trying to listen. The importance of what he heard impressed him but he was processing very slowly. He must not try too hard or he would lose it. He squinched his eyes closed and said, "If I can do this, then I can do anything I want."

"Yes," Sally reiterated before she left him, "if you can do this, you can do anything you want. You are very, very powerful."

The glow that spread through Brackin was something wonderful and precious, not merely warmth or safety, not even pleasure, but beyond all those: It was relaxation, repose. Sally had just given him the right to relax, to imbue himself with confidence. His face aglow, he watched as she nodded at him significantly and went back to her seat by the window. What an extraordinary feeling this was, how it ranged over him. The key was his power, and who could take that from him? No one, no one at all. He was too alert and ready for them to take him by surprise; they would have to attack directly. Frontal assault, that's what it would take. Terrible odds, too strong to repel. Multitudinous forces coming all at once from every direction. Hordes screaming down at him from every crevice and opening. Plug the holes. Close the circle. Brackin was sure he heard a noise outside the fire door and leaped up to put his ear to it. Too soft, too subtle they, but ever careful, ever cautious he. Everywhere they thrust he parried, keeping the circle closed. His eyes darted from window to window, skipping over the window of death, the eye of the enemy. The two women sat beneath it, on either side in perfect peace. The death watch for him.

Gaylord was watching Brackin surreptitiously as he worked. He was concerned by Brackin's sudden changes of mood. With Sally he had looked elated, excited, but now his excitement had turned round into anxiety and he was acting strangely again. Suddenly Gaylord was gripped by a shock wave of fear and nausea. He almost threw up on Mrs. Talmage's desk during one of those thank God infrequent moments of lucidity when he was completely aware of where and who he was. There was a madman with a rifle not fifteen yards from him who regularly threatened his life. Gaylord's nausea slipped into a sweat, the clammy sort when he knows without looking that he is pale and that anybody who looked at him would stop and become alarmed. Gaylord hid his face behind some papers and turned away from the others. He controlled his breathing and counted his breaths until normalcy resumed. After a bit he felt some color return, but with his blood came no solutions. He took a last deep breath and called to Brackin. "Gene, could you come over here for a bit, please? I'm sorry," he went on, holding up his chained arm, "but I can't come to you." Brackin mumbled a reply and came over to where Gaylord was, taking the seat his boss indicated. Brackin sat, patiently waiting for Gaylord to say something.

When Gaylord had called Brackin over he had nothing specific in mind. All he knew at that moment was how important it was for him to face his fear, confront that reality he had seen. Its personification was Brackin, unpredictable and unmanageable in the extreme. When the needs and desires were unknown it became next to impossible to manipulate behavior; the desireless person was free.

"There's something that's been on my mind for a while now and I decided to ask you about it right out. Is that okay?" When Brackin seemed to assent, Gaylord continued. "A while ago there was a position open as assistant department head in research. Your name was mentioned and I was asked for an opinion. I told you then what had happened, and you agreed that I was right not to recom-

123

mend you for the position. You are a very valuable employee, but did not seem to have the drive to supervise. We spoke of all that. Do you remember?"

Brackin remembered perfectly and said so. The conversation had depressed him for days. Gaylord was going on now. "What I want to know, Gene, is this, are the hostage-taking and missed promotion connected? Did I have anything to do with causing all this? Did I?"

"Oh, no, Mr. Gaylord, I told you then that you were right. I felt bad that you were right, that I had to agree with you, but it wasn't your fault. We both know that Sally has to supervise the assistants." As at the first interview, Brackin sounded and felt apologetic for putting his boss into such an uncomfortable position.

"Then this . . . ?" Gaylord said, indicating the room and its occupants.

"Nothing at all to do with that. Nothing at all."

"Is there something else I've done? As your supervisor is there some way I've inflicted harm on you? Have I unintentionally slighted you in some way?"

"Please, Mr. Gaylord, none of this is any fault of yours. There is nothing you've said or done that has hurt me in any way. I think you've been a fine boss. This has nothing at all to do with you. Nothing."

Gaylord smiled and breathed freely. How he wished for a tape recording of that conversation. He was totally without any responsibility at all. He was not to blame for this debacle and could only come out of it a hero. He would write a memo to that effect. That's it. He would write an accounting of the entire episode, clearly demonstrating the gratuitous nature of the whole mess. Brackin could have done it anywhere. Its happening at Felton, in his department, was the purest bad luck.

He stopped himself abruptly. What was he going on about? Who would blame him? Who would care if he was dead? If this nonsense worked out, he was going back to

New York and that was that. They couldn't refuse him. And if they did, well there were other outfits who had heard of him and who didn't exile rising executives so their wives could sleep around more easily. Forget this nonsense of blame and concentrate on getting out of here.

"The other thing I wanted to ask you, Gene, is when we're getting out." Gaylord noticed the quickly darkened brow and growing frown and continued before Brackin could reply. "Wait, Gene, I don't want to rush you, but I have a responsibility here, you can see that. If we're going to be here much longer, I feel I should make plans and arrangements for you and the others. Not to mention the rest of the plant. They need warning to close down; they probably don't know what to do. If we're going to be here on a Sunday, Gene, we need permission. Do you see what I mean?"

"No, I don't know. What permission? What do you mean?"

"Well, now, there's quite a few things to tend to if we're going to be here tomorrow. For example, take Mrs. Talmage. She's working overtime, sort of. I really should work that out, shouldn't I? She's paid hourly. That's got to be decided."

"I still don't know. You can take care of that later, can't you?"

"What about you and Sally? Surely you should both receive bonuses for all this. Don't you want Sally to get a bonus and a commendation? Don't you think she deserves it?"

"Yes, very much. I do."

"But how can I fill out the right forms, indicate the correct information without knowing when we're getting out?" As soon as Gaylord used those last few words, when we're getting out, he wanted to bring them back. He should have said, how long we're staying, never mentioning getting out. He always said too much. Once again he would be foiled by his own eagerness, and he could tell instantly that the error had been serious. Brackin glared at him.

"I alone have the plan, Mr. Gaylord. I alone know what is to happen and when. I'm sorry this causes you problems, but there are none you can't work out. I know you have the ability to manage all right even under these difficult circumstances." Brackin was standing beside Gaylord's desk; Gaylord in turn was looking at Brackin as if he were a madman. These were the words of a VP to a department head who was flipping out in an emergency. And Brackin was not finished, either. "We must all pull together now and do our best to maintain an even keel. I want you to know, Mr. Gaylord," and here Brackin put a hand on Gaylord's shoulder, "that I have every confidence in you as a supervisor and a person." Brackin gave Gaylord's shoulder a paternal squeeze and went back to his corner.

Gaylord sat blinking and trying to figure out what had happened. He had just been given almost the identical speech he had received when told he was going to Ohio. Hearing those words twice in one life was more than anyone ought to have to bear. It's bad enough for his subordinates to charge around with rifles and pistols taking over his office, but the additional burden of paternal talks was adding insult to injury, salt to the wounds, coals to Newcastle. It was beyond confusing, it was crazymaking. Gaylord looked on the desk before him. His eyes lit on a half-finished report concerning marketing strategy for the Canadian west. He greedily plunged himself into the figures and projections where he knew, if nothing else, he would find sanity and order.

ELEVEN

Mrs. Talmage sat in the sunlight by the window across from Sally, reading a romance. Periodically she would raise her eyes and look around her. She could see Gaylord buried behind his papers, and she knew that he was having difficulty controlling his fear. She saw when he went pale and pretended not to notice for fear of embarrassing him. But Sally seemed composed, relaxed. Several times Sally rose and went to talk with Brackin, probably to urge their release or make sure that nothing was troubling him. Mrs. Talmage was glad that Sally was able to speak easily with Brackin; it meant that she could just try and stay out of his way. Mrs. Talmage was aware that her relationship with Brackin had never been good. Every time she tried to speak with the man he seemed guilty and ill at ease. She knew she could be forbidding and had tried to contact him, but had never been able to until, finally, she gave up.

She could not see Brackin from where she sat. He was behind her and she did not want to twist around in her chair to look at him. She was managing to keep her terror at bay by reading and pretending that she was on a long lunch break. She would completely forget that she was wearing only a slip, and was thankful she had that. What if she had not worn one yesterday? She could pretend a slip was a dress, but her imagination would not go beyond that. She desperately wanted to go home, to spend about a week in the house walking about in her robe, doing some cleaning, some reading, but mostly being alone. Robert would make a great fuss over her when this was over, and that was something to look forward to. He always pampered her when she was ill or upset, and she missed him achingly. She really did not give him very much, she knew. She was a withdrawn and closed-in person, but Robert never complained, and seemed content.

Her eyes went once again to the rope jammed into the bottom of the closed window. She had a fantasy of herself, forty years younger, casually opening the window to get a breath of air and, with one standing jump, leaping out and sliding down, landing safely to spring around the nearest corner. But her bones were old, sixty-two years old, and the impact would as likely kill her as not. Still, it was nice to think that she could have done it back when.

Mrs. Talmage stretched herself and, wanting to use the washroom, turned round to tell Brackin. "Mr. Brackin," she said, "I need to go to the ladies' room." He said nothing, and just stared at her for several very long moments. She was now glad that she had never been friends with him; it showed good taste. Really, she had always thought him strange, and now the only word that kept coming to mind was creepy, which she was sure was not in fashion. Now Brackin took himself away from the corner where he fooled with his rifle and approached.

"All right," he told her, and unlocked the cuff on her wrist. "The door doesn't lock, does it?" Mrs. Talmage shook her head, no. "Okay," Brackin told her softly, "but don't lock the cubicle either."

Don't lock the cubicle. She thought, the man is mad. What did he imagine she might do? Jump down the toilet and swim away? Again she nodded her assent and went off to relieve herself. As she went she saw Brackin go to the kitchenette. As she entered the ladies' room she could hear him turn on the tap.

Mrs. Talmage entered the ladies' room and went into

the cubicle. She raised her slip, lowered her underpants and pantyhose, and sat down. She realized that except for last night when she slept, this was the first time she was alone. She thought she missed that more than anything. The fear she had experienced yesterday was diminished today. She could not really imagine anyone as ineffectual as Mr. Brackin harming anybody. She was sure he was all bluff. Still, she did not doubt he was crazy and would not be the one to put him to the test, not again. Yesterday's adventure, when he had torn away her dress, had been in the heat of anger, and she would not let her rage get the better of her again. For now, it was nice sitting here alone if only for a few minutes.

She did not hear anyone enter the washroom, but a sense that she was no longer by herself came over her immediately, manifesting itself in a crawling feeling and a tightening of her sphincters. She looked up and strained her ears to hear if she was deceiving herself or if someone had entered. She was in this state of hyper-alertness when the door to the stall slammed open and Brackin stood before her, brandishing his pistol in his right hand while clutching the rifle in his left. She let out a gasp that would have been a scream had she not been so startled. Her eyes widened in horror, her mouth stood open and useless, and she suddenly felt her sphincters loosen to let the flood of her terror escape. He was pointing the pistol at her head and smiling in a sick, sick way. Mrs. Talmage paled and began to shake her head, no no no. She could see his finger tighten on the trigger and finally squeeze it closed.

The click of the gun resounded in the silence with an echo that would stay with her for eternity, forever resounding off the tiled walls. Brackin lowered the gun and looked at her. "See," he said, "I told you I wouldn't hurt you." Then he turned and left.

Mrs. Talmage sat on the toilet, shaking. She had to get out of here. Had to. She stayed for a moment until she had regained some semblance of her composure. She did not know if anyone had heard—the click of the pistol was the loudest sound she had ever experienced—but she did not know if anyone else knew. She hoped not.

Smolen sat in the trailer counting his blessings. The meeting had ended about half past two, and somehow, he was not quite sure how he did it, he had managed to buy some time. He was pondering the Mayor's last remarks to him, wondering what he had in mind. Was the Chief on his way out? Was the Mayor going to recommend the Chief for the Mayor's post when he went to the capital? Smolen was not sure. But Kowal was right: Smolen did not want to be a deputy all his life. He wanted his own force that he could run the way he wanted, and not have all his authority dependent on an incompetent chief. There was time. A man in his early thirties was far from past it yet, but he needed the break that Kowal could give him, the support from someone up above essential to advancement. If he could get everyone out alive and throw some of the credit to Mayor Kowal, then he might well be on his way. Not that he would endanger the hostages for the sake of looking good, but if it was possible he could come out shining. It was worth keeping in mind. Chief of Police Gregory Smolen had a nice ring to it.

Smolen's reverie was broken by Joe Sloan's coughing. He looked up inquiringly. "Do you know," Sloan asked him, "what today is?"

"Yeah," Smolen answered, "it's Saturday."

"Of the Thanksgiving weekend. The Mattsfield-Winston game is today, Dep."

"Shit," Smolen exclaimed. That game was the high point of the local high school football year. Smolen had played in that game some twelve years ago, and while he had no hair-raising stories for his grandchildren, it meant a lot to him. Sloan, he knew, had a son playing in it and wanted to be there as much as he. And Brackin was keeping them from it. Baby-sitting Brackin meant they would miss the game, maybe the only event in the entire year that was sacred to Smolen. Goddamn him. It wasn't enough that he had to sleep on a cot in this crummy trailer, take shit from every political hack and busybody around, miss his wife and kids, but now he was going to miss the game. The Game. Well, the hell with Brackin. He could watch out for himself this afternoon. Maybe it was not a bad idea. Maybe Brackin needed to know that he could be abandoned, that he was not the center of the universe. Sure. That was it. He'd call Brackin and tell him he was on his own. No attention, no coddling, no keeping the world waiting for his whims. "Give me the phone, Joseph. We're going to the game."

Sally had heard the slam from the washroom, but not the click of the gun. She and Gaylord had both had their backs to the door and had not seen Brackin enter. It took her a minute to realize that he was not in the room with them, and another moment to connect the activity in the ladies' room with Brackin. As she stood and began to walk toward the door, he came out grinning and holding his pistol and rifle.

"What were you doing in there?" Sally demanded of him.

"Just visiting," he giggled.

"Joan," Sally called, "Joan, are you all right?" Gaylord had turned around and was looking concerned.

"Mrs. Talmage," Gaylord tried, "do you need help? Do you want Sally to come in?"

They heard nothing for a minute and then the door opened, and Mrs. Talmage stood holding on to the frame, pale, trembling still, and trying to moisten her mouth before she spoke. "It's all right," she whispered. "I'm just not feeling well for a moment. I'll be fine."

Sally helped her to her seat with Brackin following to fix Mrs. Talmage's chain. Sally turned to Brackin. "Tell me,"

131

she was insisting, "what went on in there. I want to know." Her jaw was set and her head held at an aggressive angle as she interrogated Brackin. Gaylord was afraid she would lose her temper and do something stupid, and at the same time was thrilled to see her turn on Brackin. She drew closer to him and Gaylord thought he might have to intervene. When the phone rang, interrupting their contest, he reached for it quickly.

"Mr. Gaylord," Smolen said when he recognized him, "this is Deputy Smolen. Let me talk to Brackin, please."

Gaylord turned back to the pair behind him. Sally was white with fury, and Brackin was trying hard to stifle his giggles. When Gaylord held out the phone to him he grabbed at the escape.

"Listen, Eugene," Brackin heard the Deputy say, "you're going to be on your own for a while. Joe and I are going to the big game. I'll be back about six to see that you get your supper. Don't do anything crazy while I'm gone."

"No!" Brackin shouted. "You can't do that. You can't go. You can't leave me alone here. You can't desert your post. You can't—"

"The hell I can't. Just watch me. You think you're the center of the universe. Well, other people have lives too, and right now I want to see the football game. So long, Brackin." Smolen hung up the phone.

Inside, Brackin was raging. He was screaming at the top of his voice, shouting at the silent telephone. "You'll pay for this, Smolen. You'll be sorry for this. You can't do this to me." He was raging around the room, the rifle held in his two hands in front of his body. He rushed up to the phone and screamed at it. His eyes wild, his head jerking, he flung himself across the room battering himself against the wall. Then cowering in the corner, he began to shout, "You can't leave me. You can't leave me. You can't leave me." His litany, terrifying and terrified, turned into a high awful wail. Suddenly, he stopped, rushed to the phone and screamed at it. "You'll suffer. You'll suffer. The life is not yours . . . not . . . not . . . not. You come back here. Here. Here." He was sobbing and moving all over the office. The others were hiding themselves, trying to become invisible to him, making themselves, willing themselves, to be invisible. Brackin spun around, looking at the room with lips pulled back in a horrible grimace. "He's there. He's there. I can tell it's a trick." Slowly now he went to the phone and picked it up. With difficulty, trying three times before he succeeded, he dialed the trailer. The phone rang. There was no answer. Still he let it ring. Still there was no answer. He looked around at the others, the handset held out with bewilderment before him. "There's no one there," he said weakly, sadly. "There's no one there to answer the phone. They've gone." Brackin was beginning to cry now and tears began to run down his cheeks. "They've left me alone. Oh, no . . . no . . . no . . . not. . . ." Brackin sank to the floor, crying and moaning.

Brackin cried. He cried for forty years. He lay on the floor, bent over double. His arms were around his belly, his legs drawn up beneath him, and he rocked himself with his sobs and cried. Rolled up on the cold floor, he cried. He looked like a large child, just too big to be picked up and held. His head was pressed against the floor and his sobs were muffled. Mrs. Talmage had begun to cry softly by the window. Sally, also crying, and the only one unchained, went to him. Kneeling beside him, she touched her hand to his face. When his sobs increased she took his head in her lap. And so he ended, his head in her lap, his moans growing softer, easier. As he calmed he began to cautiously peer out at his surroundings, anticipating reaction. But no one said a word, not even Gaylord who had managed, with manly power, to control the sympathetic tears he too had felt.

Smolen got a little less than halfway to the playing field before he pulled the car over to the side of the road. He turned around and drove back to the trailer, then sent Joe

Sloan to the game while he went back to his post. He entered and went directly to the phone.

"Brackin, this is Deputy Smolen. Wait. Please don't say anything till I've finished. I'm sorry. I shouldn't have left."

Now the shouting should start, but it did not. Brackin was exhausted from his hysterical bout. He was far too emotionally drained to call up the energy needed to raise his voice. So all he said was "Please don't do it again." And he hung up the phone.

When Brackin returned to his corner to rest, Sally decided to talk to Gaylord. She was not pleased at the idea of open conflict since real life would, eventually, begin again. And, as a matter of fact, Gaylord had just the same idea, so he was more than willing to offer conversation when Sally came over to the desk.

"That was quite a number," Sally said.

"A breakdown within a breakdown, I suppose. But then we can't expect anyone doing what he's doing to behave in an ordinary way, can we?"

"Are we acting in ordinary ways?"

"That's it. Ordinary and regular. The more routine there is the safer we are."

"Do you really think so? That you're safe, I mean."

"Who knows? I have to believe I am or I'll end up on the floor next. Would you cradle me if I had a breakdown?"

"I'm afraid," Sally said with a smile, "that there's only one way you'll find out."

"How come you didn't grab his gun?"

The question took Sally by surprise; her immediate reaction was defensive. But his tone of voice had been even and curious, not at all accusing, so she decided to give Gaylord the benefit of the doubt. "It never even crossed my mind to touch it. I didn't even think till now that I could have."

"Yeah," Gaylord affirmed, "that's what I figured. It

didn't occur to me either until it was all over. He trusts you."

"Yes, he does. Do you?"

"Any reason I shouldn't?"

"I asked you first, Larry."

"Well, it's difficult to say. You seem to have the best contact with Brackin, talk to him the most. Yet you haven't included me in anything. I don't know what you're doing with him. I don't know what's going on." Gaylord paused and looked uncomfortable. "Sally," he continued, "I think what worries me the most is you don't really seem frightened."

"Maybe I'm not. Maybe I believe Eugene isn't going to hurt us, that he's pulling this number without any intention of harming anyone."

"What if you're wrong? What if he's crazier than you think? Sally, you've got to take this seriously."

"Don't tell me what to take seriously," she replied with some anger. "I take Eugene very seriously. Much more than you do. Understand this: I want out of here. I want us all out of here. I hope when we get out we're all heroes, but most that we're alive. I've been working on his trust, getting him to open up to me, allow me freedom. Maybe it makes you feel worse, but even you can see it's for the best."

"Sure, sure, Sally, of course you're absolutely right. The more you can control him, the better off we are. You're doing a great job, we all are. Maybe we'll get promotions when we get out of here. Then you can have my job."

"You know that I was slotted for your post, then?"

"Of course. Even they couldn't throw me in here without telling me that. I hope you get it soon, Sally. Because that means I go to New York, where I belong."

"What really happened? I've heard rumors, of course, but..."

"I got in the way of my wife's sex life, which, unfor-

135

tunately for me, was with a vice president. I was in line for assistant vice president when it was decided that a stint in Ohio would do me a world of good. Not that I've got anything against Ohio, you understand, it's just not what I'm used to. When said vice president tires of my wife, which will, of course, happen eventually, then I'll be able to return."

"Just like that. There yesterday, here today, gone tomorrow. What a game. I'm sorry it worked out that way, Larry. For both of us. I think I'll go see what Joan is up to."

Gaylord nodded his goodbye and watched as she went across to Mrs. Talmage. He continued staring after her, contemplating the events that led to his being held hostage in a branch plant, a subsidiary in Ohio. What bothered him, what really gave him more and more trouble all the time, was his increasing inability to accept his own story. There were too many holes in it, too many improbabilities to convince a corporate infighter like himself. He knew perfectly well that if someone else had told him the same story he would have expressed his sympathy, clucked over the abuse of power, and still wondered what really happened. He knew what really happened. He had blown it. And he had blown it for precisely the same reason he had blown all his other great opportunities. He was too damn eager, too damn ambitious, too damn willing to use anything he could to get what he wanted. And he was not really good enough. That was the hard one.

Lawrence Gaylord was not a fool. At some point in New York there had been a meeting. Armour, the VP with his wife, had suggested sending Gaylord to Ohio. At least three other VPs had known the real reason. But no one, no one at all, had said, What? How can we send him to Ohio, we need him here. And the reason no one said that was that it was not true. He just was not the super–high-powered executive he wanted to think he was. No one would miss him in New York. No one would worry about someone's saying, Gee, if only we hadn't sent Gaylord to the sticks we wouldn't be in this hole. No one.

He also knew that if it were carefully examined, the roots of the affair between Armour and his wife could be traced back to him. He was the one who urged her to be nice, to make him happy. He was the one who accepted invitations well after he could see what was happening. He started his wife on that path, how should she know when to stop? And if that was what he wanted, then why should she? Only it didn't work out that way, did it? He was not seen as smart, but as greedy. No one thought he was clever, just creepy. The man who would give his wife for an office near the top. Well, that was fine at his level, but beyond that a man had to have more than a sexy wife. And he didn't.

Gaylord was an expert at blaming others. He knew that the gossips would wonder if the hostage-taking would have happened if Gaylord had not made everyone work on Thanksgiving weekend. They wouldn't really believe it, but they would wonder. He was sure enough of that to have thought of a dozen different ways of fixing the blame. But the truth was that he was finished. This had happened in his department while he was on probation. He, Lawrence Gaylord, had a senior subordinate on the extreme edge of a breakdown and had not known it. He needed powerful connections to get out of that one, and he did not have them. Just the opposite. I've done it again, he thought, and with flying colors this time. He was in a hole with only his greed and big mouth and dumb ambition to thank for it. The best thing that could happen to him would be not to get out of this at all.

Gaylord's rage at himself made his muscles bunch and cramp. He wanted out of here very bad. Maybe he would have a breakdown. He had a sudden urge to charge at Brackin and try to take him. One run across the room before anybody knew what was happening. A great leap onto the man, knocking him senseless, beating him quiet. Gaylord stirred in his seat and measured the distance. But he was firmly chained to his chair and could not very well carry the chair in one hand and take Brackin with the other. And anyway, who was he kidding? He wouldn't go up against VP Armour, job or no job. This was it. He'd never leave Ohio and he knew it. Maybe one last promotion to clear the way for Sally, but that was it. Not even an assistant VP, just a department head. In the sticks. Forever.

The wave of self-pity that flooded through Gaylord was strong, and he fought back the tears that had come when Brackin was on the floor. He had forsworn crying long ago. And the only time he had violated that personal covenant was the night before he left for Ohio. His wife had been out and he was all alone in his den. He had sat sobbing, incapable of doing anything to save himself or redeem himself. And then his wife had returned and he heard her stop at the door to his den, listen to his sobs which he was unable to silence, and then go on to bed. He had suicidal thoughts that time, just like now. The child imagining the grownups' misgivings when they find out what he had done. Wouldn't they be sorry. But the only one who was ever sorry for Larry Gaylord was himself. And far, far too often. If he could only . . . Enough. This was it. He had made his own luck. It was time to grow up.

He shook himself like a dog waking. It was just about half past four and he was tired. He saw Sally and Mrs. Talmage sitting together talking. "Hey, Sally," he called out, "since you're so mobile, how's about making some coffee for the unfortunates?" Sally acknowledged that as a good idea and went off to the kitchenette. Coffee would be good now.

* * *

Smolen was sitting alone trying to figure out how to get those people out. And that was the way he wanted it. No Garlas to railroad a massacre, no politicos making speeches; just careful, slow police work totally geared to saving lives. If Garlas wanted to waste Brackin, that was his business and he was welcome to find a way to do it. But not in Mattsfield. Not in Smolen's town. If he could only think of some trigger, some way of getting them out. If he could just solve the puzzle of Brackin. Go figure why a man would suddenly grab three people he works with day in and day out as hostages and never even make a demand. Was he going to live there with them? Was he planning to make them his family and keep them locked in that office forever? And what if he was? What would Smolen do then? How long could he keep Garlas in check? How long could he allow it to go on? He imagined Brackin taking them into their second or third month, like Iran, with daily reports in the papers about the latest negotiations. Only this wasn't Iran. It was Mattsfield and if that sonofabitch didn't come out soon, Smolen was going to have to go in and get him. He was going to have to go up there and knock on the fucking door and say, Open up, Brackin, it's me, Deputy Smolen, and hope to hell that Brackin didn't blow his head off. Smolen was quickly making himself sick. There was no way he wanted to go up there because he knew how it would have to be done. Slow and careful, one man, one gun, him.

He looked around to see if there was any coffee in the pot when he was startled by Ida Crane standing in the doorway. "Damn, Ida," he exclaimed, "you keep scaring the wits out of me. What are you doing here, anyway?"

"I was at the game but I got caught. I ran into two fellows from the wire services, and they made some pointed remarks about where I was and where I was sup- posed to be. So here I am. I brought some coffee."

"You're a mind reader," Smolen said as he took the

coffee. "Ida," he went on after a moment, "suppose he just plans to stay in there indefinitely. What if it's my play? What if it's up to me to make a move?"

"Do you think that's what's happening? Do you think he wants to stay there forever?"

"No, I don't. I think he's too uptight. He's too easily rattled, too confused. I've got a feeling myself that tomorrow's the big day, that he's just going to up and let them go. I don't know if he'll come out with them, but that's his choice. If he's not holding anybody in there, he takes his chances."

"If you think he's coming out, what are you worrying about?"

"What if he doesn't, Ida?"

"Right, Greg. What if he sprouted wings, held the lot of them in his teeth, and flew to Australia?"

Smolen laughed. "Hell, Ida," he said, "then it would be out of my jurisdiction." He finished his coffee and looked again at his friend. "Would you like me to call him? Then you could have one of your This Reporter Was Present stories."

"It's the least you could do for me, young man. Get on the phone."

Smolen dialed while grinning at Ida Crane. His expression changed when all he got was a busy signal. Nonplussed, he held out the phone and said simply, "It's busy."

"Well," said Ida, "at least now you know they're home."

"Who is this? Who are you?" Brackin demanded of the voice on the phone. "Why have you called here?"

"Yeah, right, hold there just a minute," the voice instructed. "Yes," the voice resumed, "hello there. Am I speaking to Eugene Brackin?"

"Yes, this is Eugene Brackin. Who are you?" Sally had come near, and Gaylord and Mrs. Talmage were watching with quizzical looks. None of them seemed pleased by a rupture in their routine.

"Now then, Mr. Brackin, I'm with WNNK News and we have a few questions for you. First of all, are the hostages all safe?"

"Uh, yes, they're safe." Brackin held his hand over the phone and looked first at Sally, then at Gaylord. "It's newsmen. Do I have to talk to them?"

"No," they said together. Neither could guess why they said no, but there was no question in their minds that they did not want to go on display.

"Tell them," Gaylord said, "that all information has to come from the police." Brackin liked the sound of that and nodded his approval.

"Now listen here," Brackin began, "if you want any information you'll have to get it from the proper authorities."

"Is it true that you are keeping the hostages naked?"

"What?"

"Naked, without clothes."

"I have never. No. Absolutely not." Again Brackin turned to his captives who, following his cue, were already adopting an outraged air. "They think I've taken your clothes away. They think I'm a savage. They think I'm a sex pervert," he exclaimed incredulously.

Sally grabbed the phone away from Brackin. "Now listen here, you. Mr. Brackin has harmed no one. He is treating us perfectly well and we are in no danger except from fools like you. As for taking our clothes away, I never heard anything so ridiculous in my entire life." Sally swept around the room with her arm to gain the vigorous assent of the assembled, all of whom were nodding their confirmation. Her eyes jerked back to Joan Talmage who, having apparently recovered from her misadventure with Brackin, was nodding and, incensed with the rest, stood, chained up in her now crumpled beige slip. Sally could

141

not stop a smile and, for the first time since the incident, Mrs. Talmage evinced public awareness of her attire.

"Are you a hostage? Are you one of the hostages?" The reporter on the line was frantically trying to get Sally's attention. "What's it like in there? Is it true he's raped you? Have you been beaten?"

"Sir," Sally replied, "you are a jerk. No harm has been done to anyone. Now will you kindly get off the phone as we need it for the police."

"Listen, lady, just put it down and don't hang up. We won't hang up either and then we can record everything you say in the room. We'll tape every word till it's all over. It's a unique opportunity."

Sally held her hand over the phone and turned to the others. "They want to leave the line open so they can tape everything. These guys are stark raving mad. I've got a better idea," she said into the phone again, "why don't you take the phone and stuff it—"

"Sally!" Mrs. Talmage cried. "Just hang up on them."

Sally put the receiver down on the cradle, and they all began giggling with the exception of Brackin who was genuinely upset that they would suggest such things about him. He went to the phone in order to tell Deputy Smolen about the incident but could not get a dial tone.

"The phone won't work now," he said. He was clutching the handset tightly, both hands choking it into acquiescence. "We're cut off," Brackin said shrilly. "What should we do?"

"Hang it up," Mrs. Talmage instructed, once again in command. "Hang it up, Mr. Brackin, and I'll explain." Brackin put the phone down. "They made the call, you see, so if they don't hang up the phone the connection remains intact. If they never hang up we can't use the phone. Please let me try." She sounded now exactly as she did during a normal working day. There was a problem and she was ready to go at it. She began walking cross the room toward the phone when the chair she was dragging behind her snagged in a table, and she was jerked back like a dog on a lead.

"Here," Brackin offered as he went to her side, "I don't think you need that on just now." So saying, he uncuffed Mrs. Talmage so that her chain was not attached to any fixture. She smiled her gratitude and went to the phone.

"Hello? Is anyone there? Will someone please respond to the phone?" There was no answer. "It is illegal to tie up someone's line by refusing to break a connection. If you do not immediately hang up the telephone I will open a window and personally report you to the police." For several moments nothing happened, and then, at last, there was a satisfying click as the receiver was replaced. All three witnesses burst into applause.

They were still standing about when Smolen got through. Mrs. Talmage, still flush with victory, answered the phone with a lilt and a cheery "Good afternoon, can I help you?" Smolen looked at the phone with some slight surprise and announced himself. Mrs. Talmage greeted him warmly and, after making inquiries about his health and well-being, related the recent adventure to him. Smolen said he would see what could be done to prevent a repeat and asked to speak with Brackin. Mrs. Talmage indicated the phone call was for their jailer, but Sally stood up and stepped toward the phone.

"Is it the Deputy?" she asked Mrs. Talmage.

"Yes, it's Deputy Smolen."

"Let me talk to him first." There were no protests to this request so she received the phone. "Deputy? This is Sally Laird. How are you?"

"I'm just fine, Miss Laird. How are you?"

"I'm doing very well, thank you, Deputy. I do want to speak with you for a moment, though." Sally settled herself on the edge of the desk and crossed one leg over the other. She knit her brows and pursed her lips over on one side of her face while she thought for a moment. "I was the person who spoke with the radio people when they called. The accusations they made were very distressing, Deputy. They were talking about our all being nude, raped, and who knows what else. You can't let that go on."

"Well, I'm very sorry, Miss Laird, but that sort of thing is bound to happen in situations like this one. People will always think the worst; they like to get excited, I guess."

"Well, what are you going to do about it?"

"There isn't much I can do, Miss Laird. Protecting the reputation of kidnappers is not a prime job of mine."

"What about my reputation, Deputy? What about Mrs. Talmage's? How do you think we'll be treated after this with all that sort of crap floating around?" She turned to her companions at this and gave a wink while receiving nods of encouragement. Before Smolen could continue she began again: "And please remember, Eugene has not been convicted of anything, so accusations in the press are unfair. He has not harmed any of us. No one has been hurt, raped, beaten, starved, or otherwise abused."

"Would you like me to hold a press conference? Do you want me to tell them that you're being well treated? Would that do it? There's little else I can do, Miss Laird."

Sally turned to the others with a large, satisfied, close-mouthed smile. "Certainly," she said, "a press conference making it clear that we are all being well treated might help. Yes, a good idea, Deputy."

"Okay, then. I'll set it up right away. Just as soon as you tell me exactly how that dress got outside the window."

Sally hesitated before agreeing to Smolen's demand, but decided that he might be able to do more if he knew the truth. So Sally told him the story and answered his questions until Smolen was satisfied that no one had been molested. Now, he told Sally, he was ready to speak with Brackin.

"What for?" she asked him.

"I beg your pardon?"

"What for? What do you want to talk to him about?"

"Well, what difference does that make? I just want to talk to him, that's all."

"The last time you spoke with him, Deputy, you left him quite upset. I see no reason to badger him just because you have nothing better to do. So, if you won't tell me what you want to talk about I won't let you speak with him."

Smolen was stuck. He had not any specific reason for contacting Brackin other than keeping in touch and trying to determine his state of mind. He really didn't know what to say at this juncture. He looked over at Ida Crane who was listening on the headphones connected to the tape recorder and gave a helpless shrug. He turned back to the phone and spoke to Sally. "I really didn't have anything special, Miss Laird. It's just important that I keep in touch with what's going on in there. You are all my responsibility, after all. Please let me talk to Brackin and I promise I'll try not to upset him. I can understand that you don't want him upset and I'll be careful."

"I'll ask him if he'll speak with you, Deputy; hold on." So saying, Sally put Smolen on hold and turned to Brackin. "He wants to talk with you, and he's promised not to upset you; but he really has nothing in particular in mind, Eugene. Personally, I see no reason for you to do what he wants. What's to be gained from talking to him?"

"Hang on," Gaylord interjected. "Smolen is the Deputy Sheriff and if he wants to talk with you, then you should." Gaylord turned from Brackin to Sally trying to transmit to her the message that she was going too far and should just shut up. She got the message but was unimpressed.

"Bullshit, Larry. Smolen doesn't care about Brackin and probably not us either. All he wants is this to end so they can open the plant on Monday and he can be a hero. He has nothing to gain being nice to Gene except to manipulate him into letting us go."

Gaylord blinked at Sally. He'd become a bit confused,

and his mouth worked for a moment before he could say anything. "Sally," he began hesitantly, "we do want to get out of here. I mean, that is the idea. After all," he continued with a smile in Brackin's direction, "while Gene is treating us very well, I'd still rather not be held hostage. You should keep that in mind."

Sally got up off the desk and walked over to Brackin. She answered Gaylord while speaking directly to Brackin. Standing just two feet from him with their eyes locked, she said, "I know perfectly well that we all want to leave here. I know perfectly well that Eugene will make sure that we do leave here. But it is Eugene Brackin, this man here," she said while she glanced at Gaylord and pointed at Brackin, "who will let us go. He is the one we have to depend on, not Deputy Smolen." Turning to Gaylord now, she continued, "Don't forget that for a minute, Gaylord. Our salvation lies with the man right here, no one else."

Gaylord was about to charge in on this claim but was stopped by the intensity of Sally's eyes, which were quite wide and slightly protruding. He turned instead to Brackin who, Gaylord was distressed to note, stared at Sally with a puppy-dog look full of devotion. Gaylord suddenly grew frightened and used the silence to try and settle his sudden vertigo. Mrs. Talmage seemed to be feeling much better, but when she lacked something specific to do she seemed to Gaylord somewhat vacant, almost hollow. This meant there were only two people to depend upon, Sally and himself. And Sally, he tried to persuade himself, was doing an excellent job of winning Brackin's confidence. That was what she must do and she was the best one to do it. Gaylord was just nervous because he had to depend on Sally. She could be trusted. There was nothing wrong with her. This was just her way of getting Brackin on her side. The anxiety that had centered in his stomach was little appeased by these thoughts and less yet by Sally's actions. She went back to Brackin, and relaxing her body she spoke to him with a soft affection.

"Gene," she said, "I'll never be the one to tell you what to do. If you want to talk with Smolen, then go ahead."

Brackin looked at her and seemed to go deeper into trance. He gave a little sigh and shook his head, no. Sally smiled a sweet warm smile and gave his hands a squeeze. She went back to the phone, took the Deputy off hold, raised the receiver and then let it drop, cutting him off. Sally smiled at everyone and went back to her chair by the window. Curling up in the seat she tucked her legs beneath her and hugged herself gently. The day was beginning to fade into dusk and Sally felt the ebb of her energy synchronous with the sinking sun. How can she control this situation without depleting herself? To acquit her responsibility and go through this mission, hers, not Brackin's or Gaylord's or Smolen's, but hers. God she was tired. Sally lay her head on her shoulder and dozed.

TWELVE

A room acquires a distinctive feel when someone sleeps within it. Those who remain awake are often close to sleep themselves, and tend to rest quietly as much from their own needs as any desire to protect the sleeper. And so the three remaining inmates, two prisoners and their jailer, drew close together so they might speak without disturbing the one who rests. For a while, though, no one spoke at all. Instead they all sat around Mrs. Talmage's desk silently watching Sally nap. As they watched, they relaxed and the muscles in their faces eased as their shoulders drooped and their legs twitched with relief.

"I don't wonder she's asleep," Mrs. Talmage said quietly. "This is an exhausting experience."

"It certainly is," Gaylord concurred. He turned his eyes to Brackin and raised them in question. "Aren't you tired?"

"Oh, yes. Very much."

"Had you expected it to be like this?" Gaylord asked.

"I hadn't really known what it would be like, Mr. Gaylord."

"How long did you plan all this, Eugene?"

"A year. I first thought of it a year ago."

"Did you know you were going to do it as soon as you thought of it?" Mrs. Talmage asked.

Brackin looked at her and smiled slightly. "No," he answered. "I thought of it a long time before I decided to do it. Mostly I didn't think I would."

"When did you know for sure that you were really going to do it?" Gaylord asked in his turn.

"At about four thirty yesterday afternoon when I locked the front door. Before then I wasn't at all sure I would go through with it."

Gaylord and Mrs. Talmage looked at each other with pained expressions. They were both exhausted and at the moment felt weariness far more than fear. Surely it was not just five o'clock, certainly it was near midnight. Gaylord laughed at himself and asked Brackin where he had gotten the idea. Brackin explained that it just came to him one day while he was walking home from work. It seemed right that he should do it, right that he should undertake a venture like this even though it frightened him terribly. And it was very difficult making the preparations, buying the supplies, getting everything together. At first he thought he was doing it all just for something to do, a hobby, sort of, to pass the time. And then, when he had arranged everything just so and knew that he really could do it if he wanted to, he began to doubt. Could he do it? He had never done anything really scary. He had always been terribly afraid of people, always did what he was supposed to. Could he actually do this thing, go through with it?

"But that's not a reason for doing something, Eugene. What did you want to prove, to accomplish?"

No, Brackin insisted. There was no goal, no end result, no reason other than its seeming like a very fine idea.

"But look at the consequences. You might get killed; at least you have to go to jail or hospital."

Brackin shrugged.

"But what about us? One of us might get hurt."

There was no way that could happen as long as things went according to plan. If it all worked out correctly, no one would be harmed except perhaps himself, and that possibility he had already considered. His first concern had been to make sure everybody would be all right.

"But, Eugene, nothing ever goes just according to plan."

Brackin rose and walked silently across the room to the desk in the far corner. He sat on top of it with his legs drawn up and his arms circling his knees. From this position he peered out over the room.

Gaylord looked across at Mrs. Talmage. "How are you doing, Joan?" he asked her.

Mrs. Talmage hesitated for a moment before she answered. "I suppose," she said, "I've been better. But, really," she went on to reassure him, "I'm all right."

"Do you think we'll get out of this alive?" he asked the older woman.

"I don't know what to think, Mr. Gaylord. I've been trying not to think about it at all."

Gaylord noticed her eyes fill and said, "I'm sorry. That was a stupid question."

Mrs. Talmage turned around and saw Sally beginning to stir from her nap. "I'm going over to be near Sally when she awakens; strange things can happen when people come out of naps." And so saying she went across and pulled her chair close up beside Sally's.

"Well," Ida Crane had said when Sally broke the connection, "they're an independent lot."

"I wish I knew what Laird was up to with that number," said Smolen. "I've heard of the Stockholm effect, when hostages become protective of their captors, but I never thought it worked this quickly."

Ida squeezed her lips together before she replied. "Another possibility," she suggested, "is that what she said is exactly what she meant."

"What do you mean?"

"Why did you call Brackin, Greg?"

"Because I need to know what's going on with that nut."

"No. That's not what you said. You called Brackin to get

me some copy for tomorrow's edition. You were going to get me an exclusive, remember?"

"Oh yeah, I remember. So what are you saying, my motives weren't pure?"

"I'm saying that Laird said exactly what she meant. You had no good reason to talk to Brackin, and their attitude is to keep him as relaxed and comfortable as possible. After all, Greg, he may get angry at you but he's only got them to take it out on."

"Goddamn, but I wish I was in there."

Had Smolen been in there he would have been bored. Nothing very much was going on, from Gaylord's perspective at any rate. He sat alone at Mrs. Talmage's desk watching Brackin perched in the corner and Mrs. Talmage with a now awake Sally over by the windows. Gaylord's fear had mostly turned to fatigue, and he was jealous of Sally's ability to nap in the midst of this nonsense. And nonsense it was. Sitting here feeling fairly relaxed, he could view the situation both literally and figuratively. And it made no sense whatsoever. He strongly hoped that Sally saw some sense in it and knew what she was doing. Looking at her, Gaylord had to admit that Brackin's choice made sense. She was an attractive woman in a wholesome, Midwest sort of way. She had an easy reachable air about her that invited intimacy and warmth, but Gaylord had never really tried to make contact beyond the business level. While there was no question as to Sally's attractiveness, her being attractive had nothing to do with being trustworthy. He could not understand how she could remain so calm, so aloof. He hopped back and forth, thinking at one moment that she was carefully manipulating Brackin to let them out, and at the next fully believing that she was almost as mad as Brackin. Maybe he should have put a move on her, but he had decided to forswear office romances forever.

151

Right now, he had to admit to himself, he regretted that decision. Sally's legs were tucked up underneath her, and her cheeks were still flushed with pink from her nap. She looked as warm and cuddly as any woman Gaylord had ever seen. Mrs. Talmage, sitting just next to her, was leaning in and nodding. Once again Gaylord found himself drawn to the older woman's shapely legs as he was struck by the dissonance between her lacy slip and composed manner. Imagine, Gaylord thought, if I'd been made to walk around all day in my underwear. I'd never be able to pull it off so well. Gaylord had a sharp image at that moment of him standing in his undershorts, a very brief snug type, he remembered, in a pale blue. With a sudden jerk Gaylord pulled himself back to reality. He was suddenly aware of being aroused again and that would not do at all. Hostages are not supposed to have hard-ons, though it was nice to know he was still alive.

The two women, by themselves, had been chatting in a desultory fashion for a while. Sally was questioning Mrs. Talmage about her career. As Sally's questions drew Joan Talmage further and further back she grew more and more distant, her eyes seeking and finding visions from the past. Sally asked about Joan Talmage's first full-time job. Where was it? What was it like? Mrs. Talmage gave out the details as best she could. What it was like to be a working woman in Ohio at that time, what was possible, how it was different from now. Sally listened carefully, trying to gain a flavor of what it must have been like. She threw her mind back now to something Mrs. Talmage had said a while ago. "You said you left college early in your second year. Why did you leave?"

"Oh, it's a long story, not very interesting, I'm afraid."

"Did you want to leave?" Sally persisted.

Mrs. Talmage laughed a small laugh and shook her head. "No, not at all," she said. "College was wonderful. It was everything I'd hoped it would be. There were two of us from Mattsfield, myself and Ida Crane. We were good friends and went off to college together. We entered regular programs, not teaching or home economics courses, and fought for the best grades in the class. We'd march around in trousers, smoking cigarettes, going to meetings, and generally trying to outrage people. By and large we succeeded."

"Then what happened? Why did you stop? And are you still friends with Ida Crane? I didn't know you knew her."

Mrs. Talmage looked at Sally and then down at the floor. What was this sudden intimacy born of imprisonment and hope? Was it real? And did it matter? "Do you know, Sally, I've always admired you. Your independence, assertiveness; spunk, we used to call it. Had I done what I'd intended I might have been like you; I would have liked that."

Sally watched Mrs. Talmage with surprise as tears filled the older woman's eyes. "Joan, what is it? You can tell me." Sally reached her hand out to Joan Talmage and placed it on her arm. She held her head at an angle and sat silently waiting.

Joan Talmage sat up and sniffed. She shook herself once or twice and, without looking directly at Sally, began to speak. "When I was at college, in the last part of my first year, I met a young man from a very good family. We spent a good deal of time together, but had to part for the summer. Well, we wrote letters once a week or more, and there was no one here in town except my old school friend Robert Talmage and Ida. All the other girls suddenly seemed very silly or very burdened. Most of the girls I was in high school with had children if they were married, the rest were in tiresome jobs they would never leave. So my thoughts were no more in Mattsfield than was my heart.

"When school began again in September it was wonderful. We were very much in love, and being a very modern young woman I decided not to wait for marriage. Who could think about marriage and mores in 1939? Can you imagine what it was like, Sally?"

Sally nodded. "It wasn't the same thing, but the Vietnam War certainly was a big factor in my life. We were all against the war, but all the boys I knew were threatened by the draft. It gave a sense of urgency to everything."

"Yes, Sally, exactly, a sense of urgency. There was no time for us to build anything since it was all coming down. And, too, I very much wanted to be daring. Well, I was. And . . ." Mrs. Talmage choked, momentarily unable to continue. Her eyes welled again and she fought for control. "I'm sorry, Sally, but I've never talked to anyone about this, not really even with Robert."

Sally had brought her chair right up so that their knees were almost touching.

"Take your time, Joan."

"I became pregnant," Mrs. Talmage began again in a very controlled way. "I discovered I was pregnant in early November of my sophomore year. I told my boyfriend, and he told his father. Arrangements were made right there in Cleveland. In those days it wasn't as easy, and it was very expensive, but it was possible."

"Oh God, Joan, it must have been horrible."

"Well, yes it was. But the doctor was very nice, and it all seemed very clean, and so on, no dirty back rooms or anything like that. And, after all, I was a new woman, able to take care of myself and above sloppy sentimentality, a realist. Still, I was sick at heart about the whole business. I remember going to the doctor's office in the afternoon. You had to go in the afternoon for an examination and to pay so in the evening there wouldn't be a lot of money around, and I had to sit in the office with pregnant women who were having their babies. They were all so happy. They all wanted to chat with me and involve me, but I kept looking away. It was all I could do to keep from getting up and running for all I was worth.

"The doctor was an older man, really very nice. He took the money, five hundred dollars, and examined me. Mostly asked me questions. I came back at six o'clock that night and the whole thing took less than an hour. He gave me some pills and that was that. I threw the pills out on the way home."

"You threw the pills away?"

"I thought they were just painkillers, Sally," Mrs. Talmage answered, with a glance at Sally to see if she could understand. "And I wanted whatever pain was involved, whatever was coming. Only they weren't painkillers, they were ergot to stop the bleeding and prevent infection. To this day I wonder whether I ever heard him tell me about them. So I went home without my pills, sick, lonely, weak, and scared out of my head. I'd moved out of the dormitory in September and didn't have a roommate, so I was all alone. My boyfriend was nowhere to be found. His father had quickly arranged for him to spend his senior year somewhere else."

"Shit," said Sally.

"The bleeding was supposed to stop, but it didn't. The next day it was worse, more blood, cramps, and weakness. By the third day I was getting scared. I'd gotten chills, and I was freezing even though it was warm in the apartment. I suddenly felt that I was going to die, that this day, or the next, would be my last. I think I was delirious, at least giddy from fever, and I wanted to telephone someone to say goodbye. I didn't have a phone, nothing. So I tried to get to a phone booth to call Robert back in Mattsfield. I felt as if my life depended on calling Robert and saying goodbye, that to die before I did that would be a greater sin than the abortion. We had played together since we were small children and as different as we were, I could not imagine leaving this life without saying goodbye. I needed to know that . . . I had to tell him . . . do you understand, Sally? Am I making sense to you?" Mrs. Talmage took the tissue Sally offered and wiped her eyes. Both women were crying and Sally was holding Joan Talmage's free hand in both of hers. Sally urged her to continue.

"Well, there isn't much more. I got through to Robert, said goodbye, and collapsed. Fortunately, I wasn't able to hang up and they found me in the booth, half dead, and mostly out of my mind. I was in the hospital for almost two weeks and had to recuperate for some time after. I'd been a gymnast at college but they told me that was out of the question for a long time. So I quit. I went back to Mattsfield, married Robert, became a secretary, and ended up being held hostage with you. It was about two years after it all happened that I found out I would never have children. The infection permanently blocked my tubes so that the only child I ever conceived was the child I killed."

Sally felt as if she had just met a new person. She was amazed at how it was possible to work alongside someone and not know her at all. She sat in front of Mrs. Talmage, brushing hair away from the older woman's eyes. "Why did you never go back to school, Joan?"

"In those days it wasn't done. And besides I couldn't bear it. I felt as if I had been an enormous failure, as if everything I had believed and expected was a sham. How could I change the world if I couldn't take care of myself? I'd been a very good gymnast, I had won competitions, and all that was gone. I would have had to go around offering explanations to everyone, where I had been, what was wrong. I didn't want to face all that. So I buried myself in Mattsfield, ignored all my old friends, and married Robert Talmage, a trustworthy, secure, and steadfast man who has stood with me ever since. Other than yourself, Robert is the only person who knows what happened, and I've never talked about it with him." Mrs. Talmage felt quite small and frail sitting in the large desk chair, barely covered by her rather woebegone slip, exhausted from the emotional letdown of telling her story. "I think about the whole ex-

perience a lot. I still believe that getting an abortion was
the right thing to do. I was too young and eager to have a
child. But what crushed me in the end is that I couldn't do
it alone. If I couldn't do it alone, then I wouldn't do it at
all." Mrs. Talmage looked at Sally and then down at her
hands, which she twisted about each other. "I guess that
was a stupid attitude because all it got me was a dull life as
a secretary in a small town, married to a nice but dull man
while I nurse my bitterness."

"You are not dull," Sally insisted, "and as for bitter,
well, you got a pretty raw deal if you ask me."

"I got what I deserved."

"Don't say that. That's terrible. You were set up by a
system that's designed to save men and screw women. But
you've got to stop blaming yourself. You were a child. A
young girl who was never properly taught about birth control is suddenly all by herself, and she's supposed to know
what to do in every situation. Having lovers is not wrong,
Joan. What's wrong, what's awful, is not teaching young
women what it's all about. In your place I would have
done just the same thing. That would have been a terrible
time for you to have a baby—one you'd resent for the rest
of your life. I'd sure as hell be angry if what happened to
you happened to me."

This made Mrs. Talmage thoughtful, but finally she
turned away from Sally toward the window. It was almost
full dark now, and as Mrs. Talmage looked she could see a
darkness that stretched out forever. "It doesn't really matter, Sally. It's all old history now. If I ever come around
again in another life, I wouldn't make the same mistakes."
She turned back to Sally and smiled. "I'd probably invent
all new mistakes if I had another chance."

THIRTEEN

Brackin had been watching Sally and Mrs. Talmage most of the time they were together. He could not know what they were talking about but could sense the intimacy that had built up between them. As they sat they grew closer both physically and spiritually, and Brackin felt more and more the observer. He circled the room from his vantage point by allowing his head to roam free of his body. Slightly, carefully, cautious that no one should notice, his head lifted off his shoulders and hovered, largely invisible, above the women. Now he could find out what was going on, now he could watch as the drama took place. His head could speak if he chose and that would shock them all, but this was not the time. He let his head come down closer to hear better and sure enough they were talking about him. He knew that people often talked about him behind his back, and he knew that it was not his imagination since he could send his head to find out. He did not do this very often because it was very tiring, and besides he would forget that he could do it and then, sitting like this wishing he were not left out of some, some, some happening event thing, he would remember and let his head float free and eavesdrop. Just once he let it happen when there was no one around and nothing to listen to but just to see what would happen. What would happen if his head just did whatever it wanted to and where would it go? But that got very scary; very frightening when he thought he could not get his head back, so he never did it again except for times he needed to know if people were talking about him. They were. But his head wouldn't send him the words, just the information. Just the message: They talk about you. Mrs. Talmage is telling on you. Confirmed. Confirmed. He would be committed when it was over—when it was over his body would be committed, maybe shot. Maybe he could get his body to fly away like his head, maybe he could sail away through the sky except he did not have anywhere to go or any reason to go. It was fine here. Good here. Stay here.

Brackin got his head back and looked around. He considered calling Sally over and telling her about his head, but she would start asking him questions about it and get all excited about it. She would believe him. She always believed him. And she always wanted to know more, always understood more even than he meant. No matter what happened and what he had to do Sally would understand, know that it was right. Gaylord would just argue with him, try to confuse him and turn him around, getting it all backwards. Gaylord always made him feel like a child, young, unschooled. But not always. Mostly since this started, but not just. When they talked about the promotion or Brackin's work it would happen. Brackin would feel like he knew nothing, could do nothing, was nothing, is nothing. Nothing.

An ache of nothingness filled Brackin's gut, and he drew his arms across his belly to protect himself. When he was nothing Brackin could disappear into the past, but people could still see him. It was not real disappearing, just going away. Children always used to tell him not to go away. When he was living with all those kids, the big house, they'd always tell him not to run away even if he wasn't going anywhere. He'd be standing here like this, and another child would come along and Brackin would sink into himself like a turtle, only without a shell. When he did that he could not be hurt or reached or anything. But the people who knew him well, maybe the ones who cared, but he was never sure if maybe they were just bothering him, they would stay and pester him until he came back and stood and listened. He would stand there like this and they would stand there like that and as long as it took it would take.

Brackin was sitting Indian-style on the desk in the corner. He had taken his pistol and placed it in front of him. Deep in his reverie he moved his fingers about the pistol, playing out the drama of his recall to attention. His index and middle fingers formed the legs of the actors while the rest of his hand made up the body. Back facing back they bobbed and weaved around the pistol, reliving those early experiences. C'mon, Genie, the right hand told the left, join the living. The memory of the attention, of the concern, of the girl-woman who was his mother not sister pervaded him so deeply that he could smell her warmth and remember her voice.

Brackin was too deeply involved in his fantasy to notice Sally who had come up alongside him. She watched for a moment as his fingers danced their ballet on the desk. She saw the pistol lying there where Brackin's memory played around it. Not wanting to startle him, Sally said softly, "Hi, baby."

Brackin jerked his head up in a sharp movement of surprise. His right hand grabbed at the pistol, his eyes were widened in shock as he swung the gun toward Sally. In that fraction of a second before he squeezed the trigger his brain registered the configuration that was Sally and sent his left hand out to knock the gun out of line. He was in time. Sally turned sheet white and her knees buckled. She grabbed the edge of the desk on which Brackin sat to keep from falling and made a sound, caused by all the air being expelled from her lungs, that came out as a "Hahh." Her face crumpled as her mouth closed into a slack frown and she felt, just for a moment, as if she might faint.

160

Brackin came to with alarm. He had been playing some stupid child's game and had almost killed his best friend. "Oh my God, my God, I'm sorry. I didn't mean it. I didn't know it was you," he stammered. He clutched the pistol in both hands now, pointing it at the desk. "Please," he ran on, "are you all right? I didn't mean it. I never—"

Sally raised a hand to stop him. She moved it up and down in a calming motion as much for herself as for him. She was trying to take deep long breaths to regain control before the adrenaline spurt declared itself in tears. Sally raised her shoulders up and took yet another breath.

"Gene," she said very quietly, "you must be careful with that thing," and the inanity of the remark struck and she began to laugh. She could feel herself on the edge of hysteria and clamped down on the sound that revealed her near panic. Sally took her hand and put it on his shoulder while she looked around the room to see if anyone had noticed anything. But everyone was involved in his own turmoil and hers went unrecognized. She noticed the clock once again, its emptiness taunting her, and she thought to herself, well, I almost joined you, old clock. She was able to stand now and breathe easy. Brackin began trying to apologize, but Sally shook her head no. "It was as much my fault as yours, Gene. I shouldn't have startled you. No," she said to stifle his appeals, "it's all right, really. I'm okay." And how she wished she could believe that. "Now it's time for supper."

Across the room the phone rang, and Gaylord quickly answered it before Sally could. He wound his hands down through the arms of the chair so he could hold the phone. It was Deputy Smolen, telling them to get their dinner order ready and advising them of the press conference he had set up. It would be reported in about a half hour. It was no mean feat, Smolen told him, getting agreement for it, but he had pleaded the ladies' good names and prevailed.

"Can I assure them," Smolen asked Gaylord, "that no one has been mistreated?"

"Yes, Deputy. We're being quite well treated. What about you? Sounds like you're not getting full support out there."

"Well, let's just say that not everyone agrees with the way I'm handling it. There are people who think the solution to every problem is force."

"Good Lord, Smolen, don't let them try to come in here. We wouldn't stand a chance."

"Try not to worry, Mr. Gaylord, I'll hold them off. In the meantime I've got to get to the press conference."

Gaylord reported the conversation to the group seated around the table while he tuned in WMAT to make sure they did not miss it. "You know," Gaylord said to the assembled as he stirred his coffee, "those people out there who want to break in here worry me."

"How could anyone be so stupid as to do that?" Sally asked.

"There are always people who think they know all the answers," Gaylord said, with just a hint that he was directing his statement to Sally, "and they just don't believe that a solid, steady, cooperative response is best."

"Well," Mrs. Talmage said, "I certainly hope he can control them. They wouldn't stand a chance breaking in here."

"And neither would you," Brackin informed them.

"You know," Gaylord intoned, breaking the ice that followed Brackin's comment, "being held hostage is really very boring most of the time."

"Shut up, Gaylord," Sally said without conviction.

"I mean it," he insisted, "there's occasional fear, some anger, infrequent confrontations with police or kidnappers, but by and large this is very boring."

"You're always boring."

"Come on, admit it, you're bored too. Brackin, aren't you bored?"

"No," Brackin answered, "I'm not bored."

"Well, I am. I think Brackin should do something to amuse us; he's responsible for our welfare and it's dangerous to be bored in a situation like this one. Come on, Gene, do something."

Brackin looked around at them cautiously. He was pretty sure that Gaylord was joking, but not absolutely certain; so, to be on the safe side, he gave a little smile to show he got the joke. They were all sitting around the conference table now. Mrs. Talmage and Sally, both unchained, and Gaylord, still attached to his chair by one arm. The strain of the day, the poor sleep of the previous night showed in their faces. They all had bags beneath their eyes, and each showed strain in an individual way. Gaylord's forehead was drawn tight back across his skull so that a small vein at the side could be seen to pulse regularly. Mrs. Talmage looked white and washed out, her pale skin in stark contrast to the beige lingerie. Sally had been biting her lip all afternoon, and her eyes had taken on a peculiar darting quality as if she were concerned not to miss anything. Brackin, too, looked awful. His hair, never abundant but usually ordered, was askew as a result of his running his fingers through it. He, like Gaylord, needed a shave, but on Brackin it had the effect of making him look very seedy. This was emphasized by his eyes, which were both large and dissolute as if he were having difficulty focusing.

Mrs. Talmage broke the silence by asking what they should have for dinner. Brackin said he would like steaks again, but Gaylord told him he did not have a vote tonight since he selected the food last night. "It's only fair, Gene, to let us choose tonight. It's our turn." This seemed reasonable to Brackin, and he went to his lair of desks to play with his rifle.

"What would you like, Joan?" Sally asked.

"Oh, I really don't care. Anything is fine with me."

"I could really go for some Chinese food," Gaylord said. "There's that takeout place on Cleveland Street that's not bad."

"I don't want that," Sally replied. "I want Italian food. Some veal and spaghetti."

"Too heavy, Sally. Look, I'm the boss. Why don't we do it in order of hierarchy? Yesterday Brackin had his choice because he's the one with the gun, and today I get mine because I'm the boss. Tomorrow you get yours, then Mrs. Talmage. Makes sense doesn't it?"

"It might if you were the boss, Gaylord, but I'm not so sure you are anymore."

Mrs. Talmage listened to this exchange with fascination. She had been wondering all day just who was in charge, after Brackin, that is. Everything seemed topsy-turvy, and she did not like to be confused. She had just decided to respect the old order of things, and here was Sally telling her it might not be that way anymore.

Gaylord was neither upset nor surprised. He had said what he did precisely to get Sally's reaction, and it was just what he expected. "Well," he said, "do you feel better now that you've got that off your chest?"

"Not yet. You have no special authority here, Gaylord. As soon as we were taken hostage we became three people stuck in a jam. You're not anything."

"Well," Gaylord said with a smile, "I wouldn't go that far."

"I would. No one here takes orders from you, not even for dinner. I want Italian food. Is that all right with you, Joan?"

"Oh, yes," Mrs. Talmage answered her, "that's just fine, Sally."

"Be careful, Joan," Gaylord said with an edge to his voice, "maybe you should be calling her Ms. Laird now."

164

"No, Gaylord," Sally said, "but it would be a good idea if you gave other people some credit once in a while."

"Oh, absolutely," he responded. "Italian food is fine, just fine."

So Sally collected the orders for four veal parmigiana with spaghetti, salad, garlic bread, and called the trailer to give it in. Then she sat down at the table and told Gaylord to get WUZY on the radio. She wanted, Sally told him, to get the worst report, not the cooperative one WMAT would offer.

The WUZY announcer informed them that the report from Mattsfield on the hostage-taking would begin after a few commercial announcements. When the reporter came on, she reminded everyone that the hostages had been held since late Friday afternoon. The Mayor answered the first questions by informing the audience that the hostages were well, and that there were no plans to enter the office. Police were hopeful of a breakthrough, but no firm times were given.

"In response to a question about Eugene Brackin," the reporter said, "Deputy Chief of Police Smolen made the following comment: 'Brackin seems quite stable. He is generally low key unless excited. He is treating the hostages very well, and seems determined not to harm them in any way.' He was next asked if it was true that the hostages were being sexually abused, a charge which Deputy Smolen vigorously denied."

"All right," said Sally, "at least they got that straightened out."

"At this point," the reporter announced, "a question was asked about a dress that was alleged to be lying on the ground outside the building. Under intense pressure Deputy Smolen admitted that there was a dress but insisted that the hostages, with whom he has personally spoken, have assured him that they are not being mistreated. Asked if the hostages might have been forced to say that they were well, Deputy Smolen could only reply that his own impression was that they were not being coerced."

"Shit," Sally said.

"The next questioner was WUZY's own Al Drake, who asked if it wasn't true that there was severe disagreement among the police as to the handling of the situation. The Mayor denied such disagreement. Here is Al Drake. 'Come on, Mayor, isn't it true that you've hamstrung Lieutenant Garlas? That you're not using the HIKS squad? Isn't it pretty cheap to risk lives so the local cops can grab some glory?' "

"Wow," Gaylord said, "he's a real darling, isn't he?"

"The Mayor denied this allegation," the reporter went on, "and became quite agitated when Al Drake asked if there was a connection between the handling of the hostage-taking and rumors that the Mayor was being considered as a candidate for lieutenant governor. Here is Mayor Kowal. 'Any suggestion,' " the hostages heard the Mayor say with heat, " 'that there is a connection between my political aspirations and the way in which the police are handling this affair is the rankest sort of yellow journalism. I have not been asked to run for the post of lieutenant governor, and if I had it would have absolutely nothing to do with this operation. It is entirely in the hands of the proper authorities.' The Mayor concluded the press conference at that point. Back to WUZY headquarters, in Cleveland."

The Cleveland announcer informed them that an Al Drake editorial would follow the seven o'clock news. Gaylord turned the volume down and asked Sally what she thought about the press conference.

"I think it stinks. No one could have known about Joan's dress except the police, so it means that one of them tipped off the press. This was supposed to help us, not let everyone think we're running around without clothes on.

If Smolen wasn't sure it was safe, he shouldn't have held the conference."

"But you're the one who insisted, Sally."

"But he's the one who was supposed to make sure it was all right."

"Look, Sally, you can't expect everyone to do just what you want in a situation like this. He has only so much control. There's that guy Garlas out there, he's the guy who really scares me. Anyone could have blown the whistle."

"Well that's too damn bad. He better straighten it out, and he better keep Garlas in check or someone's going to get hurt."

Gaylord looked at her with his head tilted to one side. She had risen and was standing with her hands on her hips facing him. "Is that a threat?" he asked her. But instead of answering him she responded to the phone, which had begun to ring.

It was Joe Sloan at the trailer telling them that their dinner was ready and would be sent up in the basket. "All right," Sally said, "but tell Smolen to call me as soon as he gets back. I want to talk to him."

Dinner was a pleasant affair, though not as light and chatty as the night before. They spent most of their time gossiping about Felton employees, though Gaylord did take a moment to tell Sally that he was enjoying the Italian food. The rich food was filling him up and relaxing them all, more so than a Chinese dinner would have, he confessed. They had just finished eating when the phone rang. This time it was Sally who answered.

"Felton Products, Hostage Department, can I help you?"

"Miss Laird? This is Deputy Smolen. How are you? Was dinner all right?"

"Oh, yes, Deputy, dinner was fine. It was before dinner when we were listening to the radio that was not fine. I

167

thought you were going to take care of everything, Deputy. That press conference was supposed to clear our names, not inform the world that we were naked."

"I know, Miss Laird, and I'm very sorry that got out. There was a leak somewhere. I don't know how they got that piece of information."

"And what's this about the police not agreeing? Is this Garlas trying to get us killed or something? Can't you control anything that's going on out there?"

"He's under control, Miss Laird; he can't do anything without my permission. He was just sounding off and someone heard him, that's all."

"That's all? And suppose Gene believed him and decided to make an example of someone so he would be taken seriously? Does one of us have to get killed before you'll believe him?"

"No, no, it's nothing like that—"

"Just remember, Deputy, that we're getting out of here soon if you don't bungle it, and when we do, a lot of reporters are going to want to talk to us and know what it was like. I have no patience with your excuses or apologies, and if you've put our lives in danger then that's what I'll tell them. Think about it."

"Miss Laird, I'm doing everything within my power to see that Brackin is not riled, and to get you out safely. I'm sorry if it's not easy, but things aren't so soft out here either. And this time I've got to talk to Brackin."

"No."

"I'm under heavy fire out here, Miss Laird. You heard that for yourself. I'm the man with the responsibility, and if I can't honestly tell them I'm in contact with Brackin and that he still sounds all right, I won't be able to hold them. I already apologized for that episode with the game this afternoon. Believe it or not, I thought it might do some good, but I realized that it was dumb. Before that happened Brackin and I had some valuable talks when—"

"All right, all right, Deputy," Sally interrupted, "I'll let you talk to him."

Smolen held on while Sally handed the phone to Brackin. He had been completely honest with her except for one thing. He had not mentioned that the Mayor had promised him the Chief's job if Smolen could pull this all off by Monday with them smelling good. He tried to force that conversation from his mind as Brackin said hello.

"Hello, Brackin. It's good to talk to you again. How are you?"

"I'm fine, Deputy. How are you?"

"Well, the pressure is really starting to build up around here, Gene. The press are giving it to us pretty hard, you know. Hostage-takings are not very popular these days. You can understand how people feel, can't you?"

Brackin waited a moment until he realized that Smolen meant him to answer the question. "Well, yes, I suppose so."

"Right, Gene, what if everybody did it, huh?"

"That would be terrible, Deputy. But I'm the only one who's doing it."

"Of course, Gene, of course," Smolen responded. He was determined to keep his promise to Laird and not rile Brackin. He was convinced they were not getting out to-night, and he was certain that he couldn't talk Brackin into changing his mind. So what did he want from him on the phone anyway? Commitment. Promises for tomorrow, guarantees about when this would end. "Gene," he said, "will you be letting everyone out tomorrow before or after breakfast?"

Brackin looked around him at his hostages. They were all trying to pretend that they were not listening, but he knew they could hear every word. "After," he answered quietly, "and I don't want to talk about that. I want to hang up now."

"One last thing, Gene, about the press conference. You

heard me tell the media that you have been very nice, that you haven't hurt anyone, that you're very considerate to the hostages, but I don't know what they'll do. The radio and TV and newspapers all have to make money, and they'll make more if they call you names and get everyone angry at you. Do you understand what I'm talking about?" When Brackin said he did, Smolen went on. "So I want you to remember that I am behind you, but unless you cooperate with me and come out soon, I won't be able to protect you, that's all. I'll be here all night if you need me, Gene. I'll probably call later so tell Miss Laird that you'll speak with me."

"I don't know, Deputy. I'll see later. Goodbye now," Brackin said, and hung up the phone. It was a quarter to seven and the news would be coming on soon. But until then Brackin decided he would go off by himself in his corner. He was greatly disturbed by the idea of everyone hating him, out to get him. Why couldn't they understand instead of attack? Why must people always think he is wrong or stupid? People constantly, all his life, have been at him, have been in his way. Not really. Not really at all. Who has been in his way for the last years? No one, that's who. But now they will attack and revile me because I am doing something that I must do. There is irony in that. I have done no harm here at all; no one is hurt. And, most important, the circle closes, tightens, shrinks slowly to a dot. And the dot becomes the purest of simple centers.

While Brackin stewed over these matters his three hostages were conferring at the conference table. Gaylord had a plan.

"Listen to me," he whispered to Sally and Mrs. Talmage, "I think he's getting weirder and weirder, and I think the time has come for us to get the hell out of here. There are two of us who are unchained. Mostly he doesn't pay attention to the rifle or pistol, thank goodness, and I think we can jump him."

"We?" Sally remarked, looking at his chains.

"Listen, just listen," Gaylord went on with urgency. "You, Sally, start talking to him when he gets up. But keep standing and get him with his back to us. Then Mrs. Talmage can come up behind him and hit him with something. I'll get over as best I can and try to confuse things, then I'll call the cops."

Sally and Mrs. Talmage looked at each other with disbelief. "And what," Sally asked, "will Joan hit him with? About the nastiest-looking object we have around here is a stapler."

"Good point, Sally. I should have thought of that myself."

"Why?"

Gaylord and Sally both turned to Mrs. Talmage who had uttered this last question. Gaylord looked perplexed.

"Why," Mrs. Talmage reiterated, "should you have thought of it? Because you're male? Why can't someone else think of something, especially someone female?"

"Go get 'im, Joanie," Sally murmured.

"I'm sorry, Mrs. Talmage, I meant nothing by the expression." Gaylord was perplexed by this show of dissonance from his faithful Mrs. Talmage. He knew more than ever that it was time to get out of here. "We," he said emphatically and with an inclusive smile all around, "have to finish our plan. Any ideas for a weapon?"

"What about a chair?" Sally suggested, but Gaylord could tell she was mocking him. "Joan could pick up a chair and hit Gene over the head just like in a Western. What do you say, Joan? Or maybe a desk?"

Mrs. Talmage had begun to titter.

"Don't you two want to get out of here?" Gaylord demanded.

"Eventually," Sally answered, "but I'm not sure this is the moment."

Gaylord looked at her evenly. Why did he have the feeling that she really did not want to get out, that she was involved here, attracted here? That would be crazy, and he discounted it. And as he did so he had his inspiration. "Look, I've got it. I know what Mrs. Talmage can use. If it's good, will you all give it a try?"

"Depends," Sally answered for them both. "First tell us what it is."

"In my desk drawer, the deep one, in behind the files there's a full bottle of Scotch. A nice heavy bottle that'll put Gene to sleep for a while until we get out of here."

"A bottle of Scotch?" Sally said, her eyes alight. "That's very interesting, Larry. I had no idea you were holding out on us." She turned to Mrs. Talmage. "Well, Joan, what do you think? Do you want to take a bottle of hootch and smack Gene on the head with it?" Gaylord's face fell at the way she put the question. Mrs. Talmage tittered again. "Really, if you think of it," Sally went on, "it's a terrible waste of booze. I mean, I could really use a drink. Why don't we first drink the bottle and then bonk Brackin with the empty? That would be much more ecologically sound; sort of like recycling."

"That sounds much better to me, Sally," Mrs. Talmage agreed. "Breaking someone's skull is not really my style." She gave Gaylord a look that was very close to disdain, and then pointed out that it was news time. Gaylord, resigned, adjusted the radio while Sally went to get Brackin. Soon all four were comfortably seated around the table listening to WUZY.

This report was considerably less volatile than the earlier noon report. There were no wild statements, just calm denials of rumor and assertions of confidence in local efforts. After the news the station announced that the Al Drake editorial would follow after a few commercials.

"Remember," Gaylord said to Brackin, "this guy thinks he's real cute and has the IQ of a carrot. So don't pay too much attention to what he says." And after that introduction Mr. Drake came on.

"This is Al Drake," the sneering voice announced, "and I've got something to say.

"I had the opportunity today to witness small-town Ohio politics at its worst. I was in Mattsfield for what was billed as a press conference, but was really a painting bee, and the paint they used was whitewash. Once again local politicos and law enforcement personnel sit around jawing mealymouthed nothings while crime is permitted to reign. Here's a man over in Mattsfield who can hold a whole town to ransom, keep three innocent people hostage, committing Lord knows what atrocities to good hard-working men and women while the cops do nothing.

"There are some people who think that maniacs should be treated with kid gloves—after all, it's not their fault they murder and rape, it's our fault for not understanding them. These people, I won't call them mushy-minded knee-jerk liberals because that label is too good for them, just want to sit around and beg and plead for hostages to be released, for children not to be killed, for hijackers to give up. And, we have to admit, many of these people are probably sincere, they really believe that nonsense. But that's no excuse for letting maniacs and hoodlums run our towns and cities. That's no reason for letting motorcycle thugs terrorize the countryside.

"It's been too long that citizens have had to take back-row seats to murderers and crooks and gangsters. Now is the time for our rights, yours and mine, to take a turn. Now is the time for Mattsfield to set an example for America and go in there and get those people out. And if that means someone might get hurt, well, then, there'll be one less crazy maniac left in the world. Lord knows we've got plenty to spare.

"This is Al Drake saying good night, and I've got something to say."

173

"It's nice to know," Sally said, "that he's so willing to let us die for his rights. That guy's nuts. Why do they let him on the air?"

Gaylord shrugged and said something about the silent majority, but he was really watching Brackin the whole time. He felt as if he were locked in a cage with some dangerous animal, and he constantly was on guard for signs of hunger or rage. He also realized how apt that analogy was, but that it was complicated by not being alone in the cage and not even being sure who the animals were. The headache he currently enjoyed began when Mrs. Talmage had shown signs of rebelling against his authority and throwing in with Sally. Now he did not know what would happen. And he still kept wondering at his own paranoia. Why should he think that Sally and Mrs. Talmage were on a different side than himself? Surely not for rejecting that ridiculous plan of his, and not for some female bonding that excluded him. Then for what? Perhaps for the way Sally's face got taut and her hands twitched when she spoke alone with Brackin? Maybe for the way she would sometimes look around with her eyes narrowed as if calculating something, but what? And did she really do these things or was Gaylord's fear all he was seeing? He had shut off the radio and watched as Sally went into his office and emerged with the bottle of Scotch. He was very ambivalent about the liquor. He could use a drink—that was the understatement of the year—but was wary of Brackin's drinking, and of Sally's drinking too, for that matter. But, who knows, maybe Brackin would get drunk and pass out and they could just get out of here. At all events it looked like he was going to get a drink.

The inmates of The Felton Prison for the Socially Confused, as Gaylord had dubbed them, were on their second drink. Neither Brackin nor Mrs. Talmage was a drinker at all, and Sally and Gaylord, like many people who live alone, drank infrequently. Still, all hands seemed to be relishing their tot. They were gathered around the conference table where Gaylord was expounding on conditions of entry to the Felton Prison.

". . . so it's much easier to get in than out. We have, for example, taking myself, that is, wayward managers from the big city incapable of avoiding trouble. We feature unmarried career women just beginning to feel desperate—"

"Why desperate?" Sally asked.

"All sorts of reasons. No man. No promotion. Future of growing old as a spinster in a small town. Lust for life unsatisfied. More?"

"That'll do. Pray continue."

"What else do we have here?" he went on and looked at Brackin. "Of course we are replete with kidnappers who have missions to fulfill." He said this with a smile and watched as Brackin looked to Sally for a cue to the correct reaction. Sally's grin told Brackin to laugh. "Mild-mannered gentlemen in middle age who suddenly turn round and become mysterious adventurers spouting cryptic slogans and even more cryptic explanations. Quite a zoo, don't you think?"

"And?" Mrs. Talmage prompted him.

Gaylord looked at Mrs. Talmage and pondered for a moment. "And," he said, "weary post-menopausal women trying to relocate their roots. We do a brisk trade in those."

"I imagine you do." Mrs. Talmage laughed. "I don't drink very much and I'm afraid I'm getting quite drunk. You mustn't let me drink too much, or I shall do something embarrassing."

"I certainly hope so," Gaylord said. "What point is there in getting drunk if not to do things we would never do sober? Have you ever been drunk, Gene?"

Brackin's world was floating in and out. One moment he would feel tightly bound to these three friends, then

175

revert to a mere observer permitted only to watch and not partake of intimacy. He had been on an outswing, alone by himself, when Gaylord's question came at him.

"What? What did you say?" Brackin managed.

"A mandatory exercise when getting drunk is the review of previous drunks, a toasting of times when sobriety was downed, drowned we should say, by nature's own inebriants. Come, Gene, have you ever been drunk? Tell me." Gaylord looked at Brackin with a smile, a smile of interest, Brackin thought. He really wants to know if I've ever been drunk.

"No. I haven't ever been drunk. I've drunk only infrequently. I don't drink by myself and I'm usually alone, so . . ."

"Well, you're not alone now," Sally said and placed her hand on Brackin's forearm. She turned to Gaylord and said, "God, but you talk a lot when you drink. I never knew that before." She did not know why, but Gaylord's loquaciousness was irritating her, making her uncomfortable.

"Certainly I talk when I drink. What other purpose is there if not to open the mind and free the mouth? Why, I'll wager that even the good Mr. Brackin here will become a veritable babbler when he downs this extra emergency drink I'm prescribing for him. Come now, Gene, down the hatch. Drink up and watch the magical effects." Gaylord, listening to himself, was somewhat surprised at how quickly the liquor had an effect on him. He always talked a lot when he drank, but he usually had to drink more than this to get there. It was not that he was worried about it, quite the opposite. The feeling of relaxation that filled him was a great relief, and it was likely the enormous tension that caused the quick reaction in the first place. But would it affect the others the same way? And what if it did? Was it good to let Brackin get drunk? Was it good for him to get drunk? Maybe he should just have another drink and forget about it. At least if Brackin shoots him after he passes out he won't feel it. He reached for the bottle and began encouraging Brackin again. "See, Gene, I'm not going to let you drink alone. Go on, drink up."

Brackin looked at the drink before him and shrugged. He picked up the mug—they were using coffee mugs for their drinks—and took a healthy swallow. Gaylord clapped and called him a good boy, so Brackin took another swallow. He was enjoying the attention Gaylord was giving him. It was the first time since it all began that Gaylord spoke to him without some purpose in mind, without trying to talk him into something, and he found this talkative, joking Gaylord very pleasant. Brackin took a third swallow and beamed at everyone. He could see that Mrs. Talmage was enjoying herself but Sally seemed distant and withdrawn. This gave him pause, and he was about to contact her, but Gaylord interrupted.

"Now, Gene, you have downed the statutory two cups of brew proving your manhood and good fellowship, to use the old-fashioned sexist terminology, and now you must address your friends and speak to them from your heart. It is time for a speech. Speech, speech, we must have a speech."

Sally did not know what the stupid sonofabitch was up to, but she didn't like it. All of a sudden he's right with Brackin. All of a sudden he wants to be a chum. Well she wasn't worried. She knew she could have Brackin anytime she wanted him. She watched as Brackin sat giggling while Gaylord and now Mrs. Talmage encouraged him to speak. The fools thought they could goad and plead him into what they wanted. But, she considered, perhaps a speech might be a good idea, and, besides, she shouldn't sit here like a fifth wheel. She turned to Brackin and stared at him until she had his attention. Her face was deadpan, her eyes directed right at him. When he had ceased giggling, when

177

he had stopped even smiling, when he was wishing he could tear himself from her stare and wondering what he had done wrong, then Sally smiled softly and said, "Give me a speech, Gene." And Brackin nodded to her and stood up. Sally immediately felt better, more relaxed. She poured herself and Mrs. Talmage another round and even tipped a bit into Gaylord's mug before she settled back and gave her attention to Brackin.

"I've never given a speech before," Brackin mumbled. "I don't really know what to say." He looked at each of his audience in turn and got no help at all. He was about to refuse to go on when a joke Mr. Felton, president of the company, had made at the company picnic one year came to his mind. He smiled shyly and said, "You're probably all wondering why I've called you here." This got a good response, especially from Gaylord, who roared. "I never seem to know what to say. I hardly ever need to say anything. But sometimes my head gets so full of words, but not really words, but thoughts, that I could bust." He was screwing his face up in concentration, trying to keep his train of thought from running away from him. "I never do anything. I mean I never do anything that I don't do all the time, the same things. I never do anything that I don't have to do." Brackin felt he was getting confused and didn't know if they understood him. Mrs. Talmage was forcing a smile, Gaylord was looking confused but earnest, and Sally, well, Sally was looking at him with a gleam, and that gleam told Brackin that Sally knew what he was saying before he said it. She had the eye of knowledge. "I know some of you are angry at me. And I don't want to have you angry at me. But I haven't hurt anyone. Maybe even I've helped some. Maybe you can't make sense of that. I've never done anything I haven't done before, and maybe that's why this is so important, so right. How could I learn if I didn't do it? How could you all become part of the circle if I didn't do it? That's what you have to tell

178

me." His gaze was mostly on Gaylord now. "You have to tell me how this could have happened if I hadn't done it." He took his eyes off Gaylord and turned to Sally. "Have I said enough?" he asked.

Gaylord was entranced. He was staring at Brackin and felt his words, heard his words very clearly even though he was not sure what they meant. Without thinking he looked to Sally and asked her to have Brackin speak just a bit more. Sally shrugged her shoulders and turned to Brackin. "That was a nice speech. You don't have to say more if you don't want to."

"Well, I don't really have more to say. I really love you all," he said with a deep blush. "And could I please have another drink?"

All three laughed at this, and Gaylord poured drinks all around while he turned up the radio. "Okay," he announced, "now that the speeches are over, the party can begin."

FOURTEEN

Deputy Smolen sat alone contemplating the rumor that the Mayor might run for lieutenant governor. If Kowal left Mattsfield, the Chief might run for Mayor, leaving the Chief's spot open for himself. Well, it all sounded nice and simple, a bit too simple for his taste, but at least there was a chance he could end up with his own force. He had to make sure he got the Mayor in at the end, and most important, that he, Smolen, was around at the end. It was not as if he was doing something for himself that would endanger his charges, the hostages, or the other police involved, just that he would grab any opportunities that arose. But never forgetting his first responsibilities.

His reveries were interrupted by the entrance of Sidney Garlas. "Hi, Sid," Smolen greeted him. "Feeling any better?"

"Stuff it, Smolen, I've had just about enough for today. Ever since you put one over on me at that fucking meeting this afternoon I've been nursemaiding a bunch of reporters who want to know everything when I know nothing. And if you don't stop smirking, I'm going to kick your ass."

"Easy, easy, no one's going to kick any asses around here, and I'm not smirking at you. I'm just finding some irony in the situation."

"I'll give you irony if that's what you want. There's a nut up there with three hostages and we're down here not doing anything about it. That's irony."

"That's not irony, my friend, that's life."

"Now you're a fucking philosopher. There's no end to your talents. What's the drill for tonight?"

"No drill, just settin' and waitin'. That car that just pulled up should be Ida Crane's."

"That old witch? What do you want her around for?"

"Never mind. Just remember she's a friend of mine and she's been a big help, so mind your manners."

Garlas nodded and turned to the door, but he was surprised to see not one but three people enter. Along with Ida was Joe Sloan, bearing Smolen's dinner, and another man who turned out to be Barry Newman, vice president of public relations for Felton.

"Great," said Garlas after they were introduced, "just what we needed, a civilian. You don't really belong here, Mr. Newman."

"I agree," he answered, "but Mr. Felton himself decided someone should represent us down here, and everyone else is away for the long weekend, probably pretending they don't know about it." Newman turned to Smolen whom he had briefly met earlier that day. "What's happening, Dep? Anything new? Are the good guys winning?"

Smolen did not feel any better than Garlas about having an outsider around, but he saw no way out. So while he ate his sandwiches he brought the VP and Ida up to date.

While he spoke, Joe Sloan busied himself clearing a table. Smolen inquired as to the purpose of this activity and was referred to Ida Crane. He raised his eyebrows to her and she replied, "Well, I wasn't sure if we'd have enough hands, but I brought a deck of cards and some chips. Figured you suckers could be talked into a friendly game of poker. That is, if you've got nothing better to do."

Garlas looked at Ida with new eyes. "You play?" he asked stupidly.

"No," Ida answered, "I just get games going and watch.

181

Son, I was playing poker when you were playing jacks and not walking on cracks. Dime and a quarter, three raise limit, dealer's choice, and no bullshit games—it's my deck, anything goes wild besides me and I leave."

"Lady," Garlas said, "you've got a game. Everybody in?" He looked around at the assemblage and got nods from Smolen and Sloan. Newman shrugged and said he didn't play much and hadn't for a long time, but Garlas reassured him that it was like riding a bicycle, you never forget once you've learned, so they had five hands. As Garlas pointed out, poker with fewer than five was like fishing in a swimming pool: It might keep you awake but you could not really catch anything.

"Okay," Ida began, "Seven card stud, the real game. Here we go." She dealt out two down cards to each player, then one up, reciting the card as she went round. "Four of clubs for Joe, Greg gets a lady, the Veep has the ace, and a knave for Garlas, wonder how that happened, Sid? All right, gentlemen, the Veep speaks."

"What?" asked Newman.

"You have the high card," Smolen told him. "That means you bet first."

Newman looked first round the table, then back to Smolen. "What should I do? Should I bet?"

"Always pay your respects to the ace, Mr. Newman," Ida suggested. "Lay out a dime." So Newman threw a blue one into the pot. Everyone followed suit and the next round was dealt.

"A seven for Joseph, no help. King of hearts for Greg, possible straight flush, good luck. Another ace for the Veep, a pair of aces showing; who invited him anyway? And a deuce for the knave, and a four to help my six, big deal."

"Now what?" Newman asked Smolen.

"Do you know anything about this game?" Smolen asked in return.

"Sure, I used to play it when I was younger, but never for money."

"Well, a pair of aces on the board is pretty good, so I'd bet a quarter if I were you."

"A dime would be enough," Garlas argued.

"Not for a pair of aces, turkey," Ida said. "He just wants to keep the price down, Barry, don't pay any attention to him."

Newman put a red chip in and that precipitated the departure of Garlas and Sloan. Neither Smolen nor Crane could get their straights going and Newman took the first hand. "Hey, this is fun," he said, "I'm glad the old man sent me down. Let's have another go at it."

Gaylord had been fiddling with the radio, trying to find some music that did not offend the ears without putting to sleep. He finally located a station on FM that held promise. "It's Harvest Moon Night tonight," the announcer crooned, "a night for the Big Hands and Big Sounds of days gone by. Tonight we go back in time to those enchanted evenings in college gyms, country clubs, dance halls, and living rooms when swing was king. Our companions on this trip back to the forties will be the glorious Glenn Miller and his orchestra, the incomparable Benny Goodman, the sweet and true trumpet of Harry James, and the artful Artie Shaw. To warm you up and bring you here, deliver you to the Harvest Moon Ball on this beautiful Saturday night of Thanksgiving weekend in Cleveland, Ohio, we have Glenn Miller and his orchestra with 'Chattanooga Choo Choo.' "

"Hey," Gaylord said, "not bad; will this do?"

"Oh, please leave it on," Mrs. Talmage begged. "That's my music. I haven't listened to any of that for ages." For the first time since this afternoon she felt herself relax. The muscles in her shoulder that had been hunched for so many hours seemed to give her some respite. She was smiling, genuinely this time, and was aware of her surroundings. She saw Gaylord sitting and grinning at her, Sally's calm watchful gaze, and even Brackin, whom she had not dared to look at unless she had to, seemed suddenly less fearsome. She held out her mug for another drink but found that she had to put it down before Gaylord could pour since she could not quite hold it steady. The mellow flow that filled her combined with Glenn Miller and the sweet rhythm of "Chattanooga Choo Choo" to make her body sway to the music and her heart drift to different times. "Once, you know, I asked a boy to a dance. And he accepted, too. We were very forward, we modern girls; made a lot of progress but lost it all after the war." She turned to Gaylord and struck a pose. Taking an imaginary cigar from her mouth and pretending to spit on the ground, she said, "War is hell, Gaylord, don't ever forget it." The Glenn Miller faded and another song began. Mrs. Talmage started dancing by herself and had to stop when Gaylord asked her what the song was. "That's 'Caldonia' with Woody Herman, you silly boy."

As Mrs. Talmage danced, the others watched and drank. It was like having a floor show. She moved with grace and confidence, dancing and sometimes singing, sometimes coming over for her drink, sometimes smiling at the others, sometimes entering a sphere she alone controlled. The others sat and drank and wondered. Sally beamed and gladdened, knowing that Mrs. Talmage was young again without any mistakes behind her. Gaylord was swaying to the music himself, enraptured by the sight of his faithful assistant flowing about the room in her lacy lingerie. Brackin watched with awe and envy as her movements led her through the mass of tables and chairs which had always before been just an office. She was circled for him by an aura of yellow light that protected her steps and guarded her body. His responsibility, too, was to guard her well-being, all of their well-being.

184

Mrs. Talmage danced for almost a full hour without stopping, except to sip at her drink, until the nine o'clock news came on. She sat down to rest and replenish her mug. "Harry James, Glenn Miller, even the Modernaires, this is wonderful. Thank you, Mr. Gaylord, for finding this station."

"Not at all. You dance beautifully, it's grand to watch. Can you Charleston?" This got pleas from Sally and Brackin as well.

"You children! This isn't Charleston music. This is lindy music, maybe the peabody, foxtrot, but not Charleston."

"But you can Charleston?"

"Certainly I can Sharshun," she said and looked at them all with triumph.

"Sharshun?" Sally mimicked. "Is that a new dance?" They all roared.

"You can't even say it," Mrs. Talmage accused. "You must be drunk."

"I am not," Sally insisted.

"Ha," Gaylord jumped in. "If you're not drunk, prove it. Let's see you dance. If you can dance you're sober, if not you're drunk. Right?" All hands agreed this would be an adequate test.

"But what'll I dance?"

"The Sharlshun," Mrs. Talmage chimed.

At precisely that moment the radio let forth with "Sing, Sing, Sing," and Benny Goodman's clarinet began to spread out from the steaming Latin background. Sally stood and began to dance. At first she tried to mimic a Charleston, but that soon stopped, for Benny Goodman was filling her with movement and fun. She gave up the dance she did not know and embraced the one she did. She held her hands out before her, in front and above her head, crossed at the wrists, arms limp to the shoulder, her upper torso throbbed in and out in counterpoint to her hips which beat with the slow sensuous music. As the clarinet rose high she raised her body up and along the music, straightening so that her chest came out, and then snaking back in as the solo became flighty and skittery. Then suddenly as the music picked up a wild Eastern beat she threw herself into rhythm and shook along her core.

Mrs. Talmage had dimmed the lights by turning off two of the three rows of overheads. Sally danced and hypnotized, entranced her audience. The fever rose as the drink flowed through the blood and its effects reached the cerebral cortex. At Gene Krupa's solo, Sally fastened her feet to the floor and shook. As the solo drove on she moved her concentration to different parts of her body, and she could feel the aliveness of herself in that place. She had the awareness of her audience and felt their energy as she shook. Without it she would stop. As the drum solo ended the piece, to be replaced by the soft sounds of Russ Morgan and his orchestra, Brackin rose in applause. His eyes were brimming with tears of joy and he bit his lower lip so as not to cry. She had danced for him and he loved her for it. She danced at his party. His. For him.

They stood looking at each other, Brackin and Sally. She appeared shy and embarrassed but was really being coy. Aware now of the impact the dance had on him, she waited for a reaction. As Brackin stood and watched her his elation ebbed. Now he should do something and he knew not what. She was looking like a schoolgirl at a dance and he had not done very well there at all. Why was she making him suffer this way? Why wasn't she telling him what to do? She knew he didn't know. He appealed to her with his eyes, begged her to take over, and, with a slight smile, she warmed him at once. As "The Very Thought of You" came softly into the room, she moved toward him and reached out to put her arms under his. Brackin realized she wanted to dance. Brackin knew how to dance. He had once been taught by his oldest-but-one stepsister. A very trying pupil he had been. In the past forty years he had danced on three occasions, each time for one dance. As Sally took him in her arms he raised his to her back, being careful to keep as much distance as possible between his body and hers. This was made particularly difficult since Sally had wrapped both her arms around him, and there was nowhere to put his except around her. She began to move him slowly round in an easy circle as the gentle music took them. Slowly, as they danced, they grew closer together. Now Brackin could no longer see Sally's face. This disconcerted him since he did not know where to look. One way showed Mrs. Talmage swaying by herself with a refilled mug of Scotch, sipping and dancing, swaying and imbibing. The other exposed Gaylord's sour visage with its bleary narrowed eyes and frown of concentration broken by twitchings and flutters induced by the alcohol. So Brackin closed his eyes and danced with Sally while the sweet sound of the big bands rolled by.

The announcer broke in with the call sign, time, weather, and a few commercials. All hands took the opportunity to move about and mingle. Gaylord, of course, did little requiring mobility, but Sally went to his side to console him. "I'm sorry I can't dance with you, Larry," she told him, "but you seem to be tied up for the evening."

"Why don't you get him to release me?"

"Because he doesn't trust you and, frankly, I don't blame him."

"But think, Sally, then we could have a glorious spin around the dance floor."

"Oh," she answered as Duke Ellington came on with "Take the A Train," "if that's what you want I'm glad to oblige." Sally put one hand on each side of his chair and spun him round like a top. She kept spinning him, shouting whoopee as he went round and round. Stopping him, she turned to the others and called out, "Mr. Gaylord wants to dance and he can't do it alone." Sally began to push him about the room, in and out the desks and table, wiggling her rear and now and then raising her right hand above her head to waggle her forefinger. Mrs. Talmage watched for a moment and then, grabbing Brackin's hand, she pulled him behind her to fall in place after Sally. They were all whooping and hollering in time to the music, dancing in and out, up and down, Gaylord doing his best by snapping his fingers.

As the song ended they returned to their starting point, Sally finishing with a flourish of chair spins, ending in a joint bow with Gaylord. The music was still wild and Mrs. Talmage was literally throbbing with the beat. The three others began to clap in time to her dancing, and thus encouraged she clambered onto the conference table and started to high kick, but her slip was too tight and she stumbled. Calling to Sally, she cried, "Scissors, Sally. I need fringe. Gotta make fringe." Sally crossed to her desk and got out a large pair of shears. She ran back to the table and, while Mrs. Talmage danced, she cut fringe into the bottom of her slip. The fringe went up about ten inches and allowed Mrs. Talmage the freedom she wanted. Now her legs flew and hands waved. She even put her hands on her knees in a Charleston step, who was to know? She spun and leaped, terrifying them for fear she might fall off the table, but she never even lost her balance. She hot-footed it and sure-footed it through Gene Krupa's "Drumboogie" like a star. As the music finished she heard the applause from her audience and quietly, gracefully crumpled into a heap on the table.

Sally and Brackin rushed to the table and kept her from falling off, though there was really no danger. They slid her off and carried her onto the couch in her office. Brackin held her around her chest and once again felt her breasts beneath his hands. He wished for a moment that he was alone with her so that he could explore her in this unconscious state. But Sally was busy arranging her comfortably on the couch and shooing him away. She was not perfectly steady but managed to get Mrs. Talmage resting comfortably. Brackin stood and watched, fascinated by the gentle motions of the one woman's hands on the other woman's body. Sally's tender handling filled him with warmth, and he pictured himself being tucked in by her, feeling the covers coming in around his chest and throat. He gagged and turned away.

By the time Brackin looked back at the conference table Gaylord had already secreted the paper shears in the back of his waistband. After rolling forward he had reached up as far as he could by moving his arms as much to one side as was possible. This barely allowed his fingers to reach the scissors. For a moment he almost dropped them as they slipped in his hand, but he secured them and was able to hide them away and rearrange them before Brackin turned back. His heart was beating a mile a minute and adrenaline coursed through his system, making him sweat and flush. The thump of his heart was synchronous with the bleats of anxiety in his stomach. He did not know which would come first, having a coronary or throwing up. He could see right away that Brackin had not a thought for the scissors and tried to relax his breathing and his stomach.

Relaxation would have helped Sidney Garlas as well, but he was unaware of this as a need. He had just slammed his cards down on the table and was glaring at Smolen. "Who told you to let that . . . that . . . that civilian into this game? Who the hell ever said we had to play with him? Whose idea was it, Smolen? Get him out of here."

Smolen said nothing because Ida Crane beat him to it. "If he leaves, I leave. I don't play in games where winners are chased out. Luck makes the call, Garlas, not you or I."

"Shit, Sid," Smolen said kindly, "I know you're losing a

lot to him, but it's his factory. You kick him out and he'll tell us all to go to town. What would we do if he wouldn't let us play with Brackin?"

"I don't think you have any right to be angry with me, Lieutenant," Newman said in his own defense. "I'm not doing anything wrong, just winning."

"Winning?" Garlas was incredulous. "I haven't won a hand in three hours of poker. It's eleven o'clock and you've won twenty-five dollars off me. In five and dime poker! 'Which is better,' " he mimicked now, " 'if they're all in a row or if they're all the same color?' You can't even play the fucking game and you're beating the shit out of me."

"Maybe that's not so hard to do," Smolen offered.

Garlas leaped to his feet and drew back his arm to slug Smolen, but Joe Sloan was on him before he could strike. Garlas struggled briefly but his anger had ebbed. "You think you're sitting pretty, don't you, Deputy? But this thing isn't over yet, and poker is only a game."

"Yeah, right," Ida Crane said, obviously not impressed. "So do you want to play the game or you want to make speeches? Which is it, Lieutenant?" Garlas retrieved his arm from Joe Sloan and sat down again, favoring the table at large with menacing looks. "Here they come," Ida intoned, "early hopes and suckers' bait, read 'em and weep."

FIFTEEN

Sally returned to the conference table giggling. "You throw a wild party, Gene. I haven't had so much fun since the last company picnic when Mrs. Jensen in accounting went skinny dipping and no one noticed. Hey, Larry, the bar isn't closed, is it?"

"Are you sure you haven't had enough, Sally?"

"Absolutely certain. All that dancing and taking care of Joan sobered me up. Come on, let's have another drink."

"I've had enough," Gaylord said.

"Have some more then."

"No thank you."

"I don't want to drink alone. It's not nice for a lady to drink alone."

"Brackin will drink with you, won't you, Gene?" But before Brackin could answer Sally spoke for him.

"He can't drink anymore, he's on guard."

Gaylord blanched. So now it was becoming clear. "What are you, Sally, his commanding general? Or are you just watching out for his interests?"

"You know, Gaylord, you're really a fool. Do you really want a man with a rifle and a pistol pointed at you to get drunk? Do you really want to find out if he can control himself and make clear decisions while he's loaded? You're a raving paranoid, Gaylord, and you're the craziest person in here; now drink." She poured out drinks for herself and Gaylord, pushing his mug over to him. He stared at it for a time and then, since he decided he really did want another drink after all, picked it up and swallowed. Sally smiled and raised her mug in salute. "Cheers," she said.

The liquor hit Gaylord very quickly, building as it did on a foundation of already laid booze. As he finished the mug his head went into a spin, and he put his hands on the chair and steadied his focus. He did not want to pass out. He should speak, make talk. If he was concentrating on conversation he would sober up. Just a little, not completely. This was no time for him to be sober, he thought, and laughed at his own joke.

"What's so funny?" Sally asked. She had been whispering to Brackin before Gaylord's chuckle got her attention.

"I was just thinking that this wouldn't be such a bad party if I weren't chained up. Why don't you get me released, Sally?"

"Now you know that has nothing to do with me, Mr. Gaylord. Why don't you ask Eugene? He's in charge here." Having just told Brackin that under no circumstances should he release Gaylord, she knew what his answer would be. She did not trust Gaylord not to try something stupid and ruin everything. He was irritating her in the extreme, constantly trying to take over a situation she already had firmly in control. Her grip tightened on her mug as she thought of the ways in which she had lost power to him simply because he was a man. No, simply because he had to be shoveled out of New York for his own stupidity. She was suffering because he couldn't handle his own life. Sally noticed that he had not asked Brackin to release him after asking her. At least he understood the basics here, she thought.

Brackin was fiddling with the radio, trying to find some more nice music like before. The party had gotten quiet and he wanted to pick it up again. "Here's some nice music," he announced. "Does anybody want to dance?"

"No," Sally answered sharply, "turn it off."

Brackin clicked off the radio and turned to Sally. "I just want to keep the party going."

"You can't keep a party going, Brackin," Gaylord told him. "It either goes or it doesn't. And since this one is over, why don't you let us go? Call it a party favor, huh?"

"No. Not tonight," Brackin told him.

"Come on, Brackin, you've had your fun, we're all tired. Mrs. Talmage is exhausted, I don't feel that great, Sally can't take much more, what the hell do you want, anyway?"

"I said no. Leave me alone."

"Brackin, this can't go on—"

"Shut up and leave him alone, Gaylord. Stop picking on him. He hasn't hurt anybody, has he?"

"Is that what you're waiting for? Him to hurt somebody? Maybe me, so you can get the job you want so much. Is that what this shit is all about? It makes sense, doesn't it? You ally with him, then get him to bump me off, get my job and be a hero into the bargain. Maybe that's why she's being so sweety poo, Brackin, maybe now you know why she's playing you so fine."

"Shut up, Gaylord," Sally shot at him. "When he wants your sickie little theories he'll make an appointment. Just sit there and get drunk like a skunk, that should be easy for you."

Brackin was frowning at them but they took no notice. He was upset at this bickering and did not know what to do. He tried to get their attention in order to scold them about fighting but they would not stop. Gaylord had answered Sally and she was returning the fire. He hated to see Sally like this, upset and angry. Gaylord would not stop badgering him for their release; only Sally never asked him to be let go. He watched as they threw anger and insults at each other. He went to the desk by the window and got his rifle, bringing it back to the conference table, but still no one noticed. Gaylord was shouting now and Brackin listened.

"You really think that?" Gaylord exclaimed with amazement. "You really think this is my fault. You idiot, it's his fault, not mine. Brackin is the one who did it—not me. A thousand million people have worked overtime without going crazy, a billion people work on days off without going nuts, so don't tell me it's my fault." He was shouting and looked as if he would rise and strike Sally if he could. Brackin hated violence of any kind, so he raised his rifle till it pointed at Gaylord and was going to tell him to shut up when Sally came back to him.

"You dumb prick," she said, "anything that happens here is your fault and you know it. It lays at your feet and no one else's."

"When we get out of here, Miss Laird, it's going to be your friend over there with the popgun who goes on trial, not me. He's the one to spend the rest of his life paying for this charade, not you. It'll be a state hospital till he's dead, or the penitentiary for the duration. Take your choice, but I won't be the one on the hot seat."

Sally had tears of rage in her eyes. She looked at Brackin and knew that what Gaylord said was true. There would be no miraculous escape and ending, no fairy-tale finish. He would end up behind bars, caged like an animal. Unless she could prevent it. It was not fair to punish Brackin for once in his life doing something that he wasn't given permission to do; it was unjust to blame him rather than the people who used him and ignored him. She would never use Brackin, so what right had they? It was monsters like Gaylord, parasites and vermin, who were the real animals. Gaylord should be on trial, not Brackin. "You should be on trial, not him," Sally told Gaylord. "You're the bastard who took him for granted and used him up. You're the one who should be punished, not him."

"I wouldn't talk about using him if I were you, Miss Purity. When it comes to using people I hear you're pretty close to an expert, or at least you think you are."

"And what the fuck is that supposed to mean?"

"Whatever you want it to, Sally."

"Well, don't go listening too much to office gossip, Mr. Gaylord, because the line on you is that you didn't just use your wife, you sold her for a pot of gold."

"Try again, bitch. That one won't work." But all the same Gaylord was clenching his teeth and gripping the arms of his chair so hard his knuckles were white.

Sally smiled at him, a sweet smile, as she bent closer, leaning down to whisper in his ear. "Well then, I'll tell you something else," she said in almost a whisper. "I'm going to see to it that you don't get out of here alive."

A wave of panic flooded through Gaylord as he heard the words and the way they were said. All of the control he had used, all of the reasons he had recited for remaining calm fled his mind and only his body was left to react. His panic soared to anger and he lunged for Sally.

The chains held him fast to the chair but he threw himself at her anyway. She leaped back and stumbled backwards, falling down. Gaylord was trying to get close enough to kick her, struggling with the chair, which was caught on the table, trying to push himself across the floor. Brackin came running around the conference table, shouting for him to stop, but Gaylord kept trying to get at Sally. He had reached her and was drawing back his leg to kick when Brackin fired his rifle. The explosion was terrific in the enclosed office and Gaylord froze at the flash, becoming white and rigid in an instant. Brackin shoved his chair back away from Sally and knelt beside her, torn by her sobs, and called to her.

"Are you all right? Sally, are you hurt?"

When she turned over and faced him, Brackin could see that what he thought were sobs was laughter. He rose with his hand on her arm and her laughter faded into a smile. She put one of her hands on each of his cheeks and kissed him on the mouth. Then she turned to Gaylord and spoke. "You are a criminal with criminal instincts and you are going to be tried and convicted. Judge Eugene Brackin will preside and I will prosecute."

Less than a minute after the shot had been fired Smolen knew about it. One of Garlas' men on the roof reported it, saying that it sounded like a rifle. Smolen, suddenly wishing that the trailer was not so full, went quickly to the telephone. He recognized the voice of Mrs. Talmage when she answered the phone.

"Mrs. Talmage," he said with urgency, "this is Deputy Smolen. What's happened? There's been a report of a shot."

Roused by the noise of the shot, Mrs. Talmage had automatically risen and answered the phone on her desk before anyone else could reach it. "Robert?" she asked. "Is that you?"

"No, Mrs. Talmage, it's Deputy Smolen. Has anyone been hurt? What's happened?"

"Robert, I need to come home now. I've been working too hard. Could you pick me up? Please, Robert."

"Mrs. Talmage, listen to me, please. It's Deputy Smolen. We heard a shot. Was anyone hurt?"

"Hurt?" she said and looked around the room. "No one's hurt, but I'm tired and I want to go back to sleep now." And so saying, she hung up the phone.

Smolen dialed back immediately, aware of the stares of the poker players, aware of Garlas' eyes speculating. "Great communications you've got going there," Garlas said. "Just get him on the line any time you feel like, don't you? Heh, heh." The phone was ringing longer this time and the answerer was Sally Laird.

"What's going on in there?" Smolen demanded.

"There was an accident, Deputy. Brackin fired the rifle by accident. Everyone's fine. And now we want to go to sleep."

"Put Brackin on, Miss Laird."

"I don't know if he wants to; I think not."

"You tell him that if he isn't on the phone in one minute I'm shutting off the electricity, heat, and water. Tell him that right now."

Smolen heard some noises in the background and then Brackin's voice came through the line. "Why are you threatening us, Deputy? Nothing's happened here. My rifle went off by accident, that's what you heard."

"Brackin, someone's going to get hurt. Rifles aren't things for fooling around with. Throw it out the window now. The pistol, too."

"Don't start picking on me again. I don't want to go through that anymore. I'm finished being picked on. Goodnight, Deputy," Brackin said as he hung up the phone.

Smolen stood where he was for a moment before turning to the table. "Everyone is all right. They say it was an accident, but that's shit." He stared at the phone for a bit longer and then turned decisively. "I'm going up to the roof," he announced. "I don't know what for, but I want to take a look."

"I'm coming with you," Garlas informed him. Smolen looked as if he would protest but instead shrugged and started for the door. "Wait a minute for me," Garlas asked Smolen. "I've got to get something from my car."

"I'll meet you there," Smolen answered, and left the trailer at a trot.

Smolen went into the factory and approached the two state troopers sitting inside the door. He asked where the others were and was told that they went up to the roof as soon as the shot was reported. Smolen reached the roof and crouched low, traveling on all fours to the parapet facing Brackin's office. Six troopers faced the hostages, one at Garlas' Monster rifle, one just beside him, the others strung out the length of the roof. Smolen went to the machine and addressed the operator. "Were you here when the shot was fired?"

The operator ignored him and the reply came from the trooper beside him. "He's not permitted to speak while on the rifle, sir, but I'm the man you want anyway. I heard the shot and so did Jackson down at the end there."

"Was it definitely a shot? Could it have been anything else?"

"No, sir, it was a shot. Rifle shot, I'd say."

"Were there any screams or shouts that you could hear?"

"No, sir, nothing else, just the shot."

"And only one, correct?"

"Correct, sir."

Smolen turned to stare at the office in which a dim peaceful light glowed. Was anyone dead or wounded in there? Had the time come for a frontal assault? Tear gas could be shot in from right here, men swung in from the roof on grappling ropes. He had the equipment and the men; did he have the right time? Not yet, he thought, not yet. Tomorrow would have to be the last day, that much he knew, but then he could do it his way, talking him out, not blasting him out. He was turning to give instructions to the troopers when Garlas came up alongside him. Garlas cradled a Remington .308 rifle with a sniper scope. "What the hell do you think you're going to do with that thing, Garlas?"

"You can't let him stay in there any longer, Smolen. There's been shooting, probably someone hurt, and we've got to get them out. I'm going to shoot the bastard."

"No you're not, Sid," Smolen said softly. "Put it away."

Garlas raised the rifle onto the parapet and sighted through the scope. "He's bound to walk across the room sooner or later, and when he does I'm going to end this stupid business."

"No, Garlas. If you missed he could kill all the hostages. He could go nuts."

"But he won't. You said so yourself. You said you were convinced he wouldn't kill them, that he's bluffing."

"Doesn't matter. If a shooting war starts people are liable to get hurt. He hasn't hurt anyone yet, Garlas, there's no call to kill him. I want him alive, not dead."

"You mean you want him, Smolen. You want to be chief of police."

"Someday. And if you don't get off the roof, Garlas, I'm going to put you under arrest. This is my jurisdiction, and you know I can do it. Now put down the rifle and get off the roof." Smolen had raised his voice just enough so that the two nearest troopers could hear him clearly. Garlas looked around him and then turned back to the scope of his rifle. "Move, Garlas, you've got to the count of five. One . . ."

Garlas ignored him and continued to stare through the scope.

". . . two . . ."

Garlas dropped his right hand down to his side, palm up in a conciliatory gesture. "C'mon, Greg, you don't mean it."

". . . three . . ."

Still Garlas kept his right hand low, away from the rifle. Using just his fingers, he unsnapped the strap over his service revolver. "You're making a big mistake, Smolen."

". . . four . . ."

"I can't let you do this to me, Greg. I have authority also."

". . . five."

As Smolen said the word Garlas pulled on his pistol. Smolen grabbed at his wrist and Garlas moved to swing the rifle around toward Smolen's head. But Smolen grabbed the rifle with his left hand while sticking his revolver into Garlas' side with his right. "Freeze," Smolen told him, "and let go the rifle." Garlas had no choice but to obey.

Smolen took Garlas' rifle with his free hand and moved

back a bit. "Get off the plant grounds, Garlas. I'm posting my own men at the factory entrance with orders to arrest you on sight. I'm not shitting, Sid. If you come onto the grounds I'll see you busted."

"You're a fool, Smolen, but I'm going to let you do it. I'll enjoy watching you blow this setup." Garlas moved away from the ledge and turned back to Smolen. "Tell you what, Greg, why don't you hang onto that Remington for a while. Who knows," he said, "you might even decide you need it."

Sally had put Mrs. Talmage into a chair, being careful not to move her more than necessary. "It's a good thing you woke up, Joan," Sally told her. "Gaylord just forced Brackin to fire his rifle and I think something should be done about it."

Mrs. Talmage looked at Sally with keen interest, slid back into the chair, and closed her eyes. She was not going to be deeply involved in the coming proceedings. Sally turned to the men and shrugged. "She's your jury, Gaylord; hope you believe in blind justice." She went behind Brackin and whispered in his ear. As the judge, she was telling him, he would have to see that everything was done properly, that no stone was left unturned. "He scared you, didn't he?" she asked Brackin. "He frightened you, I know, but you came to rescue me like a knight in shining armor, and you are sweet. But we must try him, and see what happens."

Brackin was not sure what Sally meant, but he nodded his understanding nonetheless. Gaylord was still looking very frightened, but Brackin did not care since he was still angry at him. Why should he attack Sally? It was Brackin who had that right around here if anyone did; if he had a complaint then he should make it, not just start attacking people. Who did he think he was, trying to kick Sally—kick her. He had a sudden fantasy of Sally and Gaylord wres-

200

tling while he tried to kick Gaylord for her. Maybe that was what she wanted. But he couldn't do that, not really. Gaylord deserved justice even if Sally did say he was an animal, and since Brackin was the judge he could not kick him. Besides, he had never kicked anybody before and it scared him.

While Brackin meditated on Gaylord, Sally was arranging the chairs. Gaylord watched as she put a chair out for Brackin, the judge, and hoped he was not also the executioner. How on earth he had landed in this circus was a mystery to him. Caged with a psychotic madman and his nutso little helper, he shrugged wryly at the fates that put him there. Sally was coming toward him and leaned down over him, one hand on each arm of his chair. She was uncomfortably close but he could not move further back in his seat. She had a calculating look about her and Gaylord wondered what she was up to.

"You know," she whispered, "you should really learn to control that aggression of yours. If it was put to better use you might not need these chains." Sally looked him in the eye, then across at either side, from chain to chain. As memories of her morning's fantasy flooded back to her, she whispered again, "What a waste."

Sally moved to turn away, but Gaylord stopped her by calling her name. "Sally," he hissed urgently, "what is all this? What's going on? What in God's name are you doing?"

Sally looked at him. Her mouth was almost in a snarl and she felt her blood hot and fast racing through her. The feeling of confusion, of not having a plan, of being part of a process she did not understand came back to her with force. Did she have to know what she was doing? "What do you want from me, Gaylord?" she asked him.

"Why aren't we working together? Why are you attacking me?"

Sally did not answer because she did not know. Her

201

hostility toward Gaylord was enormous, and she had to stifle a strong urge to slap his face. She was shocked by her rage but overwhelmed by her feeling of its rightness.

"I'm not responsible," Gaylord pleaded, "for what's happened to you. It's not my fault that you didn't get this job, and it's not my fault you're unhappy. Please, help me get us out of here."

Sally did not understand, and did not care that she did not understand. She just looked at him and said, "I wouldn't help you do anything, mister." Then she stood up, twirled around, pointed her finger at Brackin and, speaking loudly now, said, "Your Honor, I thank the court for convening under such trying circumstances and intend to be as succinct as possible." She turned her finger now to Gaylord who was looking to the sky for salvation. "That man is an animal. He tried to attack me, kick me, after unjustly accusing you, Your Honor, of being responsible. He is a gutless worm who would blame anyone except himself for what he does. A coward."

"I'd like to say a few words on my own behalf. If I—"

"Not now," Sally informed him. "I'll give you a chance soon, but first the charges. There is, of course, the charge of assault against myself, but that is the least of it. The main conviction I seek is for kidnapping."

"Kidnapping!" Gaylord shouted. "He's a kidnapper, not me."

"Shut up, criminal. He is the one responsible for this kidnapping, not you, Eugene. Gaylord is the root cause of this with his compulsive, aggressive ways. What right had he to ignore you, to treat you like a nothing? He drove you to this, he led you right there and as good as commanded you to do it." She turned back to Gaylord and demanded, "Isn't that so? Admit it."

Gaylord said nothing, just stared at Brackin who sat with a perplexed expression. When Brackin turned to look at Gaylord, the latter spoke softly. "I am nothing here," he

202

said, "Brackin decided to do it, and did it. I don't pretend to understand or even approve, but that this is Eugene Brackin's show is absolutely certain. You," he spoke directly to Brackin, "are in charge here, not me and not Sally. You have to make the decisions. You have to make the choices."

"He's conning you, Gene. Listen to me. He offered me a plan to get out of here. He wanted to get Joan and me to knock you out. He can't be trusted."

"She's telling the truth, Gene. Your job is to keep us in here, mine is to get out. You know that; that's why you're keeping me chained up. But you can't hang me for doing what comes natural. Lock me up and I'll try to get out, that I am willing to be responsible for. Are you willing to punish me for it?"

Brackin listened to Gaylord and his mind flew back to Steve McQueen in a prisoner-of-war movie where he kept escaping and being caught, escaping and being caught. He was recalling his admiration for the character, but Sally was demanding his attention. "That's bullshit, Gene," she hissed. "All he wants to do is see you locked up. He has no honor and no scruples. He'll see you locked in jail and forget about you in a flash. He's a cheap hustler."

"I'm just an honest man trying to get along, Gene. Just like everyone else."

"He's a liar and a cheat. Punish him."

"I've done nothing to harm you."

"He hurt me! Punish him."

"She's lying, don't believe her."

Sally came up to Brackin and knelt before his chair. "I need you to protect me, so he can't hurt me again. Won't you please do it?"

Brackin looked into Sally's eyes, and the need he saw there touched his heart so that he began to weep. He thought that Gaylord must be terrible for hurting Sally; even if he only scared her it was an awful thing to do. But he also cried for his position. He had promised not to hurt anyone unless they disobeyed him and Gaylord had not. "What shall I do?" he asked Sally.

Sally stood up and announced that the court had found in her favor, and that the punishment had been left to the offended. She approached Gaylord and looked down at him with contempt. He returned her stare for a moment and then exploded. "Damn it all, Sally, stop being crazy. The fun is over, ha ha ha. Now cut it out." When she only smiled at him he went on, getting redder and redder as she laughed at him. "You're fired," he screamed, "you don't work here anymore. You're fired."

Sally laughed and laughed. She kept herself from hysterics, maintained control and stopped laughing. "But all I'm going to do, Larry," she cooed, "is cut your little balls off; and you hardly ever use them anyway, so what's the difference?"

"You're not being funny, Sally, so cut it out."

"That's exactly what I intend, dear boy." She turned and looked at the conference table. "Where are the scissors? Weren't they on the table here?"

Gaylord began to sweat, but said nothing. Sally looked around the table for the scissors, muttering all the time about being sure she left them right there after making Joan's fringe, and how could they just disappear. Gaylord could feel them in his waistband and knew that his time was up. Any second now and Sally would realize he had the scissors and tell Brackin. Gaylord did not doubt for a second that she would take them away from him, turn him in, and delight in doing it. What the hell had he done? Trying to be a hero was not his line. He had almost decided to tell Sally that he had them when he saw Mrs. Talmage rise unsteadily from her seat. She slowly approached him, gripping the conference table for support. She was coming to take the scissors from him, but he was afraid to take them out of his waistband until her body shielded him

204

from Sally. He could hardly believe that even though she was drunk she was going to rescue him. His relief was abruptly halted by the chilling thought that Sally might really go through with her planned punishment. But maybe Joan could help, maybe she could bring Sally down to earth and save his neck, or balls, if it came to that. He looked up at her with earnest eyes as she stood over him now, beginning to speak.

Mrs. Talmage looked down at Mr. Gaylord, who sat with terror and pain inscribed upon him, and tried to speak. She wanted to tell him that he had behaved well, that he was in no way dishonorable. She reached out her hand to him when suddenly Sally shouted out her name. "Joan," Sally cried, "stay away from him." Mrs. Talmage turned to Sally and then quickly back to Gaylord. Her plan to help was aborted; she would be no use at all. Just then her stomach gave a horrible lurch and she felt its contents rise inside her. Paralyzed, she turned back to Sally and then back again to Gaylord and threw up all over him. The foul-smelling mass left her with relief as she heaved and heaved. Gaylord was covered with her vomit before he could push himself away, and even then, cornered by the table and caught by his chain, he could not escape the flow.

Mrs. Talmage's relief changed to horror when she was able to open her eyes, and she began to cry. Sally took her by the arm and led her to the ladies' room where she washed her off as best she could. "Don't feel bad, Joan," Sally told her, "this is a much better punishment, and if he had his choice he'd take it. You saved him really." Mrs. Talmage smiled weakly and begged to lie down, so Sally took her back to her bed.

Brackin had wheeled Gaylord into the corner and waited for Sally to return. He needed to unchain Gaylord so he could wash up. But when Sally had put Mrs. Talmage in bed for the second time that night, she had other plans. She told Brackin not to unchain him, that she would take care of it. Then she went back to the ladies' room and opened the door to the janitor's closet just inside. She lifted a big bucket from its place and put it into the work sink in the closet. She ran cold water till the bucket filled, then, with a grunt, lifted it and carried it out to the office. She went right up behind Gaylord, raised the pail, and dumped the water over him. She repeated this twice more until most of the puke had washed off him, then put the empty bucket over his head. She told Brackin to leave him in the chair. Then she took his arm and went with him into the inner office. As soon as they closed the door they could hear Gaylord tossing off the bucket. Sally laughed as it rolled over the floor.

SIXTEEN

When Smolen entered the trailer he found himself alone with Ida Crane. Newman had left, and Sloan was out setting up a watch for Garlas. Smolen knew Garlas would not try anything stupid—Sid had no desire to be a sergeant again—but Sloan had less faith.

"I think," Smolen said to Ida, "that I need some time alone."

"I was just on my way, Greg. But I wanted a quick word before I left. I listened to the tape of Joan while you were out and it worried me. No one knows for sure what happened to her back at school, and it certainly was a long time ago, but she did have a breakdown of one sort or another, and she's never been the same since."

"And you think she might be near another?"

"Don't know. But she doesn't sound good."

"Okay, Ida, I got it. See you tomorrow."

Smolen watched her leave. For a long time after she had gone he stared at the door. He turned back to the table where he had put Garlas' rifle. He had made an enemy of Garlas, something he had avoided doing for a long time. Well, he was on his own now, it was all up to him. Who knows? Maybe Brackin would prove him right and just walk out on Sunday. That's the way it should end. But the rifle, sitting there inanimate and ominous, suggested that it would not be that easy.

Brackin sat on the couch and watched as Sally paced up and down in front of him, talking and gesticulating as she marched. She seemed to him to be walking on air, floating half an inch above the floor. She did not have to move her legs, did not have to use her feet, she could slip along the air near the surface. This was very exciting to Brackin since floating was a habit of his that often scared him, but if Sally also did it then it must be all right. All right. He must pay attention to what she was saying. He knew it was important because she was trying to save him, rescue him like he rescued her. He remembered how he rescued her, how she kissed him, how she was proud of him. Maybe she would kiss him again tonight. He remembered his hand on Mrs. Talmage's breast, how soft it felt, how warm. When she was dancing he could see the whiteness of her thighs from where he sat. What was Sally saying? Why was she talking about going somewhere? He didn't want to go anywhere. Why did she want to leave him? Listen, he commanded himself, listen. But the surge of terror he felt at Sally's sending him away filled his eyes with tears.

"I don't want to go anywhere without you," he blurted.

"Of course not," Sally cooed, realizing that he was not following her. "I wouldn't let you go anywhere without me. Did you think that?" She sat down beside him and took his hand into her lap. "Do you want to get out of this mess, Gene? Do you want to leave this and start again without having to be locked up anywhere?"

Brackin thought for a moment and then shrugged. It did not really matter to him what happened after it was over. He knew that if he lived he would be taken away, but what difference did that make? He turned to Sally who sat silently beside him and said, "I don't care what happens. As long as you don't get hurt it's all right." She squeezed his hand harder and told him that if he was hurt then she would be hurt, that he had to get away for her sake. "But I don't want to go away from you," he repeated to her.

"Don't you realize that I want to go with you? We'll

both go away together. We'll go to South America. If I help you it will be easy. And they'll never know. They'll think I'm your hostage. Then when we get away we'll be together." She stroked his cheek, tilted her head, and asked, "Don't you want to help me?"

"Oh, yes, of course, Sally. I'll do anything you tell me."

Sally began to explain her plan. After breakfast tomorrow Brackin would call Smolen and tell him he was releasing two hostages, Gaylord and Mrs. Talmage, but that he was holding Sally. Then Brackin would demand five hundred thousand dollars, a half a million—in gold. It would be put in a truck which would take them to the Cleveland airport where a plane would be waiting to take them to Brazil. There would be no risk at all because Sally was on his side. These things only went wrong when the hostages did not cooperate.

Sally rose again and began to pace. She drew them a picture of Brazil with its lush jungles and beautiful cities. Dark-skinned women and exotic Latin men sitting in sidewalk cafés sipping drinks and reading papers. And no winters, just perpetual summer, an easy, easy life. The two of them, she pointed out, together always with plenty of money and plenty of time. She knelt down before him and put her head on his lap; putting his arms around her neck, she snuggled down into him, murmuring the while. "I know you can do it, Gene. No one else may believe in you, but I do. I know you can do anything you want to do." She turned her head up and looked at him. "Do you want to do this with me? Do you understand it?"

Brackin nodded slowly. His face hung in a deep tired frown, and the corners of his eyes also drooped with the weight of the day. His pale face, more ashen than usual, finally broke into a smile. "I'm not crazy, Sally, I understand everything. I want to go to Brazil with you. We'll ask for a million dollars and a helicopter. Then we'll go away together forever, if they don't kill us."

"They won't kill us, Gene. We're too smart for them. You've even made the plan better. You're so smart we can't get killed."

"But they want to kill me very much, I can feel it. There are a thousand arrows pointed at me, a million spaceships with bombs are sailing around the planet waiting for me to step outside; even angels will attack me if I show myself. But I'll go anywhere with you. We'll float together and make ourselves invisible so no one can hurt us. Is that a good idea?"

"That's a wonderful idea," she agreed as she squeezed him around the waist. She lifted herself off his lap and remained kneeling before him as she unbuttoned her blouse and unhooked her brassiere. She put both items aside and gently took his hands in hers, moving them over her breasts. "You have the most wonderful ideas," she told him. "I feel so safe with you, so sure of everything all at once. You are a remarkable man, Eugene Brackin, a remarkable man."

Sally sat next to him on the couch and he never took his hands off her breasts, even as she rose from the floor. She lifted one palm away and brought his head down, while her other hand placed her nipple in his mouth. "Yes, my baby, take it," she crooned. "Oh, how safe I feel, how warm and nice I feel." Brackin nursed at the breast as Sally stroked his back and undid his shirt, running her hands over his chest.

Brackin was transported beyond himself. Where he had floated before, he flew now. Where he had felt before, he quivered now. Sally's hands on him brought his skin alive as he felt every movement, every touch. And he was aware as he sucked on her, his mouth full of her, that he could do this. This was no accident, it was no act of charity, it was something that he wanted and could feel inside himself as a driving need expressed in noises that were only partially halted by the soft flesh in his mouth. Let it never stop.

Never. Never. It will. Not. His hand was eternally long, able to reach back through all time to touch all women and as he did so he screamed inside his skull for the flesh of it that was so rich like warmth.

Sally put her hand on Brackin's shoulder and pushed him back against the couch. His whole body lunged back at her but she shoved him down and sat astride him working at his belt and pants. She was grinning down at him and stopped her work long enough to attack his neck with her teeth, staying at his ear to mutter, Brazil. She watched as he looked amazed at his own nakedness, his eyes spinning from his loins to her face to her body to his loins. She laughed at his terror and amazement, and she laughed in her own triumphant abandon as she ravished his innocent body. She grabbed him then and shook him several times before letting go and tearing at his body, giving him feeling and feeling and more feeling. More feeling than he had ever had, and from me, she thought, from me, the giver.

Brackin was not using his hands; afraid to touch without instruction, afraid to break some rule or violate some canon, he lay not still but not interfering with whatever holy process Sally wrought upon him. His eyes ached from seeing flesh, his, hers, the movement. When she grabbed his penis he thrashed and thought he would explode as fear and ecstasy challenged his existence. I rise, he shouted in himself, and he bucked while slapping his hands on the couch. Then she took his hand and put it between her legs, jamming it hard up against her, forced between her hands and her soft and wet and he could feel could soar could rise as she put him into her and he went black not seeing as the center of the universe became the center of his soul her soul and I can will do. Then his hands clutched at her shoulders and for the second time in his life Brackin came in a woman.

Brackin was in a vortex the center of which was Sally

with himself revolving around her at greater and greater accelerations. When he finished his climax the vortex spun him out into a soft reality constructed of Sally and fuzzy feeling. When she reached down and let her hand cross his brow, the sound he made was both gentle and animal. He could see her above him, could see her lips moving, could even hear sounds but no words entered into that strange land to which he had flown. There could be no problem with escape, no reason to fear, since Sally had taught him to fly. As he fell asleep with his teacher alongside him, Brackin had a vision of the two naked birds, forgotten feathers waving around them, flying to the hereafter.

PART THREE
Sunday, November 29

SEVENTEEN

The warmth that Brackin felt as he woke in the pitch-dark room startled him. It was only a moment before he identified the source, but his adrenaline had shot and his senses come alive. Gently he steadied a hand and placed it on Sally's head to twice stroke her hair. The covers had slipped and he could watch her chest rise and fall with each sleeper's breath. He matched his own rhythm to hers and calmed himself with her presence. Soon after, he took his eyes from Sally to the unlit room.

Brackin could see in the dark. As a child he had been frightened of the dark, sure each time the lights went out that they would never go on again. The fear was with him always, even in broadest daylight, until several years ago when he learned to see in the dark. He looked around to the wall behind Gaylord's desk and stared at the calendar there. It was a picture of a boy fishing in a rowboat, rod and reel held in one hand, sandwich in the other. He could see it just as if it were projected before him on a huge screen, every detail, every nuance visible. He looked back to Gaylord's desk where he had put his rifle and pistol last night. They stood out, surrounded by a glow to let him know that they were there. The rest of the room was also clear to him though anyone else would be blind, blind to all that he could see. Brackin, as always, was comforted by this skill, this gift, and he grinned as he continued to examine his surroundings. The room was still private, still sealed off from the rest of the world, still the haven in which he and Sally remained intact, single, separate.

Brackin rose from the couch and padded quietly to the door, his nude frame sagging along. He had considered leaving it behind but was still too sleepy for the necessary concentration. Opening the door a crack he could watch and see if there was any movement in the other room. He did not need his night vision here since the single row of lights that had been left on still burned. He saw Gaylord slumped in his seat, head lolling to one side, arms still chained to the chair. As he watched, Gaylord's head snapped up suddenly, only to slump quickly down again onto his chest. The room had a faint odor of vomit, and even in the dim half light looked as if it were a battleground. As this thought passed through his head, Brackin turned back into his room, Gaylord's office, and knew that it was true, it was a battleground. But what were the warring forces? Not good and evil; they never fought, just worked together to make pain and futility. Not right and wrong; he had always been right and felt wrong, they were the same. Maybe madness and sanity. But if I'm mad, Brackin thought, then who is sane?

Sitting on the edge of the couch, Brackin pondered his madness. They must know I'm crazy. To do this I must be crazy. And everyone who does something crazy must be fixed. They'll fix me. They'll fix me by killing me. They've always wanted to kill me and now they can. I can't stop them. I don't want to stop them. The only thing they must not do is harm Sally. He rubbed his eyes and yawned. It would be nice to be in Brazil but he knew it could not happen. They can't let it happen. Of all the things they will do to me that is one they will not. Today, after lunch, I will let them go. Then I will come out and they can kill me. Again. And again.

He stretched out on the couch, being careful not to disturb Sally. She now seemed restless and there was a sheen of perspiration on her skin. Brackin moved to pull the blanket up over them and as he did Sally began to make a low moaning noise and shake her head back and forth. The noise increased in pitch and her body jerked, her hands reaching out to grab. Brackin took her by the shoulders and called her name to wake her. He had to shake her several times before she came to, and then she looked at him with despair, with a wonder that she should have arrived here from where she had been.

"You were having a bad dream," Brackin told her, "I had to wake you."

Sally nodded and pulled the blanket up to her chin as she rested her head on her arm. "I was littler," she began, "not younger, but littler, and I was climbing up a hill, a steep rocky hill. I was naked, and it was cold. I kept slipping and scraping myself. The wind was cutting me, and the stones were cutting me, and"—she began sobbing—"I just couldn't make it. I knew that I was going to fall backwards and be a cripple for the rest of my life. I don't want to be a cripple," she said as she burrowed into his shoulder, "I don't want to be a cripple."

Brackin rocked her gently in his arms, making soft noises. "Really," she said, "I'm much stronger than this. Dreams never scare me."

"It's all right," Brackin tried to say, but the words got caught in his throat so that he had to clear it before he could speak. "It makes me feel like I can help you, Sally. Try to go to sleep now."

"Eugene," she said and turned to look at his face, "we're not really going to go to Brazil, are we?"

"No," Brackin said softly, "we're not. Go to sleep now, Sally." And she did.

About two hours after Brackin's 5:30 A.M. inspection, Gaylord woke and was unable to fall back to sleep. His body ached from sleeping in the chair and from not mov-

217

ing since the previous morning. He could barely get his eyes to unglue, doing his best to get his hands up to his face to clear them out. His clothes were still damp from the soaking Sally had given him and his body was chilled from the wet. The smell that rose from him turned his stomach and he had to force back a retch. His stomach and head added to his misery by demonstrating the results of too much alcohol and too much stress. And his bladder, not the least pressing of his complaints, was about to rupture if not shortly released from the inhuman job it had been performing since sometime yesterday afternoon. More than anything else it was his simple need to pee which propelled him to seek assistance.

Gaylord rolled himself across the room to the couch on which Mrs. Talmage slept. She looks about how I feel, he thought, as he looked her over. Her hair was all askew with ragged tufts pointing every which way, and what was left of her slip was bunched and wrinkled beyond belief. It was hard to judge, but Gaylord felt that the sour odor of vomit increased as he approached her couch. Gaylord sat and watched her for a moment and knew that they must get out today if they were to keep their sanity as well as their lives. He would have to get them out or tell the cops to come in. As he thought this he remembered the scissors in his belt, tucked in during the party last night. When he was released to go to the toilet he would have to make his move, and he would have to get Mrs. Talmage to assist him. Maybe now she would not favor Sally so. But he did not want to think about Sally or try to puzzle out that little matter until he felt better.

Gaylord called out softly to Mrs. Talmage. She turned and began to snore, but then, when he had called her again, she opened her eyes and peered about. She sat up with a start and stared around her, not recognizing her surroundings. Sally had unhooked her brassiere and her slip had fallen off her shoulder so that when she sat, one

218

white blue-streaked breast hung out in front of her. Gaylord averted his eyes, and as soon as Mrs. Talmage registered his presence she grabbed for the blanket and covered herself.

"Oh my God," she said in a small voice, "I feel terrible."

Gaylord asked if she remembered last night and learned that much was with her, but many details, including all those implicating Sally, were lost. She had no recollection of the trial and, while she knew she had been sick, did not know that Gaylord had been the recipient of her gifts.

"You're wet, Mr. Gaylord. You look terrible. What's happened?"

"Sally poured water over me after you turned in last night."

"Sally? Poured water over you? Why would she do that?"

"She was cleaning me off, Mrs. Talmage. She thought it was funny."

"Why was she cleaning you off? I don't understand."

Mrs. Talmage sounded very shaky, and Gaylord did not know what to do. He needed her help badly, but she was in no shape to cooperate now. He decided the best thing to do would be to tell her everything and let it take its effect. When she had absorbed how mad things had been she would help him overpower Brackin. She would come through in a crisis, he was sure of it; she just needed to know that the crisis had arrived. So Gaylord explained to Mrs. Talmage that Sally had put him on trial, determined to castrate him, and been interrupted by Mrs. Talmage who had diverted everyone by being sick all over him. The water had washed off the damage.

Though he would not have thought it possible, Mrs. Talmage turned considerably more ashen. She seemed to swoon for a moment, then grabbed at the couch for support, fell back upon it, let her head roll forward, and began to sob. Her crying was soft and quiet, but persistent and all-pervading. She did not move, not even to wipe away her tears which had begun to course down her cheeks to slip wetly onto the blanket clutched about her. Gaylord called her name but she did not respond. His efforts to reach through her shock were to no avail and he could only turn away and hope that perhaps later she might come round. Why were people always going strange on him, he wondered. He had a consuming sense of isolation that wrapped him in a cocoon of sudden despair, and for a moment he considered using the scissors on himself but rejected the idea as quickly as it came. There could be no point to that unless it caused Brackin to let them go. If he was wounded, that might force Brackin's hand, but this thought too left him with a shudder.

Gaylord made his slow and painful way to his office door, now the entrance to Sally's boudoir, he realized. Well, he consoled himself, there would be a reckoning after this, a settling of accounts that would rid him of her and her insane arrogance. But now, if he was lucky, she would be asleep for some time yet. When he reached the door he opened it with one hand but did not look in. He wanted to rouse Brackin, not enrage him, and Gaylord had no idea what was going on anywhere anymore so he had elected for caution. He softly called out Brackin's name, telling him it was time to get up.

Brackin could hear him and, indeed, wanted to get up. He was an early riser, and he had been lying in the same position for several hours now. But Sally still slept, and to move would be to disturb her, and it would also mean removing her warm breasts from his chest. Resting on the bed, drifting in and out of sleep with her female softness against him, had a tremendous calming effect upon him. Never had he felt so rested, so peaceful, so clear about what must be, what must not be. Today was certainly the last day of his crusade. He was saddened by the thought of leaving the office and ending this affair with his friends; there were so many things he still had to do, to say, to listen to. But he was never heard anyway. Never completed anything. Never accomplished anything. Except this. This he had done. He had a vision now of his parents whom he had never seen, but he knew nonetheless they were his parents. They floated up above the doorway and smiled warmly at him in their kind and loving way, expressing their approval and pride in the way he managed such an arduous task. Now he had finally shown what he was worth, and the heavy ropes could be undone, the anchors could be lifted, and he could sail away on a soft breeze of glory.

He heard Gaylord again, still calling him, softly but insistently. He was going to whisper out to him to go away when Sally stirred beside him. She opened her eyes and said nothing for a moment until, hearing Gaylord, she told Brackin to go out, she would get up shortly. So Brackin rose, still hearing Gaylord who called out to him in a stage whisper, "Time to get up, it's morning. Rise and shine."

Joe Sloan found Deputy Smolen slumped over in his chair, head hanging down onto his chest. "Dep," he said softly, "it's eight o'clock." Smolen opened his eyes and nodded at Sloan. "You been there all night, Dep?"

"Yeah," Smolen answered while stretching the kinks out. "Mostly thinking, Joe. Everything all right outside? You get any sleep?"

Sloan told him that everything was under control and, yes, he had caught about four hours in his cruiser. Smolen approved and told him to stay around the plant, but to send someone over to get breakfast for the hostages. Sloan said, sure, and Smolen was once more alone.

It had been sometime in the middle of the night that Smolen had decided that today had to be the last day. It was not just the Mayor, he was not that concerned about grabbing the opportunity, but he was losing his sense of what was going on in there. He was going to have to do it.

He was going to have to go up there himself and get Brackin out. In all the years he had been a policeman his life had been in danger only very rarely. This was going to be the most dangerous thing he had ever done. But maybe, just maybe, he could talk Brackin out. He'd have to give him a call soon and see what was happening. It was time to get tough.

EIGHTEEN

Brackin, dressed and presentable, had emerged from Gaylord's office. As soon as he entered the main room he could see that Mrs. Talmage was in terrible shape. She still sat sobbing on the couch, muttering to herself. He approached and asked what was wrong, if she was sick. Brackin was scared that her condition might be his fault and sought reassurance that he was not to blame, but his questions received no reply. He turned to Gaylord who had wheeled over and asked, "What's happened? Is she sick? I never hurt her, you know that."

"Oh, no," Gaylord replied with sarcasm, "you did nothing. Just kept her locked up for forty-eight hours, got her drunk and sick, that's all. Brackin, you fool, she's half crazy with fear and exhaustion. And you want to know what's happened." He wheeled around and pushed himself to the corner near the men's room, then beckoned to Brackin. "Listen to me," he said when Brackin had stumbled over, "you are as much responsible for the condition of that woman as if you had beat her with a club. She needs rest and attention, medical attention, and if you don't see that she gets it then you are breaking your promise not to hurt anyone. Now I need to go to the can very badly. You let me go while you think that over."

Brackin nodded dumbly and, after taking out his pistol to cover Gaylord, carefully unlocked him, then sat with his gun pointing at the door to the men's room while Gaylord, stiff and pained, made his way. Brackin watched him with-

223

out feeling. Gaylord was always making him responsible for everything, always trying to blame him for this or that. Sally had told him that Gaylord used him to escape his own responsibility, that Gaylord was afraid of the world and hid behind Brackin. He had done nothing to Mrs. Talmage except when she had attacked him, so how could it be his fault? Brackin's fists balled, his stomach tightened, and his eyes welled with tears of pity at the blame he was forced to shoulder, the weight he was made to carry, the onus that lay upon him. Unfairly. But before he could begin to cry he started to giggle. It was a small giggle, more like a titter, that rose through him as he recollected Mrs. Talmage dancing on the table. How could they blame him? He hadn't made her dance. He hadn't made her drink. He went back to where she sat huddled on the couch, sobbing and muttering, moaning and groaning. Brackin did not do that sort of thing. He always had it a lot worse than she had it now, but he didn't roll into a ball and sob. If that was all she was good for then she got what she deserved.

"Stop that stuff," he told her, but she went on sobbing. He reached out and suddenly slapped her, not too hard, across the face. That was what they did in the movies. And it worked. Mrs. Talmage stopped crying and stared at him with wide-open eyes, eyes that seemed to grow larger and larger as he watched. He reached out again and pulled the blanket from her. "You don't need that," he said, "time to get up." When the blanket was gone he could see, staring at him like a third eye, the breast that had fallen from her slip. He saw it wink at him, invite him, and he reached out to touch it, to say good morning with his index finger. Good morning smiling breast. But Mrs. Talmage gave a jerk at the blanket and was covered again, sobbing harder than before. Now Brackin stood away and stared at her. "I didn't hurt you," he insisted. "I did nothing to you. You did it."

When Brackin heard the door to the men's room he whirled around, grabbing for his pistol. Gaylord immediately raised his hands above his head to show that he had no ideas, no crazy notions. He had known that he would not be able to do much alone. In the washroom, after the blessed relief of the urinal, he had repositioned the shears so that he could get at them more readily, but still had no idea how he could use them. Cleaned up a bit he still smelled like a cheap flophouse, but the water had refreshed him. Some way or another he had to effect their release today; he could not take it, Mrs. Talmage could not take it, and Sally also seemed to be growing stranger with every hour. But he didn't know how to do it. Sally would be no help. No help, that was an understatement. She was really going to castrate him last night, she really did hate him fiercely. Gaylord had not permitted himself to think about Sally until he entered the washroom, and when he did so he tried very hard to retain his control. Yet as his mind ran through last night's debacle his rage grew and he was glad she was not there with him. Her cruelty drove away the pity he tried to feel; her enjoyment of her power over Brackin, and through Brackin over him, was sadistic and sick, and he was sure she should be put away, locked up as tight as Brackin. And he would see to it with pleasure.

Brackin signaled for Gaylord to sit in his chair. When they were together, Gaylord asked Brackin if he had thought things over. "You can't blame everything on me, Mr. Gaylord. I'm not responsible for whatever people do. Just for what I do. Now I'm going to chain you up again."

"Wait. I've had a very bad night. Please just put one chain on. Just lock up one arm. I give you my word that I won't try anything. I haven't so far, have I? Really, it won't do any harm."

"I don't know."

"It will show that you really are considerate, that you

225

really don't mean any harm. Please, Eugene, I can't stand being chained like that any more."

Brackin thought for a moment and then smiled. There was something nice about Gaylord supplicating him in this way. And it was true what he said, that he had not tried any tricks on him. And it would show that he was concerned for everyone's welfare. Brackin looked over to Mrs. Talmage; she was just trying to make him feel bad with all that crying. "Stop that noise," he called to her, but she ignored him. "All right," he said to Gaylord, "I'll just chain the one side, but it will be your right arm."

"That's fine, Eugene, I just want to be able to move a bit more. For my circulation." And anyway, you maniac sonofabitch, Gaylord thought, I'm a lefty.

The phone rang as soon as Brackin had secured Gaylord, and he was the one to answer it. The caller was Joe Sloan who wanted the breakfast order. Brackin gave it to him after some deliberation and consultation with Gaylord who was able, to Brackin's relief, to remember what everyone had eaten the previous day. Brackin believed that breakfast was an important meal and knew that people could get cranky if they had to eat something they did not like for breakfast. When the order was in he went back to the office to check on Sally.

Sally was sitting up and smiling at him when he entered. He loved her sweet smile and wondered if anyone was as innocent as she. He went to the couch and sat beside her where she had indicated. She raised her hand to his face and held it there; for several merciful minutes she was touching him, and as long as she did so he was at peace.

"Did you sleep well?" she asked him.

"Oh, yes." He blushed and looked away. "I liked sleeping with you beside me."

"And I liked having you inside me," Sally replied and put her hand casually down to his lap.

Brackin blushed some more and told her that breakfast

226

was on its way, but Sally wanted to sit with him. "Tell me what you would do if we were in Brazil," she asked him. "Tell me the very first thing you would do." But he just kept blushing and could say nothing. "Then I'll have to tell you, won't I?" Sally said with a movement of her disturbing hand. "The very first thing you would do, if you know what's good for you, is make love to me. Do you like making love with me, Eugene? Come on, I demand an answer now or my feelings will be hurt." Brackin managed a nod, but Sally was not assuaged. "I want to hear words, Eugene. Tell me the words so I can feel them."

Brackin looked behind him and then toward the door. He looked down at the floor and then up at the ceiling. Sally increased the pressure on his thigh and repeated her demand. Brackin looked at her with a fleeting glance, afraid to settle on those haunting eyes, and said, "I like it very much."

"What do you like very much, Gene? I don't know what you're talking about." With this a tighter squeeze.

"I like making love with you very much."

"Now look at me and say it."

Brackin turned to her eyes and was immediately swallowed up in the open pools of brown. "I like making love with you very much. Love. With you. You."

Sally smiled a large smile, a smile of sweet affection, a smile of you and me-ness, and drew his head down to hers for a long, rich kiss. "You will always be mine," she told him. "Don't ever forget."

Without prompting this time, Brackin answered, "Never."

While Brackin and Sally were saying good morning to each other Gaylord was making another attempt at enlisting the aid of Mrs. Talmage. With his increased mobility he hurried over to her couch to take advantage of whatever time he had while Brackin was back in the office. Her sobs had diminished greatly but her mutterings had not ceased, so Gaylord did not know what to expect. Beside her, he gently said her name, "Joan, Joan," but got no response. He tried again with more urgency. "Joan, you've got to listen to me, pay attention, it's important." Still she kept her eyes cast down and mumbled into the blanket. Gaylord took the scissors out of his pants and waved them in front of her, keeping one eye on the office door. "Look," he hissed, "dammit, look at this. I've got the scissors. You can get him. He won't expect you. You can save us, Joan. Do you hear me? You can save us."

Mrs. Talmage looked at the shiny scissors which glinted back at her as Gaylord turned them in his hand. "Save us?" she said absently while imagining the bright shears covered with blood. "I can't save us," she said more clearly now, her voice gaining timbre. She looked at Gaylord with an earnest demeanor, almost pleading with him to understand. "I can't save us," she repeated, "I can't kill again. I need to go home."

"What do you mean, again? You never killed anyone, but you've got to kill Brackin. He won't let you go home. I can't do it; he won't let me get near him. You've got to do it, Joan, do you understand?"

"I've killed enough in my life, Mr. Gaylord. I just want to go home. Oh, please, just let me go home. I don't care if you fire me. I don't care about anything, but I need to go home." She was clutching the blanket up to her chin and holding her head to one side in a gesture of supplication.

Gaylord was desperate. There was no way he could kill Brackin and Mrs. Talmage was his only hope. She was obviously in a state of shock and near, he feared, a breakdown, but he had no choice. "You can't go home, Joan, it's not possible."

Mrs. Talmage looked to the window and again saw the flagpole line swaying gently just three feet away. If only the window were open; if only she were thirty years

228

younger. She tried to pull herself together. "When I tell Mr. Brackin," she said to Gaylord, "how badly I need to go home, he will certainly permit me to leave."

Gaylord did not know what to do. She was under a terrific strain and he did not know how much more she could take. "Look at you," he insisted, "you can't go home like that. And it's Brackin who did it. It's Brackin who took your dress. Joan, you've got to kill him."

Something in this illogic affected Mrs. Talmage, and she moved her head down while lifting the blanket to look at her clothes. Her beige slip was in tatters, having been cut from the bottom for fringe as well as having been worn unprotected for forty-eight hours. She looked at her feet where her toes stuck out of her ripped and laddered hose. She looked at her chest and hurriedly covered her still-exposed breast. She groped for her mirror in her handbag and was confronted with an almost unrecognizable face. She was chalk white and her skin hung loose and lifeless on her bones. Her hair was all askew, hanging in tufts every which way. Her face shuddered as a tear spilled over her eye, and she began to cry softly and then sob again. "I need to go home," she whimpered. "I haven't been home in a very long time. I really must go today." When Gaylord tried to say something to her she averted her face and waved him away with her arm, crooning and crying, whimpering and sobbing. Gaylord knew that she would be no help this morning.

Deputy Greg Smolen had just got off the phone with the Mayor who had been imploring him to conclude the hostage-taking, and to make sure that he, the Mayor, was there at the finish. The voice that startled him was Ida Crane's.

"Pretty thick with the politicians these days, aren't we, my boy?"

"Don't you know it's rude to eavesdrop?"

229

"Not if you're a reporter, Greg. Then it's your business."

Greg told her that he was getting Brackin out today. When she asked him why it had to be today, he explained that there was too much going on in there he did not know about. Shots had been fired last night, as she knew, and he felt that he might lose control of the situation if he did not act. "It's gone on long enough, Ida. I'm going up there. Soon. He's had two nights to play his games, that's as long as I'll give him."

"I hope you know what you're doing."

Brackin and Sally emerged from the inner office hand in hand. Sally quickly let go when she saw Mrs. Talmage and rushed to the couch. "Joan," she said as she knelt down beside her, "what's wrong? Are you all right?"

Mrs. Talmage looked at her blankly before answering. She reached out and grabbed Sally's hand, clutching it tightly, and said, "I want to go home. I need to see Robert. I haven't seen Robert for a very long time. Sally," she said with a sob, "I just have to go home."

"Yes, of course. Yes, you need to go. We'll see what we can do. For now just sit and have a rest." Sally backed away from the couch toward Brackin. "She's very bad, Gene. I think she should get out soon."

"Maybe later," Brackin said, not wanting to admit that this day would be the last.

Sally was going to argue when Gaylord stood up. "Good morning, madam, I hope you're pleased with the results of your handiwork," he said while pointing to Mrs. Talmage.

Sally looked at him and laughed. "As far as you're concerned I am. God you smell. Don't you ever wash? Did you wet your pants or something?"

"Look at her," Gaylord demanded. "You've reduced her to that, you arrogant fool. Never mind what you've done to me, never mind your sadistic cruelty, just look at Mrs. Talmage. You've made a weeping wreck out of her."

"Don't try and lay that on me, Gaylord. You're the one

who got us into this mess in the first place. You're the one who was so eager to set the world's record for efficiency that you treated us like machines instead of people. And how did you get unchained?"

"I'm not unchained," Gaylord said while holding up his right hand, "just a little less chained. I hope you don't mind, Warden."

Sally frowned and went back to Brackin who had sat down at the conference table to play with his rifle. He was feeling bad about giving it up. He was beginning to get used to the noise and shock of firing it, and he knew that after he went out he would never hold another again. A feeling of anxiety pervaded him whenever he thought about going out, and for that reason more than any other he was loath to speak of it. He would just do it at the right time. No one needed to know except himself. It was his business and no one else's. Maybe Sally. Sally could know but that was all. He watched her approach and noted the unhappy look she wore. Trouble. He did not want trouble on the last day. Everything had gone so fine, so smooth till now, it must not be spoiled. If it was trouble he would hide. He would hide under the table or back in the office. He would take Sally back into the office and go back onto the couch and go back into her arms and go back to sleep forever. Back until he forgot everything he ever knew. Sally was talking to him about Gaylord. Gaylord had to be chained. All the way. Chain Gaylord up or he'll do something stupid. He can't be trusted. You must do it. I must do it. It is important.

"We're too close to the end now to take a risk of his getting hurt. All I'm concerned about is his own welfare, and yours, of course," Sally spoke quietly but firmly. "He's a very frustrated man and a coward to boot. There's no telling what he might do. I don't think he's very stable right now, Gene, and we don't want to be responsible for any crazy stunts he might decide to pull, do we?"

The words floated around him, the conflict driving away

the peace attained this night. The anxiety was clutching at him and he wanted Sally to go back to bed with him, show him how to make love. But she waited for his answer and he nodded, but she still stared at him with the waiting look until he said, "Yes, I'll chain him." Then she smiled and touched his cheek.

"Do it now," she said.

Brackin was stuck to the chair, unable to command his movements, unable to respond to Sally's demand. He would chain Gaylord. Really he would, but in a minute. He would do it in a minute. Sally stood away, waiting for him to rise, to follow her finger to Gaylord. He stared at her with all his eyes, soaked in her form and essence. Maybe they could go to Brazil. Maybe they could dance in South America. The anxiety gripped his stomach with a wrench, twisting until he almost doubled over. When the phone rang right behind him he jumped from the pain back to the world, startled out of himself.

Brackin reached for the telephone before Sally could. He wanted anything that would delay chaining Gaylord. Gaylord would hate him for the chains, and Brackin did not want that. So he leaped at the phone with a quick hello.

Smolen, surprised at the fast answer, responded with a querulous "Who is that?"

"It's Brackin, who's this?"

"Oh, Brackin, you startled me. It's Deputy Smolen. Good morning. How are you?"

"Fine, thank you. What do you want?"

"Come on, Brackin. You know perfectly well what I want. Today is the day. You're coming out after breakfast. I'm letting you have breakfast as a sign of my good faith, to show you how much I'm willing to let you have. After a nice meal you're going to come out. That's the deal."

"I don't have to make any deals. I can make my own decisions."

Smolen clenched the phone and held himself back from shouting. "Of course you can make your own decisions, Brackin. I know that. What have you decided? Tell me."

"I don't know yet," Brackin temporized, "but it's up to me. And it won't be after breakfast. It may not be today."

"Brackin, we had a deal. You promised it would be today."

"I did not. I never promised that."

"You're a liar. You're a liar and a cheat."

"That's not true. I never promised you anything."

"You did, Brackin, you promised. I even have it on tape. Do you want me to find it and play it?"

Brackin was sweating and the phone was becoming slippery in his hand. He never lied in his life, not even once. Did he tell Smolen that he would let them out today? He had no memory; but what if he forgot? Maybe he did. "I don't remember telling you anything," he said.

"Well look, Brackin, if you can't be trusted, then we're changing the rules. No more being so nice. No more being so friendly. I've been going to bat for you a lot around here. There's a whole bunch of people who think I should be a lot tougher with you, but I've fought them off. You know what I told them, Brackin? I told them you could be trusted. I told them that if Eugene Brackin says something you can depend upon it. How do I look now? Pretty foolish, huh? But that's all over now. From now on it's dog eat dog."

"But I don't remember telling you anything," Brackin pleaded.

"Well, I remember just fine. You're coming out right after breakfast."

"No, no. That's not right. We can talk later. We can talk after lunch."

"There's gonna be no lunch, Brackin."

Brackin was squeezing the telephone with both hands. He rolled his head around and moved his shoulders as if he were trying to see Smolen. He wanted to tell him, to explain that they would really come out after lunch, that he meant to do it, release everyone. Say goodbye, farewell, and close the circle. Seal it. Float on through the circle. But he couldn't. He couldn't say that. He couldn't say it was over. He could do it. He knew he could do it. But he couldn't say it. The words hurt too much.

"Send in breakfast and then we'll talk," Brackin pleaded.

Smolen was essentially pleased with the way things were going. He was sitting in the chair at the table with the phone, stretched out with legs crossed at the ankles. Now he sat up and stroked the stubble on his chin, then said, "How can I believe you anymore, Brackin? You already lied to me once."

"I mean it. Really I do. Send it in."

"Only breakfast. If you don't cooperate with me, then you're going to be responsible for everyone's hunger. And I'm also turning the lights, heat, and water off. Nothing to drink. Toilets that don't work. I'm getting you out of there, Brackin, whether you like it or not."

"You can't make me. No one can."

"I can, Brackin. And I will."

"No."

"Yes."

"No," Brackin shouted and slammed down the receiver. "I'm not ready yet," he said to the telephone. "I can't do things before I'm ready. It makes them wrong."

NINETEEN

Smolen placed the phone back on the cradle and turned to Ida Crane who was sitting near him with the earphones on. "I don't like it, Ida. He doesn't want to come out. Suddenly I don't know if I can trust him anymore. The Mayor will have my ass if it doesn't end today, and then there's your friend Joan."

"He did say it would end today, didn't he?"

"Yeah. He said that yesterday. But he sounds jumpy this morning."

"I don't envy you, Greg. I wouldn't trade places with you for anything. I wish I could help you, but I can't."

Smolen turned away and looked again at the rifle. "Maybe Garlas is right, Ida. Maybe I'm being too soft."

"Well, I am worried about Joan," Ida said slowly, "but I'd hate to see her hurt. If you think hotting things up would get anyone hurt then stay loose."

"Right. Stay loose. Loose enough so the Mayor hands the whole thing over to Garlas who'll fill the place with tear gas and try a bust-in. Damn." Smolen slammed his fist onto the table. "Look, Ida, I'm going up to the roof. Breakfast is arranged and I'm going to see what things look like from up there." He walked to the door, stopped, turned around, went back to the table and picked up the rifle. "I'll be back in a while," he said, and left.

After Brackin slammed down the phone he turned to look at the others. They would be angry, he knew, wanting

235

to know what went on, but they hardly noticed him. When he had picked up the phone Gaylord had approached the table, and in order to keep him away Sally had gone to the other side before he could cross. She had ordered him to stay away, telling him that it was none of his business. They had begun battling and had not stopped. Mrs. Talmage, Brackin could see, was still on the couch weeping. Why did they all have to get so strange? Why couldn't they all stay sane, normal? Last night the party had been so good. So nice. He couldn't depend on anyone. Mrs. Talmage was no good, making all that noise, looking so awful, making him feel bad. Stop it or I'll kill you, he screamed to himself. I'll shoot your head off. I'll stamp you out. And Gaylord was always picking on Sally. Always trying to run things, make him feel bad, make trouble. He could be dead too. Two shots for these troublemakers. One for Smolen. Maybe he wouldn't let anyone out. Maybe he would go out with his rifle shooting. Never take me alive. Or dead. And even Sally could have helped to keep Gaylord quiet. But she didn't like him. Only me. Brackin thought, she only likes me. But none of them were paying any attention to him at all. He clutched his rifle hard.

"You're sick," Gaylord was shouting at Sally. "You really would have done that last night. You really get kicks out of terrorizing me. You're a goddamned sadist." He was standing three feet away from her with fists balled and shoulders hunched.

"You believe everything you tell yourself, don't you, Gaylord? No wonder you're such a creep."

"When we get out of here you're finished. I'm going to report everything to the cops and see you locked up with your nutso boyfriend."

"Such aggression. You really should learn to control yourself, you know. It's very bad for your heart." Sally turned round and sat on the conference table. "I should have cut your balls off last night, Gaylord, it would have

236

been a service to womankind. A symbolic sacrifice on the altar of sisterhood."

"You are sick, Sally."

"But you're lucky. I couldn't even find the damn shears." Suddenly suspicious, Sally asked, "Where were they, anyway? Why couldn't I find them?"

Gaylord involuntarily averted his eyes at the question, evoking a curious glance from Sally. "You know something about them," she said to him. She left the table and approached Gaylord. "Do you know where they are? Are you up to something I don't know about?"

"I don't know what you're talking about."

Sally turned a fiery red and spoke to him in a hoarse whisper. "You arrogant creep, if you try anything, or pull any stunts I'll see you dead." Sally turned and began to search frantically for the shears. "Where are they, goddammit," she spit. She turned to Mrs. Talmage and asked her where they were but got no response. She grabbed the woman's shoulders and shook her. "Joan," she demanded, "where are the scissors, where are they? Do you know? Pay attention, for God's sake."

Mrs. Talmage looked at her through a mist. The scissors? She had seen the scissors. "Yes," she mumbled, "I know where they are."

"Where? Tell me."

But Mrs. Talmage said nothing.

"Joan, listen. If you tell me where the scissors are I'll get Brackin to let you go home. Otherwise you'll have to stay here. You'll have to stay here and not go home. Tell me where they are."

Mrs. Talmage looked round the room until her eyes found Gaylord. She said, with a pout, "He's got them."

Smolen crouched on the roof looking over the ledge at the windows. He could see nothing. He stared at the prison in which the hostages were locked. He felt the heft of the rifle which was cradled in his arms. Garlas wasn't right, but maybe he wasn't all wrong either. So far Brackin had been calling all the plays with Smolen just able to put pressure on over the phone, when, that is, Sally Laird would let him. He could be a thousand miles away instead of around the corner and still be doing as much. Brackin had no sense of his presence. The man probably didn't even really believe in him. A phone call once in a while, a tussle over the electric wires, but no real contact, no real impact. That's what was driving him nuts.

Smolen raised the rifle over the parapet and sighted on the center window. It consisted of eight large panes of glass. Four in the upper part, four in the lower. One cross piece in each half. If he shot out the upper cross piece it would make a lot of noise and mess, but no one could possibly get hurt. Maybe, he thought, it was time to make his presence felt.

"Gene," Sally was urgent, "Gaylord's got the scissors. Hurry." She ran up to Gaylord and grabbed for his free hand as he reached for the scissors in his pants. But even with two free hands she was no match for him and he was able to get them out. He pushed her away, the scissors in his fist, but she just came back at him, clawing and struggling for them. They fell back onto his chair with Sally on top of him trying to pry open his hand. Gaylord shoved her away again, and when she came back at him he was holding the scissors like a knife. He held her now with his chained hand, squeezing her shoulder with all his might, but still she struggled. Sally grabbed his chained arm and bit him as hard as she could. Gaylord screamed and raised the scissors high above him to strike.

"Now, dammit," Smolen commanded himself, "shoot."

The bullet hit the wooden center of the window, spewing glass all over the room. The noise was shocking. Glass hit the floors and walls with a crashing jangling shocking impact. Mrs. Talmage screamed. Gaylord threw Sally to the floor and began to move toward Brackin, calling out his name and shouting that it was over, all over. He still held the shears in his left hand, which was out before him pointing toward Brackin, who was shooting his rifle out the shattered window from which the shot had come. Suddenly Gaylord was jerked back by Sally who had grabbed the chair he dragged behind him. She pulled it back as hard as she could as she screamed to Brackin, "Eugene, the shears, he's got the shears. He'll kill you, kill you. Watch him. He's coming."

Brackin swiveled back, his eyes wide as they locked with Gaylord's. He'll kill me, Brackin screamed to himself, kill me. Watch him kill me. Kill him. Him. Shoot him. He shot.

Brackin looked to where Gaylord's head had disappeared. And suddenly the room was red. Mrs. Talmage was still screaming. A high, steady, piercing scream with eyes closed and hands over ears. Now she stopped and opened her eyes. As she did so she saw the window through which the first shot had been fired. The glass had come away completely. She stood and stared at the window, and then spread her arms out before her.

"I'm coming," she shouted, and began to run for the window, much too fast for anyone to stop her. In a single leap she was out and flying forward, grabbing at the flag-pole rope as she reached it, then, with a sickening noise unlike any other ever heard, she hit the ground.

Brackin raced to the window and looked down. He could not tell if she were dead or alive. A wail reached his lips and tears reached his eyes as he saw her lying there.

Trooper John Shaughnessy had been on duty in front of the Monster's video screen for two hours. In his trancelike state it took him only two seconds to have the rifle's cross hairs positioned. Exactly three seconds after Brackin reached the window a small hole appeared in his forehead and he was dead.

TWENTY

It was many hours later as the light was beginning to fade that Deputy Chief of Police Greg Smolen and Ida Crane sat in police headquarters in Mattsfield. They were sitting together drinking coffee, not saying much, just sitting and staring. When Joe Sloan came in they both looked up expectantly.

"She'll live," he said of Mrs. Talmage. "She's broken both her legs pretty badly, and they've got her under sedation, but the rope stopped her from killing herself." He sat down at the table and opened the third coffee container. "And Sally Laird, who's fine but shaken, was promoted to Gaylord's job by old man Felton himself. It was like he was pinning a medal on at bedside." Sloan looked at Smolen who nodded his thanks and turned morosely back to a study of the table. "C'mon, Dep," Sloan tried, "losing one of three hostages isn't so bad. If you hadn't moved they might all be dead."

"Two people died," Smolen said, his voice exposing his total exhaustion. "Two people who didn't have to die."

Ida Crane stirred and roused herself. "No one knows who has to die, Greg, certainly not you."

Smolen reacted aggressively, putting his hands on the table and thrusting himself forward. "I was in charge, and while I was in charge two people died. It's as simple as that."

"Nothing," Ida said softly, "is as simple as that."

MICHAEL A. GILBERT was born in Brooklyn, New York, in 1945. He is now associate professor of philosophy at York University in Ontario, Canada, and lives with his wife and son in Toronto. *Office Party* is his first novel.